Warrick saw the exact moment Raina became aware of how close they stood, the moment she realized that one more step, one little tug from him, could bring their bodies into full contact

Her pupils darkened, turning almost smoky. Those voluptuous, pillowy lips parted on a soundless breath.

They stared at each other. The electricity crackling between them was enough to power every tool and machine in that garage.

As Warrick watched, her eyes sank to his throat, following the movement of his Adam's apple as he swallowed. Her gaze lingered there for a moment before dropping lower. Warrick's heart thudded as she stared at his bare chest, her eyes filled with a smoldering, naked hunger that knocked the air from his lungs.

"Kiss me," he asked, hoarse with need.

Raina raised her eyes to his meet his.

"Please," he whispered huskily.

At the first touch of her wa[illegible] a jolt of pure need sizzl[illegible] groin. She tasted lik[illegible]ng it was as though she [illegible]ent her entire life. Warrick su[illegible]. Kissing Raina was unlike anything he [illegible]d.

In a dim corner of his mi[illegible] voice reminded Warrick that this woman was his enemy, a woman who could not be trusted. But in that moment he didn't give a damn about old feuds. All that mattered was quenching the fire in his blood.

Books by Maureen Smith

Kimani Romance

A Legal Affair
A Guilty Affair
A Risky Affair
Secret Agent Seduction
Touch of Heaven

MAUREEN SMITH

is the author of twelve novels and one novella. She received a B.A. in English from the University of Maryland, with a minor in creative writing. As a former freelance writer, her articles were featured in various print and online publications. Since the publication of her debut novel in 2002, Maureen has been nominated for three *Romantic Times BOOKreviews* Reviewers' Choice Awards and twelve Emma Awards, and has won the Romance in Color Reviewers' Choice Award for New Author of the Year and Romantic Suspense of the Year.

Maureen currently lives in San Antonio, Texas, with her husband, two children and a miniature schnauzer. She loves to hear from readers and can be reached at author@maureen-smith.com. Please visit her Web site at www.maureen-smith.com for news about her upcoming releases.

Touch of HEAVEN

Maureen Smith

To my husband, Lorrent
Life with you has been a touch of heaven

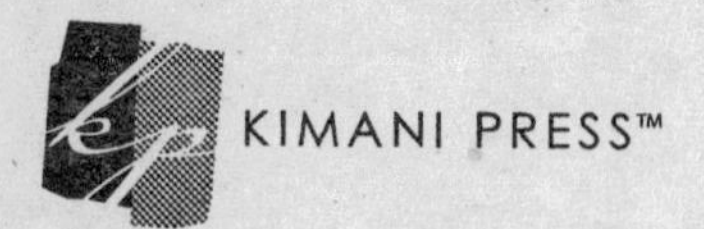

ISBN-13: 978-0-373-86135-4

TOUCH OF HEAVEN

www.kimanipress.com

Printed in U.S.A.

Dear Reader,

Warrick Mayne has never met a challenge he could resist. He overcame crime and poverty to become a multimillionaire and the successful, dynamic CEO of Mayne Industries. When he sets his sights on an acquisition, nothing stands in his way.

When he chooses the location of Raina St. James's day spa to build his new headquarters, he has no intention of backing down. In fact, he relishes the idea of demolishing Raina's business as payback for the way she destroyed his sister's life twelve years ago. As far as he and his family are concerned, Raina is public enemy number one. Warrick will show her no mercy…or so he thinks.

He doesn't count on how irresistibly beautiful Raina has become, or his body's powerful reaction to her. Years ago he saw her as nothing more than his baby sister's sidekick—plain and forgettable. But there's nothing plain or forgettable about the woman who now stands before him. Every time Warrick gets anywhere near Raina, the chemistry between them is so explosive it takes his breath away. Soon his thirst for revenge will take a backseat to his fierce, forbidden hunger for her. Although he feels guilty for betraying his sister, nothing will stop him from claiming the woman he loves.

Except, maybe, Raina herself.

I hope you will enjoy Warrick and Raina's story as much as I enjoyed telling it! Please share your thoughts with me at author@maureen-smith.com.

Until next time, happy reading!

Maureen Smith

Chapter 1

"Good morning, boss."

Raina St. James stepped through the doors of Touch of Heaven Day Spa and smiled at the attractive young woman seated behind the circular reception desk. Although Raina had been in business for nearly two years, being addressed as "boss" still gave her goose bumps on occasion.

"Good morning, Nikki," she cheerfully greeted the receptionist as she approached the large desk. "How's everything going?"

"Great! We're already at full capacity and it's barely ten o'clock."

Raina grinned. "Now *that's* what I like to hear first thing on a Monday morning. Got any messages for me?"

Nikki Kramer passed her a small stack of phone messages. "I put the rest through to your voice mail."

"Thanks, Nikki," Raina said, her high heels clicking on the gleaming marble floor as she left the lobby and headed toward her office near the back of the small building.

As she walked, she passed wood-paneled walls adorned with tranquil seascapes and bamboo light sconces that provided warm, ambient lighting. Soft, serene music wafted from hidden speakers throughout the spa, and the scent of fragrant oils and candles blended in a soothing aromatherapy that delighted customers.

As Raina took in her surroundings, she felt a deep sense of pride wash over her. Located in a trendy neighborhood near downtown Houston, Touch of Heaven was a full-service day spa that specialized in therapeutic massages, waxing, facials, body wraps and treatments, manicures and pedicures. The staff included ten dedicated professional massage therapists and estheticians who had become like family to Raina. They served as sounding boards for her, letting her bounce new ideas off them, celebrating her accomplishments and commiserating with her when setbacks occurred. They were the backbone of her business, and Raina appreciated each and every one of them.

Just as she reached her office, the intercom on her cluttered desk buzzed. Raina hurried across the room to pick up the phone.

"Raina, you have a visitor in the lobby," Nikki informed her.

Raina frowned. A visitor? Unless she was mistaken, she didn't have any appointments scheduled until late in the afternoon. She planned to spend the morning catching up on paperwork and reviewing vendor contracts before heading out for a lunch date.

"Who is it, Nikki?" she inquired.

The receptionist paused before responding apologetically, "He'd rather not say."

What? Raina thought, her frown deepening.

"You mean he wouldn't provide his name?" she clarified.

"That's correct."

Raina shook her head, bemused. She couldn't imagine who on earth would show up at the spa to see her and refuse to identify himself. An obnoxious salesman? A disgruntled customer? The blind date she was supposed to meet for lunch?

Only one way to find out.

"Tell him I'll be out in a minute," Raina instructed the receptionist.

"Yes, ma'am."

Heaving an impatient sigh, Raina stuffed her handbag into the bottom drawer of her desk, then left the office and made her way back to the front of the building.

As she neared the lobby her steps slowed.

A tall, broad-shouldered man stood with his back to her, one hand thrust casually into his pocket as he studied a framed newspaper article mounted on the wall.

Raina stared at him, her nerves instinctively tightening. *No. It can't be.*

But as the man turned slowly to face her, her heart jammed in her throat.

Memories assailed her at once. The packed courtroom. The grim-faced jury foreman who stood and announced the devastating guilty verdict. The room erupting in cheers that were drowned out by loud, angry protests and anguished sobs from the defendant's family and supporters.

Raina remembered burying her face in her father's shoulder and squeezing her eyes shut to block out the painful image of her best friend being led away in handcuffs.

She remembered being ushered out of the courtroom amid obscene taunts, threats and insults hurled at her from every direction. *Traitor! Sellout! Lying bitch! You're gonna get yours!*

She remembered dodging rabid reporters who shoved their microphones in her face and shouted questions at her.

But most of all, Raina remembered the cold, lethal fury reflected in the eyes of the man who now stood before her. It was a look she had never forgotten.

Even now, twelve years later, a shudder swept through her at the memory. Her arms lifted, folding across her chest in an instinctively protective gesture as she stared at her visitor.

Her sworn enemy.

Warrick Mayne had always been way too attractive for his own good, with his impossibly broad shoulders, endlessly long legs and athletic build that had made him a natural star on his high school and college basketball teams. Instead of the cornrows he'd once sported, his short black hair was now cut in a straight hairline across his forehead. He had the same sharply planed cheekbones and straight nose, the same square jaw, the same full, sensual lips framed by a neatly trimmed goatee, and his dark-chestnut skin was as smooth as ever. But time had added a maturity, a certain sophistication that tempered the hard edge he used to wear like a chip on his shoulder. Even his wardrobe had undergone a transformation. He had traded in his Timberland boots and baggy jeans for Ferragamo loafers and a charcoal Italian suit worn with a snowy-white shirt open at the collar. The absence of a tie drew Raina's gaze to the strong, masculine column of his throat before she realized she was staring and forced herself to look away.

"What are you doing here?" she managed to say with a composure she didn't feel.

Instead of answering, Warrick inclined his head toward the framed newspaper article he had been reading when she'd appeared in the lobby. "Nice write-up about your spa," he said, his voice even deeper than she remembered. Deeper and darkly intoxicating.

Raina dismissed the unwelcome thought, as well as the compliment he had paid her. "You haven't answered my question," she said frostily. "What are you doing here?"

Those dark, piercing eyes raked over her in a slow, deliberate perusal that left her feeling exposed—which had probably been his intent.

"Is there somewhere we could speak in private?" he murmured.

Raina stared at him. She could not imagine what she and Warrick Mayne could possibly have to say to each other after all these years, and after everything that had happened. The last time she'd seen him, he had looked her straight in the eye and told her to stay the hell away from him and his family.

Raina had every reason to send him packing. She didn't owe him a damn thing. But just as she opened her mouth to tell him so, she remembered that they had an audience.

Nikki was openly watching them, her eyes alight with unabashed curiosity. When Raina caught her eye, the receptionist quickly glanced away and busied herself with straightening items on her already tidy desk.

Not wanting to cause a scene in front of her employee—and provide any more fodder for gossip—Raina turned back to Warrick and said tersely, "We can talk in my office. This way, please."

Without another word she spun on her heel and led the way back to her office. When they reached the room, she waved Warrick into the lone visitor chair before rounding her desk to sit down.

She watched as he swept a dispassionate glance around, taking in the modest furnishings, bare walls and cluttered desk. Raina knew her tiny, nondescript office was nowhere near as glamorous as the plush corner suite Warrick occupied as president and CEO of a large engineering firm in Philadelphia. She knew that the small window that afforded her a view of the parking lot was laughable in comparison to the panoramic view of the downtown skyline Warrick enjoyed from his own sixtieth-story office. But she didn't care. She had spent a fortune on the day spa's upscale decor, state-of-the-art equipment and top-tier products, because only the best would do for her customers. What did it matter what her office looked like, a room she only used for completing paperwork, making phone calls and storing extra supplies?

Raina was so preoccupied with her defensive line of reasoning that it took her a moment to realize that Warrick was no longer inspecting her office. Instead those hooded, dark eyes were watching her with a silent, probing intensity that made her face grow uncomfortably warm.

"You look good, Raina," Warrick said softly. While her cheeks flamed hotter, he added, "The years have been good to you."

Raina did not miss the trace of cynicism in his deep voice. The unspoken accusation hung in the air between them. She had no right to be enjoying life while his baby sister Yolanda remained incarcerated, a travesty for which he and his family still blamed Raina.

Ignoring an all-too-familiar stab of guilt, Raina leaned back in her chair and smoothly crossed her legs. "For the record," she said coolly, "it wasn't necessary for you to withhold your name from my receptionist. Did you think I would refuse to see you?"

"You might have." There was a hint of mockery in the sensual curve of Warrick's mouth. "I decided not to take any chances."

"I see." Raina pursed her lips, studying him in shrewd silence for a moment. Although Warrick occupied the visitor chair, anyone observing them might have thought *he* was the one in control, the one with the upper hand. Reclining in the chair, his big hands clasped loosely in his lap and one long leg stretched out in front of him, he exuded the innate confidence of a man who was sure of himself in any situation. A man accustomed to getting what he wanted.

Which was what troubled Raina the most about his sudden appearance that morning. For the life of her she could not imagine what had brought him there. But whatever it was, something told her she wasn't going to like it.

"What can I do for you, Warrick?" she finally asked.

He pinned her with a direct look. "I want to buy your property."

Raina frowned, staring at him uncomprehendingly. She couldn't have heard him right. "I beg your pardon?"

Warrick held her gaze without blinking. "I'm relocating my company headquarters to Houston. I've chosen this location as the site of my new office complex."

Raina felt the blood drain from her head. A knot of dread settled in the pit of her stomach. *Just when everything seemed to be going so well...*

"I came here to make you an offer," Warrick continued in the same calm, implacable tone.

Raina clenched her jaw so hard her back teeth hurt. "That won't be necessary," she said tightly. "I have no intention of selling my property to you or anyone else. But thanks for your interest."

An amused gleam lit his dark eyes. "Don't you want to know how much I'm offering before you turn me down?"

"No," Raina said flatly. "I don't care how much you're offering. It makes no difference to me. This property is not for sale."

Warrick reached inside his breast pocket and pulled out a white business card. As Raina watched, he wrote a figure on the back, then leaned forward and slid the card across the desk to her.

"Maybe you need more time to consider," he said silkily. "I can come back tomorrow after you've had a chance to review my offer and discuss it with your people. I think you'll agree that what I'm offering is more than generous."

Raina bristled at his arrogant, condescending tone.

Holding his gaze, she reached for the business card and picked it up. Slowly, deliberately, she tore it into several pieces, dropped the little pile of paper on the desk and slid it back toward Warrick.

He shook his head at her with a soft, mirthless chuckle. "You always did have a flair for the dramatic, Raina."

She just looked at him.

"You should know," he said evenly, "that we've already begun contract negotiations with Ralston Development, the owner of the shopping center next door. The Ralston brothers are not as opposed to selling their land as you are. In fact, they're very open to the idea of being able to turn a nice profit during these difficult economic times."

Raina kept her expression neutral, though a dagger of alarm had shot through her at his words. If the neighboring landowner sold out to Warrick, it was only a matter of time before Raina would be pressured to do the same. She knew it, and so did Warrick.

She glared resentfully at him. "I find it interesting that, of all the locations in Houston you could have chosen for your megacomplex, you chose *this* one. The site of my business."

Warrick lifted one broad shoulder in a lazy shrug. "What can I say? My area research team evaluated the entire city and concluded, for a number of reasons, that this particular location best suited the company's needs."

How convenient, Raina thought bitterly. She didn't buy his explanation for one damn second. There was only one reason Warrick Mayne wanted to buy her out, and it had nothing whatsoever to do with business. This was personal. He wanted to punish her for testifying against his younger sister. He wanted a pound of Raina's flesh. More, if he could get it.

Shoving aside the unsettling thought, Raina raised her arm and glanced pointedly at her watch. "If it's all the same to you, Warrick, I have a ton of paperwork I'd like to get to as soon as possible. I trust you can find your way out?"

He looked at her, a solitary muscle twitching in his jaw. With a supreme effort she returned his gaze without flinching.

After another tense moment he unfolded his long, powerful body from the chair and made his way to the door. His walk resembled something between an unhurried strut and a prowl that Raina had always found mesmerizing.

Unfortunately, nothing had changed.

At the doorway Warrick paused and glanced back at her, a glint of steel in his dark eyes.

"I know you have your reasons for refusing to consider my offer," he said in a deceptively mild voice. "But there's one thing you should know about me. I didn't get where I am by playing nice or learning to take no for an answer. I play to win, Raina. You'd do well to remember that."

Raina raised a defiant chin and said with icy disdain, "I wish I could say it's been a pleasure seeing you again, Warrick, but I think we both know better."

His mouth curved in a sharp, feral smile. Without another word he turned and strode out of the room.

Raina waited several beats before releasing a deep, shaky breath and pressing a hand to her roiling stomach.

She knew she had not seen the last of Warrick. But that was just fine with her. Because what Warrick failed to realize was that Raina was no longer the insecure, guilt-ridden teenage girl who had shown up on his doorstep and begged his forgiveness and understanding twelve years ago. She would not be bullied or bribed into selling her property to him just because he wanted to satisfy an old vendetta against her. She'd worked too hard and sacrificed too much to fulfill her lifelong dream of owning a business. No way in hell would she throw everything away by selling out to the highest bidder, especially if that bidder was Warrick Mayne.

It was bad enough she'd once lost her heart to him.

She'd be damned if she would let him take anything else from her.

Chapter 2

Warrick Mayne's cell phone rang as he climbed into his sleek black Bentley luxury sedan parked in front of the day spa. He reached inside his breast pocket, removed the Bluetooth BlackBerry handheld and stabbed the talk button.

"Mayne," he growled.

The phone line was filled with a low, knowing chuckle. "I take it things didn't go too well with Miss St. James this morning."

Warrick scowled. "What do *you* think?"

Stephon Fuller, who had served as vice president and chief operating officer of Mayne Industries for the past seven years, laughed. "That bad, huh?"

"Worse." With an impatient flick of his wrist, Warrick turned the key in the ignition. The engine purred to life, dumping a frigid blast of air into the car. Although it was barely ten-thirty in the morning, the temperature had already soared to a sweltering eighty-five degrees, which made him question his sanity for returning home at the height of summer. The heat, coupled with the oppressive humidity, was an entity most Houstonians learned to live with, like bumper-to-bumper traffic and underachieving sports teams.

"How did the conversation go?" Stephon asked dryly.

Warrick snorted. "I don't think you can call what Raina and I had a *conversation*. For one thing, it lasted all of five minutes. Once I told her what I wanted, she basically told me to go to hell."

"Damn." Stephon pushed out a deep breath. "Looks like you underestimated just how much that spa means to her."

Warrick frowned. The only thing he had underestimated was how beautiful Raina St. James had become over the past twelve years. When she'd appeared in the lobby that morning, he hadn't recognized her at first, and for several stunned moments he'd found himself at a complete loss for words.

He had never seen Raina as anything other than his younger sister's sidekick—a skinny, aloof girl with a mouthful of braces who was a constant presence at his family's house. The woman who'd approached him that morning was a Nubian goddess poured into a stretchy tangerine dress that clung to her shapely hips and thighs and revealed a mouthwatering expanse of long, curvaceous legs. Her gleaming golden-brown skin looked kissed by the sun. Her shoulder-length dark hair was fashionably cut in long, breezy layers that accentuated the sensual contours of her face. She had a slim nose, high cheekbones, and dark, slanted eyes that had always struck Warrick as feline. But had her lips always been so full and lush, so damned tempting? And had her voice always been so low and throaty?

The moment he'd seen her, he'd been caught off guard by the sharp jab of lust that speared through his groin. His reaction to her had been visceral. Powerful. Not at all what he'd expected to feel for a woman he had spent the past twelve years hating.

"Do you think she wants more money?" Stephon asked, breaking into Warrick's thoughts.

"I doubt it. She doesn't even know what I'm offering. I wrote it on the back of a card, and without giving it a second glance, she tore up the card in my face."

"Ouch." Stephon chuckled ruefully. "Maybe it wasn't such a good idea for you to make the sales pitch—in person or otherwise. You should have sent me or another company rep."

"It wouldn't have mattered who presented the offer," Warrick said darkly. "As soon as Raina found out *I* was the buyer, her response would have been the same."

There was no doubt in his mind that Raina's staunch refusal to even consider his offer was out of pure spite. After all, he was offering her more than the property's appraisal value. More than enough for her to open a bigger, better day spa in a new location.

Not that she'd given him a chance to explain any of that.

"So what's our next move?" Stephon asked, a note of impatience in his voice. "We need Raina St. James to sell in order to build on that site. And it has to happen soon if we want to adhere to our projected construction schedule. Not to mention the preliminary groundwork that still has to be done, between meeting with the planning commission and—"

"I know all that," Warrick said brusquely. "Believe me, I already got an earful from the project manager during our meeting yesterday. I know the kind of timeline we're up against. I don't need another lecture."

A lesser man would have heeded the growled warning and backed down. But Stephon—who had known Warrick since college—forged ahead, undaunted. "You have to find a way to convince Raina to sell her property to you. Maybe you need to try a different approach."

"Really?" Warrick drawled sarcastically. "And what makes you think there's anything wrong with the approach I used?"

Stephon barked out a short, grim laugh. "Because I know you, Mayne, and I've seen you in action. I've watched you lay on the charm and work a room better than a seasoned politician, but I've also watched you reduce grown men to stammering idiots if they so much as cleared their throat the wrong way. Considering the bad blood between you and Raina, I'd be amazed if you managed to be civil to her, let alone charming."

Warrick didn't bother refuting his friend's assessment. Stephon was right.

Warrick had always prided himself on being a shrewd businessman. Whether he was dealing with demanding clients, obstinate board members or cutthroat competitors, he knew how to put aside personal differences in order to achieve a mutually beneficial goal. He'd always understood that he could catch more bees with honey than vinegar, a principle he should have been able to apply to the current situation with Raina St. James.

But he couldn't.

Once he had recovered from the shock of seeing her again—all grown up and sexy as hell—the old anger and bitterness had taken over. He'd wanted nothing more than to lash out at her, to punish her for the abominable way she had betrayed his sister. He'd wanted to make her suffer, to make her feel the pain he and his family had endured every day that his sister had remained incarcerated for the past twelve years.

As Raina sat behind her desk looking down her prim nose at him, as beautiful and untouchable as Queen Nefertiti, Warrick was struck by the total lack of remorse she demonstrated. It didn't matter to her that her best friend had been convicted of a crime she had not committed. It didn't matter to Raina that Yolanda Mayne had been deprived of the same opportunities *she* had enjoyed—attending an expensive college, earning a master's degree, traveling overseas, landing a good job on Wall Street, successfully launching her own business before the age of thirty. It was painfully obvious to Warrick that Raina St. James had not lost any sleep over what she had done to his sister. She was as unrepentant as ever.

Any inclination he may have had to make nice with her had flown out the window when she had calmly and arrogantly torn apart his business card. He'd decided right then and there that he would show her no mercy. One way or another, she *would* sell her property to him.

Interrupting his thoughts a second time, Stephon said quietly, "Raina St. James has something you want, Mayne. And I know this may be hard for you to hear, but the reality is that you need *her* more than she needs you." He paused. "Maybe it's time to bury the hatchet once and for all. Maybe you should tell her you forgive her—"

"No." Warrick's tone was low and forbidding.

Stephon faltered a moment. "You don't have to mean it."

"Then why the hell would I say it?"

"To soften her up! To play on her emotions. To make her feel good about handing over her property to you. Take your pick. Hell, if I were you, I'd be doing whatever it takes to get that woman to sign on the dotted line. Wine and dine her if you have to."

Warrick scowled at the suggestion. "Tell you what, Fuller. Let *me* worry about Raina St. James. *You* concentrate on holding down the fort in my absence. Think you can do that for me?"

Stephon said dryly, "I think I can manage." Just then his assistant's voice could be heard in the background. Stephon's response was muffled as he covered the mouthpiece with his hand.

A moment later he came back on the line. "Darlene wants to make sure you're all set for the videoconference this afternoon."

"I should be. You know Mabel is always on top of those things."

Warrick had leased out space in a downtown office building for his secretary and the other three members of his transition team who had accompanied him from Philadelphia. More staff would join them once the first phase of the construction project was under way.

"How long are you going to crash at your mother's place?" Stephon asked. "For as long as you can take it?"

Warrick grimaced. "Something like that."

Every time he mentioned renting an apartment while he waited for his own house to be built, his mother tearfully protested, reminding him that it had been *his* idea to buy her a sprawling eight-bedroom house in an exclusive Houston neighborhood, forcing her to leave behind all her friends in the Third Ward. Bertrice "Birdie" Mayne complained incessantly about everything from her uppity new neighbors to her frequent bouts with loneliness, although her divorced daughter and grandchild lived with her, and every time Warrick came home for a visit, his mother was merrily entertaining a houseful of guests, just as she'd done back in the day.

"At least you have the place to yourself for a few days," Stephon said, a knowing grin in his voice. "Sending your mom, sister and niece on a Caribbean cruise was a stroke of genius."

Warrick chuckled dryly. "You make it sound like I got rid of them on purpose. I booked the cruise last year, before I even knew when I would be coming home. I was actually looking forward to spending some time with Yasmin and my niece."

"Uh-huh. Likely story," Stephon teased.

"Whatever, man." Warrick glanced at the clock on the gleaming mahogany dashboard. Ten-fifty. He still had a few more errands to run before he headed to his temporary office to catch up on some paperwork and attend the scheduled videoconference.

That evening he was having dinner with Deniece Labelle, his high-school sweetheart who had tracked him down after learning that he was back in town to accept an award (his PR team had successfully managed to keep the real reason for his return under wraps). Warrick had not seen Deniece in more than ten years, but now as he tried to imagine what she must look like, his mind could only conjure an image of gorgeous, leggy Raina in that take-me-now getup, her lush, sensual mouth slicked with gloss, her high, round breasts rising and falling above the scooped neckline of her dress.

Warrick swore under his breath at the tightening in his groin. Old grudge be damned. His body had a mind of its own.

"I gotta run," he told Stephon. "Talk to you at the meeting."

Warrick disconnected and shoved the BlackBerry handheld inside his breast pocket, wondering if Raina was watching him from her office window and deliberating whether to call security to have him removed from the premises.

Mouth twisting cynically at the thought, Warrick surveyed the small Spanish-style building, with its red-tiled roof and green canopy hanging over the entrance, the words *Touch of Heaven Day Spa* stenciled in fancy white letters.

The popular establishment was located on the outskirts of Uptown Park, a trendy retail area that boasted a collection of upscale shops, boutiques and restaurants. Touch of Heaven was adjacent to an older strip mall that included as tenants a nail salon, a beauty supply store, a dry cleaner, a gourmet deli and a junior department store. While Mayne Industries had already entered into contract negotiations with the developer that owned the shopping center, the bordering parcel of land was an entirely different matter. Raina not only owned the building that housed her day spa, but the surrounding acreage as well. Warrick's purchase of the three-hundred-thousand-square-foot strip mall was contingent upon his ability to acquire Raina's land as well. If she refused to sell to him, he would have to find another location—a comparable or better location—for his new office complex.

As far as Warrick was concerned, that was not an option.

If Raina St. James thought she'd seen the last of him, she was in for a very rude awakening.

With one last look at Touch of Heaven Day Spa, Warrick slid on a pair of mirrored sunglasses, backed out of the parking space and drove away.

* * *

Watching surreptitiously from her office window, Raina did not draw an easy breath until the shiny black Bentley disappeared down the busy street.

And then she strode back to her desk, her heart pounding furiously against her breastbone, her thoughts racing a mile a minute.

How long had Warrick Mayne been planning to relocate his company headquarters to Houston? And how had he kept such a big story out of the media? Had she missed something?

Raina drummed her manicured nails impatiently on the desk while she waited for her slow computer to boot up. Once she was online, she quickly pulled up her favorite search engine and typed "Mayne Industries." Not surprisingly, her query produced several pages of hits. Over the past ten years, dozens of articles about the prominent engineering firm had been published in various newspapers and magazines, including *Forbes, Fortune*, and *Black Enterprise*. The company had received numerous industry awards for achievements in technology, innovation and energy conservation, and had also been recognized for outstanding service, growth and community outreach by some of the most prestigious organizations in the country. The firm generated millions in annual revenue and had sustained robust stock holdings even in the face of economic turmoil and escalating oil and gas prices.

But it was the man at the helm of Mayne Industries who garnered the most attention—and adoration—from the media. To Houstonians, Warrick Mayne was a success story, the proverbial hometown hero who had overcome impossible odds to seize the American Dream.

His personal biography was the stuff of Hollywood scripts and popular hip-hop songs. He was born and raised in the Third Ward, one of the poorest, most crime-infested communities in Houston. When he was eight years old, his crack-addicted father walked out on the family and was never seen or heard from again. Warrick, the second eldest of five siblings, was forced to grow up very quickly. Armed with food stamps and a stubborn will to survive, he did the grocery shopping while his older sister, Yasmin, took care of the cooking and cleaning. While their mother held down two minimum-wage jobs, Warrick and his sister looked after their younger siblings, helping them with homework and trying to keep them out of trouble.

Warrick was always aware of the danger and violence that awaited his family every time they stepped outside their apartment. When he was fourteen, he watched in horror as his favorite cousin was gunned down in a drive-by shooting. Three weeks later, he attended the funeral of another childhood friend who had been caught in the cross fire between rival gangs.

Grief-stricken and impotent with rage, Warrick became disillusioned with life. His grades tanked, he got into fights at school and began cutting class. One night as he was making his first drug run in a borrowed car, he got pulled over by the police. The cop turned out to be the estranged brother of Warrick's father. Warrick would later confide to others that the worst beating he'd ever received was not at the hands of his mother or neighborhood bullies. It came courtesy of his uncle. Randall Mayne could have taken his wayward nephew into custody and charged him with drug possession and driving without a license, not to mention speeding. Instead he gave Warrick the whipping of his life, promising the boy that if he ever caught him breaking the law again, he would personally see to it that Warrick did serious jail time. But Randall didn't stop there.

He helped Warrick and his family move out of the projects and into Section 8 housing in a safer neighborhood with better schools. Keeping his pledge to his uncle, Warrick brought up his grades and joined the high-school basketball team. He graduated with honors and attended Texas A&M University on a full academic scholarship. After college he landed a job at a top engineering firm in Philadelphia, where he designed pipelines to draw oil and gas out of new wells developed by his company.

After getting four years of experience under his belt, he struck out on his own and founded a startup consultancy, capitalizing on a time when the oil-and-gas industry was making a strong comeback. Although success had not come overnight, with fierce determination, hard work and careful planning, balanced by a willingness to take risks, Warrick had built a thriving, successful engineering company with a clientele list that included major corporations, government agencies and some of the largest global refineries.

And now he had returned home.

Apparently he wasn't satisfied with conquering the world.

He had to conquer his old nemesis as well.

With mounting apprehension Raina scrolled through the online links, searching for an article or blurb that detailed expansion plans for Mayne Industries, absurdly hoping that Warrick had only been playing a cruel joke on her that morning.

An article in today's *Houston Chronicle* about Warrick receiving a prestigious entrepreneurial leadership award from his alma mater was the most recent news item Raina could find. She went to his company's sleek, ultramodern Web site and spent a few minutes clicking around in search of a press release or architectural scale drawings of the proposed new office complex.

Once again, she came up empty.

Whatever Warrick had up his sleeve to coerce her into selling her property to him would remain a mystery. For now.

His parting words whispered through her mind, a not-so-subtle threat: *I didn't get where I am by playing nice or learning to take no for an answer. I play to win, Raina.*

"So do I, Warrick," Raina said with the quiet, steely determination that had enabled her to survive the wounds inflicted by the Mayne family twelve years ago. "So do I."

Chapter 3

"Thank you for being so understanding about lunch earlier," said Bradford Torrance, smiling ruefully at Raina across a table covered with white linen and softened by candlelight. "I hated having to cancel on you like that. I really thought I'd be able to get away for a couple of hours, but we had an unusually high number of walk-ins this morning, and with two of our pediatricians being on vacation this week—"

Raina waved off the rest of his apology with a soft laugh. "It's all right, Bradford. You really don't have to keep explaining what happened. I know how busy things can get at a doctor's office. You're forgetting that my sister is an obstetrician. We've been in the middle of dinner when all of a sudden she gets an urgent phone call and has to rush off to deliver a baby, leaving me with the bill *and* no ride home."

Bradford smiled, his green eyes twinkling with warmth. "I can assure you that I would never stick you with the tab or leave you stranded." He paused, mouth twitching. "At least not on the first date."

Raina laughed, feeling relaxed and content for the first time that day. She'd been so preoccupied with thoughts of Warrick Mayne earlier that she'd nearly forgotten about her lunch date with Bradford Torrance until he'd called to regretfully ask for a rain check. Other than to feel disappointed that she had worn a sexy new dress to work for nothing, Raina had welcomed the reprieve, telling herself she wouldn't be much company anyway, with fears of a hostile takeover weighing heavily on her mind. When Bradford had called back a few hours later to ask if she was available for dinner, she'd almost declined.

Now, looking across the candlelit table at him, Raina was glad she had accepted his invitation. She was having a really good time. The upscale downtown restaurant had a cozy, romantic atmosphere. And Bradford, with his pretty green eyes, warm smile, smooth coffee-and-cream complexion and short, curly hair, was shaping up to be the most promising blind date she'd ever had.

Apparently the feeling was mutual.

Bradford, staring at Raina in undisguised admiration, said, "Not that I could ever forget that your sister is a doctor, considering that we work at the same hospital and *she's* the one who introduced us to each other." He smiled, absently running his finger around the rim of his wineglass. "I've been sitting here wondering how I can ever repay her for that. You're an amazing woman, Raina."

She smiled demurely. "Why, thank you, Bradford," she said, lifting her own glass to her lips and taking a sip of wine.

Raina had to admit she'd had serious reservations about meeting the doctor her older sister, Reese, had been raving about for months. Not only had past experience taught Raina to be leery of blind dates—especially those set up by her matchmaking sister—but Bradford Torrance had simply sounded too good to be true. He was a handsome, smart, caring man with a great sense of humor. He had a successful career, owned a house and had never been married. And Raina reasoned that as a pediatrician he dealt with children every day, which must mean he loved kids and would not be opposed to having one or two of his own someday.

He *definitely* had potential.

Not that she was in the market for a husband or anything, Raina hastily reminded herself. Running her own business consumed most of her time and energy. As owner and spa director, her plate remained full with marketing, sales, public relations and strategic planning functions, as well as handling payroll and managing her staff. She didn't have room in her life for a serious relationship. Still, it was reassuring to know that her options were not as bleak as she'd always assumed they were.

Bradford Torrance was proof of that.

The waiter arrived with their meals, and as they began eating, Bradford said conversationally, "So tell me more about yourself, Raina."

She chuckled as she cut into her veal tenderloin. "You mean my sister didn't already tell you my life story?" she teased.

Bradford laughed. "She may have left out one or two details. How long have you owned the day spa?"

"Almost two years. I purchased the property shortly after I moved back home from New York. I was fortunate. The owner and his wife were retiring and relocating to Florida, so they were eager to get the property off their hands. I made some minor renovations to the building, and within three months Touch of Heaven was open for business."

"That's great," Bradford said, sounding genuinely impressed. "Reese brags about you all the time. She said you've always had a head for business, which is why the spa is so successful. I think she keeps a stack of coupons in the pocket of her lab coat and hands them out to everyone she runs into at the hospital."

Raina grinned. "That would explain why most of the pregnant women who come to the spa for our maternity massages are Reese's patients. God bless sisters."

Bradford smiled at her over the rim of his wineglass. *He has a really nice smile,* Raina thought, not for the first time that evening.

Maybe, just maybe, it was time for her to start dating again.

No sooner had the thought crossed her mind than she glanced up and saw Warrick Mayne standing near the front of the restaurant. She froze at the sight of him. He looked brutally handsome in a dark Armani designer suit—he probably owned hundreds of them—that accentuated his tall, powerful build.

A ripple of excitement spread through the room as several diners recognized him. More than a few female gazes swung in his direction and lingered to openly admire him.

Raina instinctively held her breath as Warrick's dark, penetrating eyes did a slow, lazy scan of the room before coming to rest on her. Her stomach bottomed out as their gazes locked. She promptly lost track of her surroundings. The tinkle of glasses and silverware, the lively din of laughter and conversation, even the sound of Bradford's voice receded into the background. All Raina heard was her pulse pounding in her ears.

What the hell was *Warrick* doing here?

She was so unnerved by his unexpected appearance that she didn't immediately notice his companion, a tall, leggy woman wearing a low-cut black dress and stiletto heels. She was latched possessively onto Warrick's arm and looking around the room with that haughty, territorial gleam in her eyes Raina remembered so well. Deniece Labelle. Captain of the cheerleading squad, president of the yearbook club, homecoming queen, she had been the envy of every female at Jack Yates Senior High School. Not necessarily because she was gorgeous and popular and always wore the latest designer clothes. No, what girls envied the most about Deniece Labelle was that she was Warrick Mayne's girlfriend. And she never let anyone forget it, perceiving every female who crossed her path as a potential threat. Even Raina, who had never registered as a blip on Warrick's radar, had been subjected to Deniece's catty remarks and hostile stares if she made the mistake of showing up at her best friend's house while Deniece was there.

The woman had obviously wasted no time hooking up with Warrick again, undeterred by his widely publicized romances with glamorous models and actresses, short-lived affairs that had solidified his reputation as a playboy.

As Raina watched, Deniece snuggled closer to Warrick, staking her claim. He glanced down at her with a brief, indulgent smile before his gaze shifted back to Raina. They stared at each other, two adversaries locked in a silent battle of wills.

After another moment Warrick acknowledged her with a cool nod of his head. Raina cut her eyes at him and returned her attention to Bradford, who was watching her with a puzzled expression.

"Is everything okay?" he asked.

Raina smiled, but for the first time that evening it felt forced. "Everything's fine," she said brightly. "I just thought I saw someone I recognized. No big deal."

Bradford looked unconvinced. "Are you sure?"

"Positive." Hoping to distract him, she nodded toward his plate. "How's your steak? It looks delicious."

"It is. Here, have a bite."

Raina accepted the proffered forkful and moaned softly in appreciation. "Mmm, that *is* good."

Bradford nodded distractedly, gazing at her mouth. "Want some more?"

Raina laughed, shaking her head. "No, thank you. I'm fine."

"Yes, you certainly are," he murmured.

They exchanged teasing grins across the table.

Raina asked Bradford a question about work, then gave him her undivided attention, determined not to let Warrick Mayne ruin what had been a perfectly pleasant evening before his arrival.

"How long are you staying in town this time, Warrick?"

The question was posed as nonchalantly as possible, but Warrick knew better. Chuckling softly, he reached for his glass and took a sip of cabernet sauvignon before responding, "Angling for an exclusive, Niecy?"

Deniece Labelle huffed in protest. "That is *not* fair! Just because I happen to be a journalist and you happen to be one of the biggest celebrities ever to come out of Houston doesn't mean I have to want a story from you!"

Warrick raised a dubious brow at her. "No?"

"No."

They stared at each other across the table.

After several moments Deniece's pouty red lips curved into a sheepish grin. "All right," she conceded. "Maybe I *was* digging around for a little information. But can you really blame me? Like it or not, Warrick, you're a huge media draw, and as a member of the press, I'd be derelict in my duties if I didn't at least *try* to get a story out of you."

"Well, now, we can't have that, can we?" Warrick drawled, grinning as he leaned back in his chair and lazily regarded his dinner companion. Deniece Labelle was as gorgeous as ever, with her creamy mocha skin and cover-girl looks. Her dark hair had been cropped into a short haircut that emphasized her long, sleek throat. More than once Warrick's gaze had been drawn to the enticing swell of her cleavage, spilling from the plunging neckline of her strapless black dress. The sultry looks she had been giving him over dinner made it clear she wanted—no, *expected*—Warrick to be peeling off the sexy little number before the night was over. He was only too willing to oblige. For old times' sake, of course.

Interrupting his reverie, Deniece pointed a manicured finger at him, her light-brown eyes narrowed in warning. "Don't you dare make fun of me, Warrick Mayne. I'm still mad at you for not keeping in touch all these years! Do you have any idea how embarrassing it is to have to rely on *Essence* and the Internet just to find out how my high school sweetheart is doing? Those jerks at the paper are always making jokes behind my back, saying I'm not even memorable enough to warrant a phone call from you whenever you're back in town."

Warrick shook his head gently at her. "Since when does Deniece Labelle give a damn what people think of her? Who cares what those losers say? They're probably just jealous of you because you're an intelligent, beautiful, accomplished black woman, not to mention an award-winning journalist. How many of them can say that?"

Deniece gave him a grateful smile, and for a moment Warrick caught a glimpse of the vulnerable girl he'd met twenty years ago, the one who used to tease and torment others to mask her own insecurities.

"You're right, Warrick. I know I shouldn't let those idiots get to me. They wish they were *half* as talented as I am."

Warrick grinned. "Damn straight."

Deniece gazed at him, her smile softening. "I miss you, baby. You're the only man who ever really took the time to get to know me. The *real* me." She hesitated. "I guess the main reason my coworkers' jokes bother me so much is that deep down inside, a part of me thinks they're right. I *wasn't* memorable enough to remain in your life after high school."

"That's not true," Warrick said, suppressing an inward groan. Why did women always have to get so touchy-feely? "What happened to us had nothing to do with you being memorable or not. We went our separate ways, Niecy. We grew up, grew apart. It happens all the time. You know that."

Deniece shrugged one bare shoulder. "Knowing it and accepting it are two different things," she said gloomily, toying with her salad.

Watching her, Warrick mused that only a woman could order a salad at a restaurant renowned for its prime steaks. He thought about the fashion model he had dated briefly last year. Wherever he took her, no matter how fancy the restaurant, she'd always ordered a salad. He didn't get that. Maybe because he was a man, or because he had grown up dirt-poor and had learned early in life not to take anything—especially food—for granted. Whatever the reason, he'd always appreciated a woman with a healthy appetite. Unfortunately, most of the women he'd dated over the years had come up short in that area. They were either too nervous and self-conscious around him to eat, or they cared more about looking glamorous at the dinner table than enjoying a good meal.

Raina St. James didn't seem to have that problem.

Earlier as he and Deniece were being escorted to their private table, Warrick had watched as Raina's dinner companion fed her a bite of his steak. She'd closed her eyes for a moment, savoring the meat with a rapturous expression on her face that had made his gut clench, a reaction obviously shared by her date, who had stared at Raina like he wanted to devour her right there.

Throughout dinner Warrick had found his gaze straying back to the couple, unable to stop himself. From where he sat he had a clear view of their table. They were now sharing a large bowl of tiramisu, laughing and gazing into each other's eyes like a pair of lovesick teenagers on their first date.

"Well, well, well," Deniece intoned mockingly. "Looks like Little Miss Thang finally got herself a man."

Dragging his gaze away from the nauseating spectacle across the room, Warrick lifted his glass and gulped down the rest of his wine. He could care less about Raina St. James's love life.

"It's about time," Deniece drawled, sounding vaguely amused. "I was beginning to wonder."

A waiter materialized just then, refilling Warrick's wineglass with an elegant flourish. After he had moved off, Warrick looked at Deniece, patiently waiting for her to elaborate on her comment. When she said nothing more, he told himself to let it go. But his curiosity got the best of him.

"You were beginning to wonder what?" he prompted.

Deniece smiled at him, a glint of vicious satisfaction in her eyes. "I was beginning to wonder how long she planned to pine away for you."

Warrick frowned in confusion. "Who?"

"Raina."

"Raina?"

Deniece nodded. "I remember the way she used to stare at you all the time, watching you like an adoring little puppy begging to be noticed by its master."

"Raina?"

"Yes, *Raina.*" Deniece shot him an exasperated look. "Why do you think I always gave her such a hard time?"

Warrick chuckled dryly. "No offense, Niecy, but you gave *everyone* a hard time."

"That's not true," she said defensively. "Only the girls who were up to no good. And Raina St. James definitely fell into that category. She had a crush on you, Warrick."

He barked out a laugh. "Nah, not Raina. She was just a kid! She was only, what, *eleven* when you and I started going out? Come on, Niecy. She was six years younger than us. What could she possibly do for me?"

Deniece rolled her eyes heavenward, muttering under her breath, "Men can be so dense at times."

Warrick flashed an insolent grin. "If you're telling me you felt threatened by an eleven-year-old girl," he teased, "then you've got a lot of nerve calling someone else dense. Besides, you're seriously mistaken about Raina. It wasn't like that at all."

Deniece held up her hands in mock surrender. "Fine. If that's what you choose to believe, Warrick, be my guest. But *I* know the truth, and so does Raina. Anyway, it doesn't matter now. Even if she stripped naked and threw herself at you, I know you wouldn't give her the time of day. Not after what she did to Yolanda."

Warrick stiffened, the grin fading from his face.

Noting his reaction, Deniece immediately realized her mistake. She blew out a deep breath and shook her head. "I'm sorry. I didn't mean to bring up such a painful subject."

"It's all right," Warrick said quietly. "You know Yolanda's never far from my mind."

Deniece nodded sympathetically. "When does she get out?"

"October ninth. One hundred three days and counting." Warrick's chest tightened as he thought about the long anticipated reunion with Yolanda Mayne, a day that promised to be as emotionally charged for his family as the terrible, heart-wrenching day his sister was found guilty in court.

"Have you had a chance to visit her since you've been back?" Deniece asked, picking up her fork to resume nibbling on her salad.

Warrick shook his head, his expression grim. "Not yet. She's asked the family to limit our visits to once a month."

Deniece frowned. "Once a month? Why?"

"She said she's getting more anxious as her release date approaches. It's becoming harder and harder for her to see us for brief, limited periods of time. She said she gets really depressed afterward. So she decided it would be better, for her sake, if we visited less frequently." He paused, reflecting on how difficult and painful that decision must have been for Yolanda, who, as the baby, had always thrived on the love and attention lavished on her by her family.

"My mother asked me and my brothers to wait until she and Yasmin return from vacation in a few days so we can visit Yolanda together as a family," Warrick said.

Deniece offered a tentative smile. "Will you tell Yo-Yo I said hello?"

"Of course." There was only one person Yolanda Mayne never wanted to hear from again, and it wasn't the woman seated across the table from Warrick.

He frowned, his gaze drifting back to the table where Raina and her date were now lingering over coffee. As Warrick watched the couple, Deniece's words replayed in his mind.

Deniece was wrong. Raina St. James had never had a crush on him. He would have picked up on something like that, although, admittedly, he'd never paid much attention to any of his baby sister's friends. His older sister's friends—definitely. But not Yolanda's. Besides, Raina had always struck Warrick as cool and aloof, and more than once he'd gotten the impression that she thought she was better than him and his family. He'd seen the way she watched him and his brothers as she passed by the crumbling basketball court where they were playing, her nose wrinkling in distaste at their crass language and the misogynistic rap music blaring from their stereo. Warrick remembered her looking the same way the very first time Yolanda had brought her home from school, when they were ten years old. Raina had taken one look around their ramshackle house filled with hand-me-down furniture, outdated appliances and scuffed floors, and had turned up her nose in disgust. Warrick hadn't been at all surprised when Yolanda confided to him that Raina's parents didn't approve of their daughter hanging out in a Section 8 neighborhood. What had surprised him was how often Raina had come back. For whatever reason, she had seemed to prefer spending time at their house over her own—a single-story brick home with large windows and a tidy yard in one of the few middle-class suburbs in the Third Ward. That was about all Warrick had ever seen of the place, as he'd never stuck around long enough to be invited inside whenever he dropped Raina off at home.

Yolanda had usually tagged along for the ride, but on the few occasions when she'd been forced to stay behind to finish her chores, Warrick had been stuck trying to make small talk with Raina, who had gazed out the window and answered in monosyllables until Warrick finally gave up and turned on the radio to fill the silence.

He sure as hell didn't remember Raina staring at him or giving him the slightest impression she wanted attention. It had been just the opposite.

The more Warrick thought about it, the more he was convinced that Deniece was seriously delusional. Raina had never had a crush on him. And he thanked God for that.

The warmth of Deniece's hand upon his brought Warrick back to the present. He pulled his gaze from Raina's table and looked at Deniece. She had finished eating and was smiling seductively at him.

"I was going to say penny for your thoughts," she murmured, "but considering how much you're worth, you would probably charge more than that."

Warrick chuckled, lacing their fingers together on the table. "Wanna know what I was thinking? I was wondering whatever happened to the country girl who used to throw down with me, the girl who could eat a platter of ribs, brisket and sausage with a helping of potato salad and beans without batting an eyelash."

Deniece smiled, shaking her head at him. "I'm not seventeen anymore, Warrick. My metabolism isn't what it used to be, so I have to watch what I eat nowadays. Unless you *want* to be embarrassed to have me on your arm the next time we appear in public together."

Warrick gave her a soft, teasing smile. "Who says there's going to be a next time?"

Deniece laughed, a low, sultry sound. "Oh, there will be. Trust me. I might not be able to eat barbecue the way I used to, but I can assure you that there are *plenty* of other things I can do just as well, if not better." Leaning close to Warrick, she purred in his ear, "By the time I get through with you tonight, baby, you'll wonder how you could have stayed away so long."

Warrick needed no convincing. Without another word, he signaled for the check.

If Raina thought she'd be able to escape the restaurant without having to deal with Warrick, she soon discovered otherwise.

She was standing in the foyer waiting for Bradford to retrieve his car from the parking garage when a low, rumbling voice drawled, "How was dinner?"

Raina spun around, startled to find Warrick directly behind her. He stood so close she could smell him, soap mingled with the subtle fragrance of a very expensive cologne. So close that she could feel his heat and the masculine energy that surrounded him like a crackling force field, electrifying her senses. Blindsiding her.

She took a hasty step backward, her face flushing when those sensual lips twitched. She started to tell him it was rude to invade other people's personal space, but she didn't want to sound uptight, nor did she want to give him the satisfaction of knowing he'd rattled her. Because he had, damn him.

"Dinner was fine," she said curtly.

A faintly mocking smile curved his mouth. "Yeah, I could tell."

Bristling, Raina glared up at him. "What's that supposed to mean? Were you spying on me or something?"

"Maybe."

Raina didn't know how to respond to that. Really, how *could* she respond? "Where's your date?" she asked instead.

"In the ladies' room. Yours?"

"He went to get the car."

Warrick raised one thick black brow, an amused gleam in his eyes. "Too cheap to pay for valet parking?"

"No!" Raina said vehemently, incensed because the same thought had occurred to her. Especially in light of what had happened a few minutes ago. When the bill had arrived, Bradford had suggested offhandedly that he and Raina split the tab. She'd been too stunned to protest, nodding mutely and reaching for her purse. She'd have to process her feelings later, after the shock wore off.

And speaking of Bradford, she thought, what on earth was taking him so long?

"How long have you been dating that pretty boy?"

Raina was so startled by the question that it took her a moment to recover and respond. "None of your damn business," she snapped.

Warrick chuckled softly, and Raina realized that he was deliberately baiting her, trying to get a rise out of her. And she was playing right into his hands.

Deciding to fight fire with fire, she made an exaggerated show of glancing around the elegant foyer and saying sweetly, "Gee, I wonder what's taking Deniece so long? Maybe you should go check up on her. You know, to make sure she's not bent over a toilet puking up that enormous salad she had for dinner."

Warrick inclined his head, his eyes glinting with amusement and a trace of grudging respect. "Touché."

Raina felt a perverse twinge of satisfaction.

It didn't last long.

"I find it interesting," Warrick said very casually, "that you noticed what my date was eating from all the way across the room. Were you spying on us or something?"

Raina blinked, heat crawling up her neck and spreading across her cheeks.

Warrick's mouth curved in a slow, triumphant grin.

Raina pivoted abruptly and walked to the opposite end of the foyer, looking out the window at the circular driveway bustling with the arrival and departure of luxury vehicles. Well-dressed men and women swept through the doors of the restaurant and were ceremoniously ushered to the dining room by the maître d'.

Where the hell was Bradford?

Raina stiffened as Warrick came up beside her at the window. What did the infuriating man want?

"I have to say, Raina," he murmured, his deep, dark voice brushing across her skin like a whispered caress, "you've really come into your own. I can't get over how beautiful you look."

Raina's stomach bottomed out.

She turned her head and found Warrick staring down at her, his hooded eyes roaming across her face in a way that did dangerous things to her pulse. There was a time she would have given anything to have him look at her the way he was looking at her now, to hear him say the things he was saying to her now. But it had never happened before, and over time she'd been forced to relinquish the fantasy to hard, cold reality. And the reality was that Warrick Mayne despised her and blamed her for his sister's downfall. And now he wanted to punish her by putting her out of business.

She must never, ever forget that. If she let down her guard even for one second, this man could—and would—destroy her.

"Nice try, Warrick," she said sardonically, "but it's going to take a hell of a lot more than cheap flattery to get me to hand over my property to you."

The barest hint of a smile curved his lips. "I wish I could say I was only trying to flatter you," he said softly, "but I meant what I said. You *are* beautiful, Raina. Incredibly beautiful. Only a damned fool would deny the obvious."

Her heart thudded. She swallowed, unable to look away from him. He gazed back at her.

"Well, well, well. Isn't this a touching little reunion?"

Raina glanced around sharply to find Deniece Labelle standing there. She was frowning, her eyes narrowed as she divided a speculative look between Raina and Warrick.

"Deniece," Raina murmured with a polite nod.

The other woman moved closer to Warrick, linking her arm possessively through his. As she looked Raina up and down, her red lips curled in a smirk, as if she'd seen something amusing.

For one awful moment Raina felt like she was twelve years old again, standing at the front door of Yolanda Mayne's house after her sister had dropped her off for Warrick's high-school graduation cookout. Raina was carrying a gift-wrapped present she'd handpicked for Warrick and wearing a brand-new sundress she'd thought was so pretty. Until Deniece opened the door, took one look at the bright flowers bordering the hem of her dress, and burst out laughing.

Raina gave herself a mental shake, dismissing the humiliating memory.

"So," Deniece began conversationally, "how's business, Raina?"

"Can't complain," Raina answered neutrally, knowing it was a loaded question. Deniece Labelle could care less about Raina *or* her business. Judging by the malicious gleam in her eyes, it was clear she had an ulterior motive for asking the question.

Raina didn't have to wait long to find out what it was. "I'm sorry to say that I've never been to Touch of Heaven," Deniece said snidely. "I only patronize the Uptown Day Spa around the corner. It's a bit pricier than your spa, but, well, you get what you pay for."

Raina flashed a cool, narrow smile. "I'm sure that's what Warrick will be saying when you wake up together tomorrow morning."

Deniece's face pinched with anger.

Before she could retaliate, one of the valets stuck his head through the door and said, "Mr. Mayne? Thank you for your patience, sir. Your car is ready."

Raina watched as Warrick escorted Deniece outside to the gleaming black Bentley waiting at the curb. He helped her gently inside and closed the door, then tipped the young parking attendant, whose eyes widened appreciatively at the generous offering.

Before climbing behind the wheel Warrick paused, his dark gaze returning to Raina where she stood inside the foyer. Their eyes met.

She lifted her chin.

Warrick winked at her, then ducked inside the car.

Her stomach was still fluttering when the tinted passenger window slid down halfway. Deniece gave Raina a look of vicious triumph before the Bentley rolled away.

A moment later Bradford pulled up across the street and waved Raina over, because the restaurant's driveway was reserved for valet-parked vehicles only. He apologized profusely for the delay, citing a heavy volume of traffic in the parking garage. Raina could only smile and nod, wondering how what had started off as such a promising evening had ended so abysmally.

Chapter 4

When Raina arrived at the office the following morning, she had a voice-mail message from Tyler Ralston, the owner of Ralston Development. He left his cell phone, office and home phone numbers, asking Raina to call him back to "discuss an urgent matter."

And so it begins.

Heaving a deep, resigned sigh, Raina dialed the office number and was put through immediately to Tyler Ralston. "Why, hello there, Miss St. James!" he greeted her, his voice a broad, gravelly drawl that reverberated across the phone line. "Thanks so much for returning my call."

"No problem. What can I do for you, Mr. Ralston?"

He guffawed. "No need to be so formal! We've been neighbors for two years now. Just call me Ty."

"All right," Raina murmured, resisting the urge to roll her eyes toward the ceiling. "How can I help you?"

"Well…since you asked. I understand that Warrick Mayne was in the area yesterday. I was just wondering if you had an opportunity to visit with him."

This time Raina did roll her eyes. *Visit with him?* As if she'd had Warrick over for tea and scones?

"As a matter of fact," she said evenly, "I did have an opportunity to speak to Mr. Mayne."

"Good, good. Then you already know all about his plans to relocate his company headquarters to Houston. Did he show you the architectural drawings of the proposed office complex? It's quite impressive. Over three hundred thousand square feet of office space, a high-tech laboratory, an atrium, a five-star restaurant, an Italian-style courtyard, even a fountain out front."

As Tyler Ralston babbled on, Raina wondered if Warrick had put the man up to making his sales pitch for him.

"Unfortunately," she interrupted Ralston's gushing recitation of the planned facility, "I didn't get a chance to view the architectural renderings, but I'm sure the new office complex is every bit as lovely and ultramodern as you say it is, Mr. Ralston."

"Oh, it is. Most assuredly." He sounded a little piqued. "But I don't understand why you didn't get to see it for yourself. Mr. Mayne and his people came out to my office just last week. Did an entire presentation for me and my brother. Took us out for dinner and drinks afterward. Really gave us the royal treatment."

"Yes, well, Mr. Mayne and I didn't get quite that far," Raina said sardonically. She didn't want—or expect—Warrick to wine and dine her. There was nothing he could say or do to convince her to sell her property to him. And he must have known that when he showed up at the spa yesterday minus "his people" and the bells-and-whistles presentation.

"Perhaps you and Mr. Mayne can reschedule a time to—"

"I'm afraid not, Mr. Ralston." Raina refused to call the man Ty.

"Why not?" he demanded. "Why don't you want to set up another meeting with him?"

"Because it's not necessary," Raina said in a calm, carefully measured voice. "As I explained to Mr. Mayne, I'm not interested in selling my property. To him or anyone else."

"Well, that's just crazy talk," Ralston scoffed. "Do you have *any* idea who Warrick Mayne is? Do you have *any* idea how much he can pay you for that piece of land you're sitting on?"

"I'm well aware of who Warrick Mayne is and how much his company is worth. It's not about the money for me, Mr. Ralston. I happen to enjoy running my spa. It's in a great location, and business is very good."

"That may be so, Miss St. James, but with all due respect, a company the size of Mayne Industries can do a helluva lot more good for this community than your little spa ever could."

Raina bristled. "That's your opinion."

Ralston snorted rudely. "Think again. Mayne Industries already employs over two thousand people. The new headquarters will accommodate close to five thousand. That means the creation of new jobs, which stimulates economic development and growth in the community. Furthermore, Miss St. James, having a high-profile company like Mayne Industries headquartered in Houston can only attract more corporations, and like it or not, that, too, is good for the local economy. I can assure you that Warrick Mayne will have no trouble convincing the planning commission, *or* the general public, that the presence of his company in Houston is best for everyone."

By the time Tyler Ralston had finished speaking—or, rather, lecturing—Raina could feel the onset of a headache. She pinched the bridge of her nose and drew a deep breath, striving for patience.

"Are you finished, Mr. Ralston?" she said levelly.

"Not by a long shot!" he blustered. "Now you listen here, young lady. I knew the couple who owned that property before you. Knew 'em for twenty years. And I can tell you right now that *they* would've had the good sense to recognize what a golden opportunity this is!"

"With all due respect," Raina said mockingly, "the last time I checked, Mr. and Mrs. Schuler's names no longer appear on the deed to this land. *Mine* does."

"Not for long if I have anything to say about it!" Ralston flung back.

"*Excuse* me?"

"You heard me, Miss St. James. My brother and I may have agreed to sign a confidentiality agreement about this deal until it's finalized, but you'd better believe I'm going to do whatever it takes to help Mr. Mayne build at that location—with or without your cooperation!"

Raina leaped from her chair, outraged. "Are you *threatening* me, Mr. Ralston? Because that sounded an awful lot like a threat to me!"

He faltered for a moment, as if realizing he may have gone too far. After another moment he said in a lofty, reprimanding tone, "I have no respect for small-minded business owners who put their own selfish interests above the needs of the community."

Raina's temper flared. "And *I* have no respect for greedy, opportunistic land developers who claim to care about the needs of the community when all they really care about is fattening their own pockets. Goodbye, Mr. Ralston!"

Raina slammed down the receiver.

How dare that man call her selfish, she fumed. The unmitigated gall! *He* was the one willing to sell out to the highest bidder. *He* was the one who would profit from displacing the tenants who occupied the shopping center next door. Where the hell did he get off lecturing *her* about serving the needs of the community? He didn't know the first thing about her. She was *not* small-minded or selfish. She—

A gentle knock at the door made Raina bark, "Who is it?"

The door opened slowly. A petite, dark-skinned woman stood in the doorway holding two lattes and staring cautiously at Raina, as if she were a venomous snake poised to strike. "Is, um, this a bad time?"

"Yes," Raina growled, waving the woman into the visitor chair. "But come in anyway."

Tina Deveaux entered the small office and walked over to the desk, her wide hips swinging. "I brought you a latte," she said in her lilting Caribbean accent, "but you look like you could use something stronger."

Raina snorted, dropping heavily into her chair. "Tell me about it."

Tina passed Raina the cup and settled into the visitor chair, sweeping her long, braided hair off one shoulder. "I have thirty minutes to kill before my first appointment. Since I was off yesterday, I thought I'd pop my head in and see how the boss lady is doing. Not too good, I see."

"No, not really," Raina admitted. She took a sip of the iced latte and let out an appreciative sigh. "That hits the spot. Thanks, Tina."

"Don't thank *me*. Thank Dalisay at the deli, who makes the best lattes in Houston, as far as I'm concerned."

"No argument there." Raina drank some more.

Tina frowned. "When I was over there, Dalisay told me they might be leaving soon. She said the landlord informed her and her husband yesterday that he might not renew their lease at the end of July."

Raina scowled, incensed to realize that Tyler Ralston was not waiting until the deal with Mayne Industries was finalized. The arrogant bastard was proceeding as if the sale were a foregone conclusion. Damn him. And damn Warrick Mayne!

"So it *is* true?" Tina prodded, noting Raina's furious expression. "Their landlord *is* planning to sell the shopping center?"

Raina hesitated, then nodded grimly. "I'm afraid so."

"But why?"

"Because he's a selfish, greedy businessman whose only concern is making money," Raina grumbled.

Tina's perfectly sculpted brows knitted together. "I don't understand."

Leaning her head against the back of her chair, Raina pushed out a long, weary breath.

Tina Deveaux was one of the first massage therapists Raina had hired after opening Touch of Heaven. Tina, a licensed masseuse with several years of experience in the salon industry, had been going through a painful divorce and struggling to raise her infant son alone when she had applied for the job at the day spa. Raina had known, even before she'd looked at her résumé, that Tina was the type of employee she was seeking. Not only was she knowledgeable and professional, but she had a way about her, an irrepressible warmth and charisma that immediately put people at ease, which was an essential quality in the service industry. From the outset she generously shared her knowledge and expertise with Raina, who, despite having an MBA from Columbia and five years of marketing and advertising experience on Wall Street, soon realized she had a lot to learn about running a day spa. In many ways, Tina had as much invested in Touch of Heaven as Raina did. For that reason, she deserved not to be kept in the dark about anything pertaining to the spa's possible future.

Releasing another deep breath, Raina said, "Last week Ralston Development was approached by a wealthy buyer who wants to build an office complex at this location."

Tina stared at her, her frown deepening. "The buyer wants to tear down the shopping center?"

"Yes. But not just the shopping center. The spa as well."

Tina's dark, almond-shaped eyes grew wide. "Oh no! You're joking, right?"

Raina shook her head, her lips twisting cynically. "I wish. He came to see me yesterday to make an offer on the property."

Tina leaned forward in her chair, her gaze intent. "What did you tell him?"

Raina gave a mirthless laugh. "What do you think I told him? I told him I have no intention of selling my property. And then I showed him the damn door."

Tina laughed, clapping her hands together. "Thank God!"

"You know I'm not interested in selling the spa, Tina. This place keeps me sane."

"You and me both. You know I love my Julien dearly, but coming to work gives me a welcome break from picking up toys, cleaning up spills and chasing down naked little boys who don't want to get a bath!"

Raina laughed, thinking of Tina's adorable but rambunctious three-year-old son. "How *is* the little man doing?"

"Oh, same as usual. Getting into everything he can, wherever he can. My mother's taking him to the zoo and to a water park today, so he should be good and worn out by the time I get home this evening."

Raina shook her head, incredulous. "*I'm* worn out just thinking about that itinerary. God bless your mother."

Tina grinned. "She had me when she was very young, so I sort of returned the favor and gave her a grandchild while she's still young and active enough to enjoy him."

Raina groaned. "Please don't ever tell my mother that. She's still wondering when Reese and I are going to put our careers on hold and get to work giving her grandbabies. I keep reminding her that it might help if we could each find a good man first."

Tina sucked her teeth. "I know that's right. Don't even *get* me started on my no-good ex-husband, who only comes around when he thinks I might be seeing someone else. Then all of a sudden he becomes the most loving, attentive father to Julien." She rolled her eyes, waving a dismissive hand. "Anyway, getting back to the buyer we were talking about before. Who is he?"

Raina grimaced. "Just some out-of-state tycoon," she answered vaguely.

Tina nodded. "When I came in this morning, Nikki told me you had a visitor yesterday. A man, she said. Fine as he wanted to be. Tall, dark and sexy. She said she could hardly keep her eyes off him. I got my hopes up, thinking maybe you finally had a new man in your life. But then Nikki said you weren't happy to see him, and he didn't stay very long. I guess now I know why."

Tina sounded so disappointed that Raina almost felt guilty. "Sorry to let you down," she said wryly, reaching for her latte and taking a sip.

Tina grinned, her dark eyes glittering with mischief. "Just because you don't want to sell your property to the man doesn't mean you can't accommodate him in other ways."

Raina nearly choked on her drink. "*What!*" she sputtered. "Girl, have you lost your mind?"

Tina laughed, rich and full, a sound that delighted her clients almost as much as her soothing, capable hands. "I'm just saying, Raina. A man like that doesn't come around every day. Tall, dark and handsome. Rich enough to buy up all this land and build an office complex. Nikki said his suit must have cost at least five grand and he was driving a Bentley, for God's sake. She looked for a wedding ring and didn't see one. You think a man like that would still be available if we were back in Saint Croix?" She laughed again, as if the mere idea were preposterous. "So who *was* he, Raina?"

Raina frowned. "I already told you—"

"No, I mean what's his name? Hell, if you're not interested, let *me* give him a call!"

Raina reached for a folder on her desk, mumbling, "His name is Warrick. Warrick Mayne."

Dead silence filled the room. Then Tina sucked in a sharp breath, her eyes widening in shock. "Warrick Mayne was *here?*"

"In the flesh," Raina muttered.

"Why didn't you say so!"

"I just did."

"No, why didn't you say so at *first?*"

Raina frowned. "What difference does it make?"

"What *difference* does it make?" Tina stared at her, shaking her head in incredulous exasperation. "What am I going to do with you, Raina St. James? Do you know who that man is?"

"Yes," Raina said through gritted teeth. "And if one more person reminds me, I'm going to—"

"Warrick Mayne is the president and CEO of one of the largest engineering firms in the country! He's worth, like, eighty million dollars. Two years ago, they named a street in Houston after him. And don't you remember when he was featured on the cover of *Essence* last year? The girls and I were sitting around drooling over his pictures and arguing over who should get to take home the magazine since it was sold out in every newsstand around the city. You finally stepped in and said it was the property of the spa since you specifically bought it for the waiting area, even though when the magazine disappeared a couple weeks later we all figured you probably took it home for yourself."

"I did not!" Raina protested.

Tina grinned slyly. "No one would blame you if you did."

"I didn't." Raina didn't need any physical reminders of Warrick Mayne lying around her house. God knows she wasn't likely to ever forget what he looked like. She had enough memories of the man to last her three lifetimes.

"Anyway," Tina continued, "I just can't believe you didn't mention his name up front. Warrick Mayne coming to the spa is a very big deal."

"Even if he *is* trying to snatch it out from under me," Raina grumbled darkly.

Tina paused. "There is that." She pursed her lips thoughtfully. "Well, he *is* a businessman. You can't blame him for trying to do what he feels is best for his company."

Raina shot her an accusing look. "Whose side are you on?"

Tina laughed. "Yours, of course! Believe me, I'm not biting the hand that feeds me. I'm just trying to see things from his perspective as well. And if you *were* thinking about selling to him—"

"I'm not."

"I know. But if you were, he could definitely make you a nice offer. A *very* nice offer."

"I don't give a damn," Raina snarled. "I don't want his money. And you're starting to sound like Tyler Ralston, so just stop it."

"All right, all right." Laughing, Tina held up her hands in surrender. "This is your spa, Raina, and you have to do what's best for you. Trust me, I'm in no hurry to start looking for another job. I really like it here, and I like working for you. We all do."

Raina smiled gently at her. "Then stop trying to break up the family. I'm not selling the property, so all of you are stuck with me."

Tina heaved a long, dramatic sigh. "I think we can live with that."

Raina chuckled dryly. "Thanks."

Tina grinned lasciviously. "But I do feel bad about you sending Warrick Mayne away empty-handed. Are you absolutely sure you can't think of other ways to accommodate him? Hmm?"

Raina scowled. She thought about the string of beautiful, glamorous women Warrick had dated over the past several years. She thought of the way Deniece Labelle had been draped all over him at the restaurant last night, the way they'd held hands across the table and exchanged intimate looks that left no doubt in Raina's mind what they would be doing afterward.

"Believe me," she said cynically, "Warrick Mayne is not suffering from a shortage of women willing to 'accommodate' him. In fact, I think it's safe to say he has no trouble whatsoever finding, ah, available accommodations."

"So true, so true." Tina sighed enviously. "Of all the days I had to be off from work. If I were here, I wouldn't have let that fine man leave without at least offering him a complimentary massage. Lord have mercy."

Raina couldn't help grinning. "We don't do happy endings, Tina. I'm not running that kind of business."

Tina snapped her fingers. "Damn!"

The two women laughed.

"But seriously," Tina said, sobering after a moment. "If you happen to run into Warrick again, could you please get his autograph, and possibly his business card, for my younger brother Alphonse? He's studying engineering at the university back home, and even *he* has heard of Warrick Mayne before. Alphonse is a huge fan of his, and I know he'd be thrilled to find out you actually met his idol." She chuckled. "You could even put in a good word for my brother. Let Warrick know Alphonse is a straight-A student who'll be looking for a job when he graduates in two years!"

Raina smiled. "Hey, that's wonderful, Tina. I didn't know your brother was an engineering major."

"God, yes. That's all he's ever wanted to be—an engineer. I guess that's another reason I admire Warrick Mayne so much. He's been such an inspiration to my little brother."

Raina's smile softened. "Well, if I ever run into Warrick again, I will definitely get his autograph and tell him about Alphonse. I don't know how much good it will do coming from me, considering I just turned down his sales offer." *And considering he already hates my guts,* she silently added.

But at Tina's hopeful look, she found herself going a step further. "I know—that is, I've *heard*—that Warrick really enjoys mentoring youth. Remember he founded that community center in the Third Ward, and his company has a wonderful minority scholarship program for high-school seniors as well as paid internships for college students."

"Alphonse would *kill* to do an internship at Mayne Industries," Tina said wistfully. "But he's already tried applying for an internship there, and the competition is fierce. Alphonse said they receive so many applications that at a certain point they have to start turning people away. He thinks his chances are even slimmer because he doesn't live in the States."

"Well, you know how it is sometimes," Raina said sympathetically. "It's not *what* you know, but *who* you know."

"Believe me," said Tina, "if I knew Warrick Mayne, I would do whatever I could to help my brother get an internship with him."

Before Raina could help herself or stop to question her sanity, she heard herself saying, "Tell you what. I, uh, know how to get in touch with Warrick while he's in town. I could give him your brother's résumé and ask him to forward it to the person in charge of the internship program. What better way to get a foot in the door than to go through the CEO himself?"

Tina's eyes widened excitedly. "Would you really do that for me, Raina?"

That was the moment Raina should have backpedaled. She should have done the right thing and leveled with Tina. She should have looked her in the eye and said, "Never mind. I spoke too soon. Warrick and I have a complicated past, and as much as I'd love to help your brother out, I'd really rather not put myself in the position of having to ask Warrick for anything."

But instead of being honest, Raina shoved her foot—already in her mouth—farther down her throat. "Of course I would do that for you. And not just for you. I'm doing it for Alphonse, too."

Tina squealed. "Oh my God! Thank you, Raina! My brother is going to be so excited when I tell him. I'm going to call him during my lunch break and tell him to e-mail his résumé to you right away."

"Now, I can't promise anything," Raina hastened to remind her. "Like I said before, I didn't exactly greet Warrick with open arms when he was here yesterday. But I know him. Er, I mean, I've *heard* that he's very committed to helping young people, especially those interested in engineering careers. I don't think he'd refuse to pass along Alphonse's name just to spite me for not wanting to sell my property to him. He doesn't strike me as that type of person."

Tina beamed with pleasure. "Everything happens for a reason, Raina. That's what my grandmother used to say, and she was right. Of all the places in Houston Warrick Mayne could have chosen for his new office building, he chose this location. You may not give him what he wants—and we won't even go there again—but God put him in your path for a reason. If nothing else, my baby brother might get an internship, eventually even a job, out of this whole thing."

Raina smiled weakly. "You never know."

Tina glanced at her watch. "I'd better head out there. My client should be arriving soon." As she stood and walked to the door, she said, "I can't *wait* to call Alphonse. He won't believe it. And wait till I tell that silly Nikki. She's going to kick herself for not recognizing Warrick Mayne yesterday."

"Actually," Raina interjected, "could you hold off on telling Nikki or the others about Warrick's visit? I wanted to let everyone know at our next staff meeting."

Tina frowned. "But that's not till Friday. Are you sure you want to wait that long? They might hear it through the grapevine."

Raina pursed her lips. "Well, so far the media hasn't reported on the story yet, so I'm hoping that means Warrick intends to keep his plans under wraps until the sale is finalized." *Which won't be happening if I have anything to say about it. And I do!*

"I don't want the others to start worrying unnecessarily," Raina continued. "If I were entertaining the sales offer, that would be one thing. But I'm not. So I think the announcement can wait until Friday."

"Okay. You're the boss." Tina winked at her. "I'll make sure no one is around when I call my brother about the internship."

"Great. Thanks, Tina."

When the door had closed behind her, Raina let out a long, shuddering groan and dropped her head onto the desk. What on earth had she been thinking, volunteering to help Tina's brother get an internship at Mayne Industries? Had she lost her natural mind? After the way she'd treated Warrick yesterday—tearing up his card and practically throwing it back in his face—she couldn't turn around the next day and ask him for a favor! How could she possibly frame such a request?

Hey, Warrick? I know you despise me and hold me personally responsible for your sister going to prison, and I know I pretty much told you to go to hell when you approached me with a business proposition, but could you ignore all that and give my friend's brother an internship at your company? And, by the way, I'm still not selling my property to you!

Idiot, Raina scolded herself, thumping her head on the desk. Not only would she have to put aside her pride in order to approach Warrick for a favor, but she'd have to promise something in return. Since giving him the one thing he wanted—her land—was out of the question, she couldn't think of anything else to offer. He and his family had already taken so much from her. Her pride, dignity, peace of mind. Her trust.

She didn't have any more to give. And the truth was that she wanted nothing more to do with Warrick. Ever.

Still, a promise was a promise.

With a deep sigh of resignation, Raina lifted her head from the desk and reached for the phone to make a call. Since she'd torn up Warrick's business card, she didn't have his cell phone or home number. And she already knew, from previous experience, that his secretary in Philadelphia guarded his schedule and personal information the way the CIA guards top-secret documents.

Raina knew who to call to get in touch with Warrick. Once she received Tina's brother's résumé, she would contact Warrick. And once she had him on the phone, she wouldn't beat around the bush. She would simply pass along Alphonse's résumé and ask Warrick to kindly forward the information to his company's internship coordinator. If he decided, out of the goodness of his heart, to do more for Alphonse, then all the better. Either way, Raina would have kept her word to Tina.

She wasn't asking for much, she reasoned. After everything Warrick and his family had put her through, this small favor was the *least* he could do for her.

Chapter 5

When Warrick pulled up in front of Randall Mayne's lakeside house that afternoon, he found his uncle inside the detached garage with his head under the hood of a 1956 Ford Thunderbird sports car.

Since retiring from the Houston Police Department five years ago, Randall had enthusiastically thrown himself into his favorite hobby of collecting and restoring classic cars. The blue T-Bird was one of many such vintage vehicles he owned.

As Warrick approached the entrance to the garage, he could hear Frankie Beverly and Maze blaring from the stereo. Randall Mayne was crooning the lyrics to "Joy and Pain" in a deep, slightly off-key baritone.

A slow, mischievous grin stretched across Warrick's face. Sauntering over to the car, he joined loudly in the chorus: "Joy and pain are like sunshine and rain..."

Randall jerked at the sound of his voice, bumping his head on the roof of the hood and swearing. Warrick grinned, watching as his uncle straightened and stepped around the fender to stare at him.

"Boy, don't you ever sneak up on me like that again!"

Warrick laughed. "You must be losing a step, old man. The cop *I* used to know could hear a cat tiptoeing across a room."

"Who you calling an old man?"

"There are only two people in this garage, and I sure as hell wasn't talking about me." Though, at just fifty-six, Randall Mayne could hardly be considered old.

Randall looked at his nephew, his expression stern. But he couldn't hold it for as long as he used to. A moment later his lean, handsome face broke into a wide grin. He grabbed Warrick, dragging him into a bear hug that evolved into a playful headlock. Warrick laughed as he endured the familiar ritual, knowing that even if he were seventy years old and president of the United States, he would still be given headlocks by his uncle.

As Randall released him a moment later, his deep-set dark eyes—identical to Warrick's—skimmed over his nephew's black T-shirt and jeans. His grin turned teasing. "Good thing you're not wearing one of those *GQ* suits. Wouldn't wanna get grease stains on your fancy threads."

Warrick chuckled, turning and walking over to the minifridge tucked into a corner of the garage. He snagged two cold beers and made his way back over to pass one to his uncle, who wiped his hands on a rag before accepting the bottle.

"I didn't know you were heading out this way today," Randall said, lowering the volume on the stereo. "I could have thrown a couple steaks on the grill."

"Sounds good. Later." Although Warrick had eaten the same thing for dinner last night at the restaurant, he wasn't about to turn down one of his uncle's juicy T-bone steaks, which had always been a crowd-pleaser at summer cookouts and family reunions. His mouth watered just thinking about it.

"So you're staying for dinner?" Randall asked.

"Of course." Sprawling lazily in a chair, Warrick took a swig of beer. "I was hoping we could shoot some hoops, but I see you're otherwise preoccupied." Grinning, he hitched his chin toward the Thunderbird. "This the new love of your life? The one you were telling me about the last time we talked?"

"Yep," Randall said, beaming proudly. "Two hundred sixty horsepower, three-hundred-twelve-cubic-inch V-eight. Did I also tell you the Fifty-six model was the rarest of the T-Birds, with a production total of only 15,631? Fifty-six was also the first year of the continental kit and the porthole window in the hardtop. Ain't she a beauty?"

Warrick ran an appreciative eye over the convertible, admiring its sleek, classic lines and gleaming chrome finish. "She's a winner," he agreed.

"Damn straight. Got her at auction for a steal." Randall chuckled. "Those amateurs didn't know what they were parting with."

Warrick grinned. He remembered, as a teenager, watching in awed fascination as his uncle bargained down the price of a used car he had purchased for Warrick to drive his mother and siblings around. The vehicle had been in fairly good condition and could have fetched a higher asking price, but Randall Mayne, with the fluid ease of a maestro conducting an orchestra, had somehow talked the salesman down. The poor bastard never stood a chance. By the time Warrick and his uncle had driven off the lot, the salesman was red-faced and flustered, undoubtedly wondering what had just happened.

Over the years, whenever Warrick found himself applying the same technique during contract negotiations with a tough client, his mind flashed back to that day at the used-car lot, and inwardly he smiled.

Randall Mayne's negotiating skills and killer instincts weren't the only things Warrick had apparently inherited. If he had a dime for every time someone had told him he was the spitting image of his uncle, he'd be even wealthier than he already was. Looking at Randall—tall and broad-shouldered, with a sprinkling of gray at his temples—Warrick realized he was seeing a future version of himself in twenty years.

He imagined his own father must have resembled Randall as well, but every time Warrick tried to recall what his dad had looked like, all he remembered was a faceless man passed out on the bed, or sofa, or floor, or wherever he'd managed to crawl and collapse after getting high.

How many times had Warrick wished that Randall were his father? Randall was the one who had stepped in and rescued Warrick when he had veered onto a collision course with disaster at fourteen, getting suspended from school and becoming involved with notorious drug dealers around the neighborhood. Warrick had often wondered how his life would have turned out if his uncle hadn't pulled him over that fateful night twenty-two years ago. There was little doubt in Warrick's mind that he would have ended up a pusher, or a junkie like his father. Or worse, dead. But his uncle had put a stop to all that, altering the course of Warrick's life forever. Randall was the one who had taken Warrick and his family out of the projects and set them up in a better neighborhood. Randall was the one who'd taught Warrick the meaning of an honest day's work when he made his nephew spend hours after school washing squad cars down at the police station, mowing lawns, cleaning storm drains and volunteering at homeless shelters. And it was Randall who had adjusted his schedule and worked overtime as needed just so that he could attend Warrick's high-school basketball games—he'd never missed one.

For as long as Warrick could remember, his uncle had always been there for him, never asking for anything in return. Even when Warrick made his first million, and other relatives began crawling out of the woodwork and hitting him up for money, Randall refused to take a dime from his nephew. He wouldn't let Warrick buy him a new house or give him the funds to retire early from the police department. Randall's stubborn pride was a tremendous source of frustration to Warrick, who, though he knew he could never repay his uncle for saving his life, wanted to try anyway. But no matter how often they argued or how gently he cajoled, Warrick couldn't persuade his uncle to take his money. Angry and frustrated, he'd finally given up.

And then, six years ago, Warrick had been attending a car auction while on a business trip to Italy. The moment he'd seen the red 1967 Ferrari 330 GTS Spyder sports car, with its powerful V12 engine and sleekly muscled body, he knew he had to get it for his uncle, whose passion for vintage cars had dominated more than a few conversations over the years. Without batting an eye at the seven-figure starting bid, Warrick had outmaneuvered several other buyers, purchased the car and had it shipped to his uncle in time for his fiftieth birthday.

The arrival of that car had done what nothing or no one had ever accomplished in Randall Mayne's life. It had rendered him speechless.

He had immediately picked up the phone and called Warrick, who was still on business overseas. Warrick, groggy from sleep, hadn't known what to make of the strangled, inarticulate noises coming through the phone line, half afraid his uncle was having a heart attack or stroke. When Randall finally got his bearings, he lit into his nephew. *Boy, how many times have I told you I don't want or need your money? And how do you expect to hang on to your fortune when you blow half of it on old sports cars?*

Warrick had silently laughed through the lecture, then swallowed a hard knot of emotion that had lodged in his throat when, at the end of the tirade, his uncle had whispered humbly: *Thank you, son.*

A year later, Randall, who had always dreamed about collecting and restoring classic cars, retired from the police force to do just that. Because he'd always been savvy with his money and had made some wise investments along the way, he'd retired with a sizable nest egg that enabled him to live comfortably and fund his somewhat expensive passion.

Watching him tinker under the hood of the T-Bird, Warrick realized that he hadn't seen his uncle this happy since his divorce had been finalized more than twenty years ago.

Chuckling to himself, Warrick set aside his beer, stood and walked over to Randall. "Rebuilding the engine?"

"Trying to," Randall said gruffly, his heavy black brows furrowed together. "This one's giving me a little trouble though."

Warrick shook his head, leaning down beside him. "It's always the beautiful ones," he muttered, and he and his uncle grinned at each other.

After Randall explained the issue he was having, the two men spent the next several minutes peering into the guts of the engine and trying to diagnose the problem. Randall, who'd been rebuilding engines since his early teens, had taught Warrick everything he knew. Warrick had spent many summer afternoons under the hoods of cars his uncle repaired for friends and colleagues, jobs Randall did on the side to supplement his income. It was under his uncle's tutelage that Warrick had discovered an affinity—and an innate talent—for taking things apart and rebuilding them, which eventually had led him to a career in engineering.

"Run into any of your old high school buddies since you've been back in town?" Randall asked conversationally.

Warrick shook his head, absorbed in an inspection of the cylinder, an original part in surprisingly good condition. "Not yet. No, wait. What am I saying? I had dinner with Deniece Labelle last night."

Randall arched a brow. "Oh, is that right? How's she doing? She writes for the *Chronicle*, right?"

"No, one of the other papers. *The Ledger.* And she's doing great."

Randall nodded. "How was dinner?"

"Good, good." *What happened afterward was even better,* Warrick silently mused. Of course, it would have been that much better if he hadn't been thinking about Raina—*Raina!*—practically the entire time. There had to be a special place in hell reserved for a guy who fantasized about one woman—a woman he didn't even like—while making love to another.

Warrick frowned darkly at the thought.

Randall shot him a warning look. "Now, don't you go breaking that young lady's heart again, War. You know her parents still blame you for their daughter not being married by now."

Startled, Warrick stared at his uncle. "Whose parents?"

"Deniece's." Randall frowned at him. "Who did you think I was talking about?"

"Deniece. Of course." His gaze slid away. "How do you know her parents blame me for Deniece being single?"

"Well, don't forget her father was the police chief before he retired. I still see him around from time to time, and he always asks me how you're doing and makes some joke about how you broke his daughter's heart after high school, how she won't settle down with any man she's dated over the years because she keeps comparing them to you and finding them lacking."

Warrick grimaced, even as Deniece's wistful words echoed in his mind. *You're the only man who ever really took the time to get to know me. The real me.*

Randall continued, "You know I'd be the last one to lecture you about your love life, considering I couldn't make my own marriage work. But when it comes to women, I like to think I've learned a thing or two along the way. You're a good-looking, intelligent, highly successful young man. As I told you when your business started taking off, all kinds of women—black, white, yellow and green—are going to be throwing themselves at you like nothing you've ever seen before. And I was right. Now, no one can blame you for having some fun. You work hard, you deserve to play hard. Hell, even *I* was impressed when you started dating that pretty actress with the long name, the one who was in that movie a couple years ago with Forest Whitaker. What was her name again?" Randall looked askance at his nephew.

Warrick actually drew a blank.

His uncle laughed, wagging his head reproachfully. "You just proved my point, son. Messing around with those Hollywood types is one thing, but when you start messing around in your own backyard, you open yourself up to a world of trouble. You've known Deniece since you were sixteen, and you know good and damn well how she still feels about you. Don't start something you can't finish."

Warrick nodded slowly. "I hear what you're saying, Uncle Randall. Believe me, I do. But Deniece and I have always been up front with each other. It's one of the reasons our relationship worked so well in high school. We understood each other. I really don't see anything wrong with two mature, consenting adults enjoying each other's company for a while. No empty promises, no strings attached."

Randall gave him a shrewd, assessing look. "Have you had any false paternity suits brought against you?"

"*What?* Hell, no! I'm not stupid. I don't take any chances."

"Good. Because when it comes to Deniece Labelle, I wouldn't put it past her to try anything to trap you into marriage."

Warrick chuckled grimly. "Don't worry, Uncle Randall. Nobody's trapping me into anything." He slid Randall an amused sidelong glance. "You know, you're the only one in the family who's never really liked Deniece. And even after all these years, you're still hard on her."

Randall shrugged, poking at the engine's crankshaft. "Maybe she reminds me a little of your aunt Clarissa. Beautiful to look at, but high-maintenance."

Warrick grinned. "Qualities you can appreciate in a car—"

"—but not in a woman," Randall finished.

The two men laughed.

After a few moments, Warrick ventured casually, "Have you seen Raina lately?"

"Not recently," Randall murmured.

Warrick looked at his uncle's face, as expressionless as his voice, and knew he wasn't being entirely truthful. While Randall had never made any secret of his dislike for Deniece, he'd always had a soft spot for Raina St. James. Growing up, Warrick remembered being both amused and annoyed that his uncle had always brought an extra treat for Raina whenever he visited the house. He'd always invited her along whenever he took Warrick and his siblings on trips to the amusement park, the beach and various sporting events. And at family cookouts, Randall had always let Raina choose the best steak or burger on the grill; when others complained about the preferential treatment, Randall laughingly explained that people whose names began with the letter *R* had to look out for one another.

Randall was the only member of the family who didn't blame Raina for what had happened to Yolanda Mayne. In fact, Randall had defended Raina from the start, much to the displeasure of the rest of the family, who viewed his stance as the worst of defections. For several months after the trial, Warrick was the only one who had remained on speaking terms with Randall. But as much as Warrick loved and respected his uncle, even *he* had a hard time understanding how Randall could so easily forgive Raina for betraying his own niece. But Randall, who'd always been the maverick of the family, had never apologized for what he believed.

Nonetheless, he didn't exactly go out of his way to remind Warrick that he still kept in touch with Raina. Some things were better left unsaid.

Which was why Warrick hadn't told his uncle about his plans to buy Raina's property. He knew Randall wouldn't approve, and although Warrick had always valued his uncle's judgment, this was one decision he couldn't be talked out of.

"Why did you ask about Raina?" Randall asked, breaking into Warrick's thoughts. "Did you happen to see her?"

Warrick hesitated, then nodded. "At the restaurant last night," he said, deliberately omitting the part about him visiting her spa earlier that day.

"Really? Raina was at the same restaurant?"

Again Warrick nodded. "She's beautiful," he murmured, the words tumbling out before he could stop himself.

Randall smiled. "She always was," he said mildly. "You just never noticed. But, then, why would you? She was just a child." Glancing up from the engine, he winked at his nephew. "And you had Deniece."

Warrick grinned, but it felt forced. "Having" Deniece last night sure as hell hadn't stopped him from thinking about Raina, speculating about whether she had gone home with that pretty boy she'd been sharing dessert with. Warrick wondered if that tiramisu was *all* they'd shared last night.

He scowled, disgusted with himself. Just because Raina St. James had morphed into a knockout, one who sent his libido into overdrive, didn't mean anything had changed between them. He still believed she was a traitor. He still detested her. The only difference now was that he needed something from her.

And one way or another, he intended to get it.

When a cell phone trilled inside the garage, both Warrick and his uncle automatically reached for their pockets. Warrick was relieved when the call turned out to be for Randall.

As head of a major corporation, Warrick rarely had a moment's peace. From the moment he got up at five every morning for his daily workout, his cell phone would begin ringing, and it would continue nonstop throughout the day. Before heading to his uncle's house that afternoon, Warrick had told his secretary that he was taking the rest of the day off and instructed her to forward all nonemergency calls to Stephon Fuller in the Philadelphia office. College buddy or not, Warrick wouldn't have made Stephon his VP and right-hand man if he didn't think the brother could handle the job.

"I have to take this call," Randall announced. Pointing at the T-Bird's engine, he grinned at Warrick. "Put those gifted, eighty-million-dollar hands to good use while I'm gone."

Warrick chuckled, shaking his head. "Still as bossy as ever. I came here to see you, and you put me to work."

Randall laughed. "Damn straight!"

After his uncle left, Warrick, still smiling to himself, went to work fitting a starter ring gear and dowels to the engine's flywheel.

It felt good to be working with his hands again, something he rarely got to do anymore. Overseeing all operational and financial functions of Mayne Industries kept him too busy to work on the complex engineering and design projects he'd once thrived on. But because Warrick liked to keep his skills sharp while keeping his company ahead of the curve, right now he and a team of his best engineers were working on a vaporization process that would reduce fuel gas consumption and carbon emissions, which would not only satisfy the global demand for clean, natural gas, but would significantly lower operating costs.

And right now, the challenge of helping his uncle rebuild the engine of a 1956 Thunderbird was too irresistible to pass up.

Before long Warrick had worked up a good sweat, a result of his exertions and the sweltering afternoon heat. He peeled off his T-shirt and tossed it in the vicinity of the chair he'd been sitting on earlier. As he threw himself back into his task, he lost track of time.

So he didn't realize how long his uncle had been gone until he heard his voice outside the garage. It was joined by another voice. A woman's. Softer, smokier.

Warrick froze, his muscles going rigid. *It can't be.*

But he'd know that siren's voice anywhere. Especially since it had haunted his dreams all night long, torturing him.

Warrick straightened from beneath the hood and stepped around the car just in time to see his uncle enter the garage. And he wasn't alone.

Walking beside him was none other than Raina St. James.

Chapter 6

The moment Raina saw Warrick standing there, her dark, feline eyes widened in surprise, although Warrick knew she must have seen his car parked out front when she'd arrived.

What is she doing here? he wondered. Had she changed her mind about selling her property to him?

They stared at each other across the distance that separated them.

Because he knew it unnerved her, and because he couldn't seem to help himself, Warrick let his gaze roam the length of her body. Today her hair was parted down the center, framing those high cheekbones and full, sensual lips. She wore a red tank top and white designer jeans that molded her long, shapely legs in a way that made Warrick long for the view of her backside, which he already knew was amazing. She had on a pair of strappy high-heeled sandals, and even the sight of her pretty feet, the toenails painted a bold shade of red, turned him the hell on.

Slowly, deliberately, he let his gaze travel back up to her face. Sure enough, her cheeks were flushed as she stared at him.

His mouth curved. Not quite a smile, but close. "Raina," he murmured.

Her chin lifted in that defiant little way he was coming to appreciate. "Warrick."

Their eyes held another moment. When her gaze dropped to his bare chest and lingered, blood rushed straight to his groin. As if sensing his body's reaction, her eyes snapped back to his face. She looked almost guilty, as if she'd been caught doing something she wasn't supposed to. Something naughty.

Warrick could think of several naughty things he wanted to be doing with her at that very moment.

Reluctantly he shifted his attention to his uncle, whose sharp, discerning gaze told Warrick he had followed the entire exchange and reached God-only-knew-what conclusion.

"You didn't tell me you were expecting company this afternoon," Warrick said evenly.

"He wasn't," Raina interjected, as if to protect Randall from Warrick's displeasure. "I called him and told him I was dropping by to see the Thunderbird."

"That's right," Randall said, smiling affably. "See, War, you're not the only one I've converted into an antiques aficionado. I dragged Raina to an auction with me a few months ago, and I think she caught the bug."

Raina laughed, a soft, husky sound that was as disarming as her voice. "You didn't *drag* me anywhere," she said to Randall. "I wanted to go. It was fun, and I learned a lot about vintage cars."

Randall tweaked her nose playfully, the way he'd done when she was a little girl. She grinned at him.

Warrick did a mental eye-roll.

"Come on over and get a closer look at her," Randall said, leading Raina over to the car.

As they drew nearer to Warrick, he saw Raina trying very hard not to look at him. Wiping his greasy hands on a rag, Warrick stepped aside as his uncle launched into a proud recitation of the T-Bird's classic features.

While Raina admired the car, Warrick admired *her*. Just as he'd thought, her ass looked incredible in those jeans. When she bent down to inspect the leather interior of the vehicle, the denim stretched tight across the roundness of her bottom, sending a sharp jab of lust speeding to Warrick's groin. When she straightened and ran a manicured hand over the gleaming chrome finish, he imagined that same hand gliding sensually over his body, wrapping around his throbbing erection, stroking up and down, before slowly guiding him into her—

"Boy, you work *fast.*"

Jerked out of his lustful daydream, Warrick saw his uncle leaning over the engine, nodding approvingly at the work Warrick had completed in his absence.

"He always did have a knack for working with his hands," Randall said proudly to Raina, who sent Warrick a furtive glance beneath her long, dark lashes. He was intrigued by the deep, becoming flush that had spread across her cheekbones.

What was *that* about?

Randall said, "Say, Raina, why don't you join me and Warrick for dinner? I was thinking about grilling tonight."

"Thank you for the invitation, but I can't stay," Raina demurred.

"Are you sure?"

"Yeah, I already have plans."

Warrick felt an unexpected stab of jealousy. "You going out with that chump again?" he blurted without thinking.

Both Raina and his uncle turned and stared at him in surprise.

"*Excuse* me?" Raina demanded. "What did you just say?"

"You heard me."

Her eyes narrowed on his face. "Not that it's any of your business," she said belligerently, "but I'm having dinner with my sister. And did anyone ever tell you it's rude to insult people you've never even met?"

Warrick gave an insolent shrug. "So arrange an introduction. *Then* I'll insult him."

Raina scowled.

"Boy, what has gotten *into* you?" Randall demanded, frowning at his nephew. But there was an imperceptible glint in his dark eyes, a glimmer of mirth, that belied his disapproving tone.

Warrick looked at Raina. "You're right," he drawled. "That was rude of me. Forgive my manners."

"Since when do you have any?" Raina retorted.

He grinned. "Touché."

Randall divided a look between them, a speculative gleam in his eyes. A hint of a smile curved his mouth. "Say, Warrick, if you get this beauty of a car up and running again, I just might let you take it for a spin."

Warrick stared at his uncle in surprise. "Really?" No one got behind the wheel of Randall Mayne's vintage cars. No one. *Ever.*

Randall shrugged. "Sure. Why not? You'd have to stay off the expressway, of course. Wouldn't want none of those crazy Houston drivers testing your patience or crashing into you. Maybe Raina could tag along for the ride, just to make sure you don't speed." He turned to grin at her. "He always did drive more safely whenever you were in the car with him. Remember how I used to ask you all the time, Does he speed or run any red lights when he drops you off at home?"

Raina nodded, smiling. "I remember."

Warrick chuckled dryly. "I drove carefully because I didn't want your old man coming after me with a shotgun."

She shook her head at him, her smile softening. "He wouldn't have done that. He liked you."

Warrick stared at her, his grin fading. He could tell by the way she quickly averted her gaze that the gentle admission had surprised her as much as it surprised him. *Martin St. James had liked him? Since when?*

"Speaking of the good doctor," Randall smoothly interjected, "how are your parents doing, Raina?"

"They're doing fine," she answered. "They've been in Paris for the past two weeks celebrating their anniversary."

"Is that right? How many years?"

"Forty-five."

"*Forty-five* years?" Randall whistled softly in appreciation. "That's wonderful, Raina. Hell, my marriage didn't last even a fraction of that time. Tell your parents I said hello and congratulations."

"I will," Raina promised with that warm, bewitching smile that was doing crazy things to Warrick's pulse.

He swallowed, and dragged his gaze away.

Randall glanced at his watch. "Would you two excuse me for a minute? I have some important calls to make."

Raina shot a panicked glance at Warrick. "I should really be go—"

"No, no, baby girl, don't rush off," Randall said quickly. "I want to visit with you some more. I just have to make some phone calls before these businesses close at five. It won't take me but a few minutes, I promise."

Raina wavered for a moment, then nodded weakly. "All right."

Warrick watched as his uncle left the garage for the second time that afternoon. And he realized, then, that Raina must have been the one who had called earlier, which was why Randall hadn't answered the phone in front of Warrick. *Sneaky old man.*

As if reading his mind, Raina said almost defensively, "I didn't know you were here. Your uncle didn't tell me, or I never would have—"

"Come," Warrick finished, mouth twitching. "I know."

Raina looked at him, biting her lush bottom lip as if to hold back a smile. "What do you think he's up to?"

"What else? He wants us to call a truce once and for all. He wants us to be friends."

"Yeah. You're probably right."

When Warrick said nothing more, Raina searched his face, an unspoken question in her dark eyes. *Could we ever be friends?*

Warrick held her gaze for a moment, then abruptly turned away and walked back over to his beer where he had left it earlier. It was now lukewarm, but he tipped back the bottle and took a healthy swig. In the middle of drinking, he glanced over and found Raina staring at him, at his throat and his bare chest, in a way that stopped him cold.

Slowly lowering the bottle, he wiped the corner of his mouth with the back of his hand and murmured, "Want some?"

Raina blinked, as if snapping out of a trance. Her eyes flew to his face. "Want some what?"

Warrick held up the bottle. "Do you want a beer?"

"Oh! Yeah, sure. That, um, that would be great. It's, like, a hundred degrees in here." She swept a glance around the garage. "Why aren't the fans running?"

"They're not working. My uncle hasn't had a chance to replace them yet." Warrick removed a cold beer from the minifridge and twisted off the cap as he walked back over to Raina. Their fingers brushed as she took the bottle from his hand. Warrick was caught off guard by the jolt of heat that shot through his veins.

Their eyes met, an undercurrent of awareness passing between them.

Raina was the first to look away, lifting the beer to her lips and taking a long sip.

Watching her, Warrick smiled crookedly. "Remember the time you were sixteen and you got drunk at my neighborhood block party during spring break?"

Raina laughed, her mortified gaze returning to his. "How could I ever forget? I woke up the next morning with the worst hangover I've ever had in my life. I honestly thought I was dying!"

Warrick chuckled. "No wonder. You must have knocked back, like, three wine coolers and two beers. And you'd never had alcohol before." He shook his head at her, bemused. "What were you trying to prove?"

She shrugged. "Who says I was trying to prove anything?"

He gave her a knowing look.

She grinned sheepishly. "All right. Maybe I *was* trying to prove something."

"What?"

"I wanted to show you and your college buddies that I wasn't a baby, that I could hold my liquor just as well as the rest of you." She grimaced. "I held it all right. Held it for all of one hour before it came back up—all over Yolanda's shoes."

Warrick grinned. "Her *brand-new* shoes," he reminded her with wicked glee. "The Nikes she'd saved up for months to buy."

Raina covered her face with her hands and groaned loudly. Warrick threw back his head and laughed.

He remembered glancing up from where he had been standing with a group of his friends and watching, in amused disbelief, as Raina vomited all over his sister's shoes. Yolanda had jumped back, cursing and shrieking at the top of her lungs. As Warrick's friends erupted in laughter, Warrick had taken one look at Raina, doubled over and clutching her stomach, and had felt an unexpected burst of sympathy and protectiveness. Before he knew it he was marching across the street and sweeping a startled Raina into his arms. He carried her back to his house, reaching the bathroom just as another wave of nausea struck. While she threw up in the toilet, he'd held back her hair and gently wiped her forehead, calling her all kinds of a damn fool. When she had finished, he walked her into Yolanda's bedroom and tucked her into bed while his sister cleaned up and changed into a fresh pair of shoes, glaring balefully at her sick friend.

After Yolanda had returned to the party, Warrick had stayed behind to keep Raina company for a while, feeling partly to blame for her condition. He was twenty-one years old, home from college for spring break. He should have known better than to allow Raina—or any of his younger siblings, for that matter—to drink alcohol. He knew that if his uncle or Raina's parents ever found out, they, too, would hold him responsible.

Not that Raina had been pointing any fingers. Warrick remembered her smiling dreamily at him and telling him how hypnotic his eyes were, saying how much she had always liked his name, asking him how he'd gotten so tall and handsome. Warrick had chuckled and shaken his head at her, assuming it was just the liquor talking. But now, in light of what Deniece had revealed to him over dinner last night, he had to wonder.

"God, I've never been so embarrassed in my life," Raina muttered, removing her hands from her face. "You must have thought I was completely disgusting and immature."

"Nah," Warrick said softly. "I thought you were kind of adorable."

She gave him a dubious look. "Sure, that's what you're saying now, fourteen years after the fact. I seem to remember you singing a different tune that night."

Warrick searched her eyes. "How much do you remember about that night?" *Do you remember the things you said to me?* was what he really wanted to know.

Raina held his gaze for a moment before glancing away, her full lips curving ruefully. "I remember enough to know I made a complete jackass of myself in front of you and all your friends, to the extent that when they saw me at your graduation a couple months later, they were still laughing at me. And I remember enough about that night to know it was the first and last time I have ever allowed myself to get drunk."

Warrick chuckled softly. "So you learned your lesson, huh?"

Raina snorted out a laugh. "Oh, yeah. Most definitely."

"Good." Warrick smiled at her, enjoying their relaxed camaraderie more than he cared to admit.

Shaking off the thought, he downed the rest of his beer and tossed the bottle in the trash, then went back to work on the car, though suddenly he couldn't concentrate on a damn thing.

Out of the corner of his eye he watched as Raina shifted from one foot to another, looking as if she were trying to decide whether to leave or stay. He found himself waiting, hoping she would choose the latter.

Finally she took a small, tentative step toward him. "Actually, Warrick, I have a confession to make."

He glanced up from the engine and looked at her expectantly.

Nervously she moistened her lips. "Okay, I didn't lie when I told you I didn't know you were over here until I pulled up. That part was true. What I didn't mention is that the reason I called your uncle this afternoon was to get your phone number."

He raised a brow. "Yeah?"

"Yeah. There's something I, uh, wanted to discuss with you."

Warrick straightened slowly out from under the car's hood. He could think of only one reason Raina had sought him out that afternoon. She had decided to sell her property to him. It had taken her just one day to consider his offer and come to her senses.

Good. Better late than never.

"Go on," he murmured when she hesitated uncertainly. "I'm listening."

Raina met his gaze for a prolonged moment, then suddenly began shaking her head. "Never mind."

Warrick frowned. "What do you mean, never mind?"

"It wasn't important. Just forget it."

"Raina—"

"It's getting late. I should go. My sister's expecting me for dinner, and I promised to stop by the bakery first and pick up dessert."

Warrick clenched his jaw. *"Raina—"*

"Could you let your uncle know I had to leave?" she said, starting to walk away. "I really wanted to wait for him, but—"

With a muffled curse Warrick reached out, grabbing her wrist to halt her retreat. As she whirled around, trying to jerk out of his grasp, her beer bottle slipped from her fingers and crashed to the floor.

Raina gasped. "See what you made me do!"

Warrick scowled.

As she clumsily tried to sidestep the spill, he instinctively tightened his hold on her wrist and pulled her toward him. "Watch the glass," he growled warningly. "You're wearing open-toed shoes."

She glared up at him, dark eyes flashing, nostrils slightly flared, breasts heaving as she struggled to slow her agitated breathing.

Warrick saw the exact moment she became aware of how close they stood, the moment she realized that one more step, one little tug from him, could bring their bodies into full contact. Her pupils darkened, turning almost smoky. Those voluptuous, pillowy lips parted on a soundless breath.

They stared at each other. The electricity crackling between them was enough to power every tool and machine in that garage.

As Warrick watched, her eyes lowered to his throat, following the movement of his Adam's apple as he swallowed convulsively. Her gaze lingered there for a moment before dropping lower. Warrick's heart thudded as she stared at his bare chest, her eyes filled with a smoldering, naked hunger that knocked the air from his lungs.

"Touch me," he commanded, hoarse with need.

Raina raised her eyes to his taut face.

"Please," he whispered huskily.

Slowly and tentatively, she lifted her hand. Warrick watched through heavy-lidded eyes as she experimentally laid her palm against his chest. A hard shudder swept through him. Her hand was soft and incredibly warm, her touch searing his skin. All the blood in his body seemed to converge upon that single point of contact before rushing, hot and heavy, to his loins.

His heart thundered furiously as Raina began to explore him, trailing her fingers over the thick cords of his shoulders and along the rigid planes of his chest. Warrick couldn't remember the last time, if ever, a woman's touch had wreaked such havoc on his senses. When her hand grazed his nipple, it hardened. Her lips parted slightly, as if she were surprised that she could elicit such a response from him. Fascinated, she brushed her thumb back and forth across the flat dark nipple, teasing and tormenting him. Warrick closed his eyes, swallowing a ragged groan. It escaped a moment later when her roaming hand slid down to his abdomen, inching ever closer to where his engorged shaft strained against the zipper of his jeans.

Warrick opened his eyes, and their gazes locked.

No words were spoken.

He lowered his head and slanted his mouth over hers.

At the first touch of her warm, luscious lips beneath his, a jolt of pure need sizzled through his veins and raced to his groin. She tasted like heaven, her mouth so soft and inviting it was as though she had been anticipating this moment her entire life. Warrick sure as hell felt like *he* had. Kissing Raina was unlike anything he had ever imagined.

Wanting to take his time and savor her, he molded his mouth to hers, exploring the soft, sensual contours of her lips. She trembled beneath him. He sank his fingers into the thick, silken mass of her hair, his other hand banding around her waist to draw her against the full length of his body. She leaned into him, her arms sliding up his chest to wrap around his neck. Warrick shuddered at the feel of her soft, round breasts crushed to his chest. As he traced his tongue over her lips and licked the inner seam, she shivered, rocking her hips against his pelvis. Warrick felt a dark thrill of pleasure.

He opened his mouth over hers, urging her lips to part, demanding it. The moment they did, he plunged his tongue inside the sweet, velvety heat of her mouth. She let out a broken moan, the sound igniting his blood. The kiss exploded. Teeth scraped. Tongues tangled feverishly, erotically. In the space of a heartbeat Warrick went from kissing her to ravaging her.

He cupped her breast, and she gasped into his mouth. Through the thin cotton of her tank top, he circled the outline of her nipple with the pad of his thumb. Her breast swelled in his hand, her nipple beaded beneath his touch. His other hand roamed down her spine, spanning her flared waist before cupping her lush, shapely bottom and holding her tightly against his throbbing erection. Her husky moan of pleasure joined his own.

He dragged his mouth from hers to nuzzle the delicate, sensitive skin behind her ear before trailing lower, raining kisses along her throat. Her skin was as soft as silk, hot and damp with perspiration. He inhaled her scent, an intoxicating blend of the light, exotic perfume she wore mingled with her own natural essence. He flicked his tongue over the pulse beating at the hollow of her neck and gently suckled her. She whimpered his name, cupping the back of his head and urging him closer as his lips returned hungrily to hers.

In a dim corner of his mind, a voice reminded Warrick that this woman was his enemy, a woman who could not be trusted. But in that moment he didn't give a damn about old feuds. All that mattered was quenching the fire in his blood.

With all his experience, Warrick had thought he was familiar with every physical sensation imaginable. But there was no precedence for this savage, insatiable need pounding through his body, making him a slave to his most primal instincts and desires. He wanted to bury himself deep inside Raina's tight, slippery heat. He wanted to devour her.

With a rough, guttural sound, he slammed down the hood of the Thunderbird, grasped her bottom and lifted her onto the car. Her eyes widened slightly, and for an instant Warrick was afraid she would come to her senses and push him away. But when he stepped between her legs, she wrapped them tightly around his waist. He groaned, the sound both tortured and relieved. Their lips and tongues fused in a hot, carnal kiss that left them both panting. Suddenly the air in the garage seemed hotter than before, thick with the musk of their arousal. A slick sheen of sweat covered their bodies, and their pounding heartbeats blended as one.

Warrick couldn't get enough of Raina. Her taste, her heady scent, the silken warmth of her skin, the voluptuous curves of her body. Sucking on her bottom lip, he rubbed his bare chest against her nipples until the friction made them stand out. She groaned and clung to his shoulders.

He could feel the tension tightening in her limbs, could hear her breath coming in short, ragged gasps that matched his own. Her hips writhed frantically against him, grinding against his erection in a manner that threatened to drive him over the edge. Through the thick fog of desire clouding his brain, he thought about carrying her inside the house, taking her to the spare bedroom he used whenever he stayed with his uncle. The king-size bed with the cool cotton sheets would be a hell of a lot more comfortable than the hood of a car.

But he didn't move. He *couldn't*. The thought of leaving Raina's embrace, even temporarily, was out of the question.

And then she reached behind him and squeezed his butt, and he sucked in a sharp breath. They rocked against each other, a slow, sensual grind that left no doubt in Warrick's mind that their love-making would be a soul-shattering experience.

Hands tangling in her hair, Warrick deepened the openmouthed kiss, his hips thrusting against her in a blatantly erotic imitation of what he wanted to do to her with no barriers separating their bodies.

Raina moaned, eagerly matching his rhythm. He reached between their bodies and cupped her mound, imagining the glorious heat and wetness that lay just beyond his touch. Raina shivered hard. And then suddenly she stiffened. Her nails bit into his back and she arched in his arms, her head falling back as she let out a hoarse, startled cry. Warrick held her trembling body, reveling in the force of her release even as moments later his own body bucked violently, shocking him, tearing a raw expletive from his throat.

They clutched each other tightly for several moments, their foreheads resting against each other's, their chests heaving as they struggled for breath.

At length Warrick lifted his head and gazed down at Raina. Her face was flushed, her hair was disheveled and her dark eyes were wide with stunned disbelief.

"I—I can't believe we just did that," she whispered.

"Neither can I," Warrick admitted huskily.

They stared at each other.

A moment later they heard Randall's voice, talking on his cell phone as he approached the garage.

With a panicked expression, Raina scrambled off the hood of the Thunderbird, batting aside Warrick's hand as he tried to help her down. She smoothed down her hair and tugged her tank top back into place.

"Raina—"

"I have to go," she said breathlessly, stepping around the broken glass on the floor as she hurried away from him.

On her way out of the garage she nearly collided with Randall. He smiled at her as he ended his call and tucked his phone into the back pocket of his blue coveralls.

"Leaving so soon, baby girl?"

Raina nodded, mustering a wobbly smile. "I don't want to be late for dinner with my sister. We get together every Tuesday, and she's a stickler for punctuality."

Randall chuckled. "I understand. Well, at least let Warrick walk you to your car."

"No!" When Randall arched a brow at her, she said less vehemently, "I mean, that's all right. I—I can see myself out." She leaned on tiptoe, pressing a chaste kiss to his cheek. "Thanks for letting me see your prize on wheels. She's every bit as special as you said she was."

Across the room, Warrick smiled at the irony of her words.

Without sparing him a backward glance, Raina beat a hasty retreat.

Randall stared after her for a moment, then turned to look questioningly at his nephew. "What in God's name did you do to that young lady?"

"Not half as much as I wanted to," Warrick muttered under his breath, low enough not to be overheard.

Still eyeing him suspiciously, Randall started across the garage. As he neared Warrick, his brows furrowed when he noticed the broken glass on the floor. "What the hell happened in here?"

"An accident. I need a shower," Warrick announced abruptly, brushing past his frowning uncle.

"What about this mess on the floor?"

"I'll clean it up when I get back."

Right after I clean up the mess in my damned pants.

Chapter 7

When Raina was sixteen years old, she had her first dream about Warrick, a sensual, fog-drenched dream that had left her with a guilty smile on her face when she'd awakened. Of all the steamy dreams that had followed over the years—and there had been plenty—none could have prepared her for the powerfully erotic interlude she had just experienced with Warrick.

As she sped away from his uncle's house like a thief fleeing a crime scene, her heart hammering against her ribs and her head spinning wildly, she felt torn between exhilaration and horror. She couldn't believe what had just happened, though the sweet, pulsing ache between her legs told her the encounter with Warrick had been all too real. After a lifetime of prayer and supplication, Raina had finally gotten her wish. Warrick had kissed her—and it had far surpassed all her fantasies and expectations.

Raina pressed her fist against her mouth to stifle the hysterical sound that bubbled up in her throat, something between a laugh and a sob.

What in the world had she been thinking?

She'd been in trouble the moment she had stepped into the garage and seen Warrick standing across the room, a smudge of grease on his rugged jaw, his impossibly broad shoulders and wide chest planed with hard, sinewy muscle that glistened with sweat. Her mouth had gone dry, and her legs had turned to water. It had taken every ounce of willpower she possessed to appear calm and collected, when all she wanted to do was fly across the room and jump his damned bones.

All bets were off once they were left alone.

Raina shivered, a slow, delicious heat curling through her veins at the memory of touching Warrick's powerfully built chest, his skin feeling like steel beneath warm silk. The heat of his mouth, the feel of those soft, sensual lips moving possessively over hers, had her wanting to climb inside him. The way he kissed—slow, deep and drugging—left no doubt in her mind that he was a magnificent lover, a skilled, patient lover who would take his time to bring her body and soul to unimagined heights of ecstasy.

Raina let out an agonized groan as she slowed to a red traffic light. She dropped her face into her hands and deeply inhaled. Almost immediately she realized what a mistake that had been, because she could still smell Warrick on her hands, a masculine musk of sweat and desire that went straight to her head and flooded her loins.

Closing her eyes, she shoved her hands between her clamped thighs as a fresh wave of arousal threatened another orgasm.

What the hell was wrong with her, getting off on a man's *scent* like some animal in heat! And not just any man, either. Warrick Mayne. The *last* man on earth she should have allowed herself to get so worked up over.

The *only* man she'd ever gotten worked up over.

She'd had no business touching him, kissing him, wrapping her legs around his waist and writhing desperately against him. They'd practically had sex on the hood of his uncle's car! If Randall Mayne had returned a second sooner, Raina would have been mortified beyond belief to be caught in such a compromising position. But Warrick had been as cool as the proverbial cucumber, leaving Raina to wonder if he did this sort of thing all the time.

Of course he does, her conscience mocked. *He's Warrick Mayne. He earned his playboy reputation as legitimately as he earned his fortune.*

If that weren't enough to convince her to steer clear of the man, the fact that he was her enemy, that he was on a mission to put her out of business, should have done the trick.

But it hadn't.

Nothing had stopped her from succumbing to temptation and melting in Warrick's arms. And now that he had discerned her weakness for him, Raina knew that he was ruthless enough—vindictive enough—to try to exploit his advantage. She couldn't let that happen.

Raina was so consumed by her thoughts that she didn't realize she had reached her sister's house until she nearly rear-ended the shiny silver Lexus luxury sedan parked in the driveway. She stomped on the brake just in time, jerking to a stop behind the car.

She breathed in deeply to compose herself, then climbed out of the car and made her way up to the large, two-story redbrick house with tall windows and surrounded by an impeccably manicured lawn.

The woman who answered the door bore such a striking resemblance to Raina that the two women, though four years apart, had often been mistaken for twins. They were both the same height at five-six, sharing the same high cheekbones, full lips and slanted dark eyes that others had been known to teasingly call "cat eyes." The two sisters had even cut their shoulder-length dark hair in similar styles. The most obvious difference in their appearance was their complexions. While Raina was golden-brown, Reese St. James's flawless mahogany skin, combined with her exotic eyes, often made her look like a Senegalese supermodel.

Raina, who had always envied her sister's complexion, had spent countless hours in the sun hoping to get darker. But all she ever got for her trouble was sunburn. Ironically, she didn't develop an appreciation for her own skin tone until one summer afternoon at Galveston Beach, Warrick, splashing and frolicking in the water with his siblings, had called out to Raina, "Hey, golden girl, you afraid of water or something?"

It had been one of those exquisitely rare moments when he had given any indication that he knew she was alive. After receiving his invitation, Raina, who had been shy about letting him see her in a swimsuit, had peeled off her T-shirt and waded eagerly into the water. Of course, Warrick hadn't spared her another glance for the rest of the day.

"Where's dessert?" Reese St. James demanded upon finding her younger sister standing on her doorstep empty-handed.

Raina blinked at her, momentarily baffled. Then as comprehension dawned, she slapped a hand to her forehead and groaned. She had forgotten all about picking up dessert on her way to Reese's house. She could thank Warrick for that.

She grimaced sheepishly. "Sorry. I forgot."

"Yes, I can see that." Heaving a dramatic sigh of resignation, Reese opened the door wider and gestured Raina inside. "I suppose I should still feed you."

"Gee, thanks," Raina muttered, shooting her sister a rueful grin as she entered the house. The hot, appetizing aroma of marinara sauce, oregano and garlic filled her nostrils. "Mmm, something smells wonderful. New recipe?"

"Of course. Got it from one of the nurses at the—" Suddenly Reese let out a shocked gasp. "Oh my God! Are those…*handprints* on your ass?"

What?

Raina whipped her head around, craning her neck to inspect her backside. To her everlasting consternation, she saw that her sister was right. She *did* have handprints on her butt. Two large, grease-stained handprints, glaringly obvious in the bright light that spilled from a crystal chandelier suspended above the foyer.

As an embarrassed flush stole across Raina's face, she mentally groaned. Of all the days she had to wear *white* jeans.

Or, rather, of all the days she had to make out with a man she wasn't supposed to be making out with.

You did a hell of a lot more than make out with him, her conscience reminded her. Her face grew even hotter as her sister continued staring incredulously at her.

"I, uh, must have sat in something," Raina lied.

Reese snorted. "Like hell! Those are a man's *handprints,* Raina, and judging by the size of them, I'd say they belonged to a very tall, strapping man." She grinned at her sister, her eyes alight with avid curiosity. "Girl, what have you been doing this afternoon? Who had his big, greasy hands all over your butt? The friendly neighborhood mechanic?"

Raina wished it were that simple. She wished she could fabricate a story about stopping at the local auto repair shop to get an oil change, only to wind up being harassed and groped by some lecherous mechanic. Why not? Those guys hit on her and her sister all the time, so it could happen, right? But the only problem with telling Reese such a story—apart from it being an outright lie that would wrongfully malign an innocent mechanic—was that her overprotective big sister would drag her down to the auto shop, and after forcing Raina to point out the offender, Reese would proceed to light into the man, ending her scathing diatribe with the threat of a lawsuit. A threat she would undoubtedly make good upon.

Unfortunately, Raina realized, there was no getting around telling her sister the truth about what had happened between her and Warrick that afternoon.

But she tried anyway. "It's really not important," she said dismissively, turning and heading for the kitchen.

"Not important?" Reese was hot on her heels, her bare feet slapping against the gleaming hardwood floor. "You show up here fifteen minutes late for dinner—with no dessert, mind you—and a man's handprints all over your ass, and you say it's *not important?*"

Raina ducked into the large gourmet kitchen and made a beeline for the stainless-steel double oven built into the wall. She opened the door and peered inside, her mouth watering at the sight of a delicious-looking casserole bubbling with cheese and marinara sauce.

"What is this?" she breathed.

"Gnocchi *di* ricotta," Reese answered, striding into the room. "I got the recipe from one of the nurses at the hospital. She says it was a staple of her grandfather's restaurant back in Italy. She made it for her husband when they were dating, and he proposed to her that very same night."

Raina chuckled. "In that case, you're wasting it on me. You should be making it for that hunky neurosurgeon you're always drooling over, the one with the dark, soulful eyes and gifted hands."

Reese rolled her eyes. "First of all," she said, closing the oven door and slapping Raina's hand away when she tried to sneak another peek at the casserole, "I do not *drool* over Dr. Carracci. How juvenile do you think I am? And second of all, he's not a neurosurgeon. He's a cardiothoracic surgeon. One operates on the brain; the other operates on the heart and lungs. *Capisci?*"

Raina grinned. "Aww, isn't that sweet? He's even got you speaking Italian."

Reese jabbed a manicured finger at her, dark eyes narrowed in warning. "Keep it up, little girl, and the closest you'll get to eating an Italian meal tonight is the takeout pizza your behind will have to order on the way home."

Raina laughed, holding up her hands in surrender. "Okay, okay! You don't have to withhold your cooking from me. Sheesh, that's just cruel, Reesey."

Her sister chuckled dryly as she crossed to the Sub-Zero refrigerator and began removing vegetables to make a salad. "Speaking of Italians with gifted hands, you still haven't told me the identity of the Leonardo da Vinci who left his masterpiece all over your rear end. You're not getting off the hook *that* easily."

Raina sighed. She should have known her sister wouldn't let the matter go. Growing up, Reese St. James had always been the more persistent of the two sisters, never settling for the simple explanations their parents gave them about everything from the existence of the tooth fairy to how babies were conceived. (And considering her fascination with the latter, it was no wonder she grew up to become an obstetrician.) Nothing ever got by Reese, and like a dog with a bone, she never let anything go. But while her relentless nature had often driven her family crazy, it had served Reese well in life, getting her through medical school and a string of bad relationships, including a painful breakup with her cheating fiancé three years ago.

Heaving another resigned sigh, Raina walked over to the large center island that boasted an electric cooktop and enough counter space to accommodate six barstools. She perched on one of the stools, reached for a gourmet cookbook—culinary arts would have been Reese's second career choice—and began flipping through the glossy pages to avoid her sister's speculative gaze.

"I was with Warrick," she mumbled into the book.

At the other end of the island, Reese paused in the middle of chopping sun-dried tomatoes. "*What* did you just say?"

Raina blew out a deep breath and repeated in a louder, clearer voice, "I was with Warrick this afternoon."

Reese's eyes narrowed on her face. "Warrick *who?*"

Raina gave her a look. "There's only one Warrick." *How true that is!*

Reese stared at her. "You mean to tell me you were with Warrick *Mayne* this afternoon?"

Raina nodded.

"I didn't even know he was back in town," her sister exclaimed.

"He is." *God help me!*

Reese set aside her knife, tomatoes forgotten. Her incredulous expression matched her equally incredulous tone. "So let me get this straight. Warrick Mayne, whom you haven't seen or spoken to in twelve years, is back in town. And you…spent the afternoon with him?"

Raina cringed, her face flushing. "It wasn't like that. Not like what you're thinking." *It came pretty damned close though!*

She hastened to explain herself. "I dropped by his uncle's house to see one of his latest classic cars. Warrick was already there when I arrived and—"

Reese shook her head. "See, that's why I've always warned you about hanging out with Randall Mayne. You just never know when one of his despicable family members—in this case, Warrick—will stop by for a visit, putting you in a very awkward position."

Raina flashed on a mental image of the position she had been in with Warrick that afternoon. *Awkward* definitely wasn't the first word that came to mind.

Reese was still lecturing her. "If I've told you once, I've told you a thousand times that your friendship with Randall is a bad idea. But, *nooo,* the two of you insist on sneaking around behind his family's back, almost like a pair of rebellious teenage lovers!"

Raina sputtered in indignation. "*Teenage lovers!* Have you lost your mind? Randall is old enough to be my father, and he's always been like one to me."

"He's not *that* old."

"He's fifty-six, Reese. I'm thirty. Trust me, he's old enough to be my father."

Reese snorted. "That didn't stop Meggie from hooking up with Father de Bricassart. Remember how romantic we thought their relationship was when we saw *The Thorn Birds* when we were growing up?"

Raina laughed, shaking her head. "This ain't a miniseries, and I'm not in love with Warrick's uncle! If anything, *you're* the one who used to ogle him in his police uniform—you and all your silly little friends. You guys are the ones who used to giggle and whisper about how fine and sexy Randall was."

Reese grinned. "*Was?* Hell, that man is *still* fine and sexy as all get out, pushing sixty or not. If he were just ten years older than me, instead of twenty-two, I might have to give him the time of day. God knows he's the only decent one in that family."

Raina said nothing. She knew that when it came to her sister's feelings about the Mayne family, there was no love lost.

Arms folded across her busty chest, Reese arched a perfectly sculpted brow at Raina. The manicured eyebrow was courtesy of Tina at the spa. The disapproving expression was very much Reese's. "Well? I'm still waiting."

"For what?"

The eyebrow rose higher. "For an explanation of how Warrick's hands wound up on your behind."

Raina scowled. "I was *trying* to explain. You're the one who interrupted to lecture me about my friendship with Randall."

Reese just looked at her.

Raina went back to flipping pages in the cookbook. "Anyway, Randall had to make some phone calls, or so he said. While he was gone, Warrick and I got to talking, and, uh, one thing led to another and…We, uh, kissed."

Dead silence.

"And?" Reese prompted.

"That's it. We kissed."

"Judging by those handprints on your butt," Reese drawled sardonically, "you and Warrick did a helluva lot more than kissing."

Raina groaned, covering her face with her hands. "All right! Fine! We kissed *and* fondled each other. A lot! We were in the garage," she explained, the breathless words tumbling out of her mouth faster than water from a spigot, "and Warrick was working on the car. It was hot as hell, and all I could think about was how incredibly sexy he looked with no shirt on. One minute we were having a perfectly normal conversation. The next thing I knew I was touching his chest, and heaven help me, it felt *sooo* good. Before I knew it we were kissing, and then we were on the hood of his uncle's Thunderbird, bumping and grinding like a couple of horny teenagers. And then…and then…"

"What?"

"I came! Right there on top of the car. Fully clothed. I came harder and faster than I've ever come in my life. And…and he did, too." Raina closed her eyes, shuddering all over again.

Once she'd gotten over the shock of her own unbridled response, she remembered being stunned to realize that she could cause a man like Warrick Mayne—a gorgeous, virile, powerful man who had slept with countless women—to lose control in such a way.

After several moments of silence, Raina uncovered her face and hazarded a glance at her sister. Reese was staring at her, mouth agape.

Humiliated, Raina mumbled resentfully, "There? I've told you the whole sordid story. Are you satisfied?"

"Are *you?*"

Raina frowned. "What's that supposed to mean?"

Reese gave her a gentle, pitying look. "You've been carrying a torch for that man ever since you were ten years old—over half your life, Raina. Now that you've finally had a taste of him, so to speak, was it everything you hoped for? Was it everything you dreamed it would be?"

Dumbfounded, Raina stared at her sister. "You…*knew?*"

Reese burst out laughing. "What a question! Of course I knew. Come on, Raina, you know you've never been able to hide anything from me. Even if you *hadn't* walked in here tonight wearing the incriminating evidence, I would have known something was different about you."

Raina's frown deepened. She had never told anyone about her feelings for Warrick. Not even Reese, with whom she had always been close. But apparently that didn't matter. Reese had figured out her sister's secret all on her own. And although Raina knew she shouldn't be surprised, she was.

She glared accusingly at Reese. "Did you read my diary?"

Reese snorted. "Girl, please. I had better things to do than snoop in my kid sister's diary. Besides, I didn't have to *read* anything. The look on your face every time Warrick was around told me all I ever needed to know."

Raina scowled. "What look? I never had a look."

"Oh, yes, you did." Reese grinned. "You tried to hide it as much as possible, and you were very convincing, for the most part. But you couldn't keep up the charade all the time. And, really, who could expect you to? You were just a little girl. Whenever you thought no one else was looking, you would stare at Warrick with such adoration, such admiration, such unrequited *longing.*" She snickered. "I didn't know whether to laugh at you or feel sorry for you."

"Gee, thanks, sis," Raina muttered darkly.

"Oh, hush. At least I never teased you about it. And I never told anyone else what I knew. I could have, you know. I could have told my friends, or Mom and Dad. I went to high school with Warrick and cheered at his basketball games, and I could have told him at any time that my little sister had the hots for him. But I never did. I didn't want to embarrass you, and I figured he already had enough girls making fools of themselves over him. He certainly didn't need another groupie, especially one who was barely in a training bra." Reese grinned. "Besides, I didn't want Deniece Labelle trying to kick your ass. Everyone knew that chick was crazy!"

Raina couldn't help laughing. "I know that's right!"

Returning to her sun-dried tomatoes, Reese said wryly, "But even if I hadn't caught you making puppy eyes at Warrick, I still would have been suspicious of you."

"Why?" Raina asked, though she wasn't sure she wanted to know.

"For starters, you always wanted to hang out over at Yolanda's house. Even though you knew Mom and Dad had concerns about the safety of their neighborhood, you somehow convinced them to let you spend all that time over there. I guess it didn't hurt that they liked Randall, and because he was a cop, they took him at his word when he reassured them that the neighborhood was regularly patrolled by the police."

"It was," Raina interjected.

"Maybe so, but at the risk of sounding like a snob, Raina, it was still the projects. There could only be one reason you preferred to hang out over there instead of your own clean, *safe* neighborhood with a lovely park and community swimming pool, and that reason had nothing to do with not wanting to hurt Yolanda's feelings. Oh, that might have been your reason at first," Reese said when Raina opened her mouth to protest, "but we both know that over time you stopped worrying about that. In fact, I seem to remember Yolanda wanting to hang out at *our* house more often."

Raina grimaced. "Yeah, at first. But she got bored too easily. She always complained that our neighborhood was too quiet and the kids were corny and too uptight. No one played loud music or sat on their porches gossiping and watching cars drive by to see who had a new ride. The girls didn't jump double Dutch or sit around braiding each other's hair, and there were no basketball courts to watch the fellas playing with their shirts off." She sighed, remembering how often she had watched Warrick running up and down the court, his muscles rippling and glistening in the sun, his teeth flashing strong and white against his beautiful dark skin as he laughed and taunted his opponents. How many times had she fantasized about what it would be like to touch him, to press her hand against the smooth, solid warmth of his chest and feel the pounding rhythm of his heart, the way she had done today?

Shoving aside the memory, Raina continued, "Anyway, after a while I got tired of hearing Yolanda's complaints, so it was easier just to hang out at her place."

"How convenient for you," Reese said with a knowing smile. "Just as it was convenient for you that we only had one car, and since Dad always had to work late and Mom didn't drive, Warrick usually had to bring you home. Oh, you used to be floating on cloud nine after he dropped you off. You'd hardly say three words to me or Mom before you ran to your room to scribble furiously in your diary." Reese chuckled, dumping the chopped tomatoes into a large glass bowl. "I think the day I got my driver's license and Dad bought me a car was probably the worst day of your life, Raina. You knew it meant no more rides home with Prince Charming."

Raina gave her sister a surly grin. "I was hoping you would think I was just jealous of you being able to drive before me."

Reese laughed. "I knew better. Just as I knew that the only reason you wanted to attend all those high-school basketball games was not to watch me cheering on the sidelines, but to watch Warrick play. And even if Yolanda hadn't always invited you, I know you would have found a way to be at all their family events—the backyard cookouts and picnics at the beach, Warrick's birthday and graduation parties. Wherever he was, you were never too far behind." She shook her head, efficiently chopping black olives. "If Mom and Dad had ever suspected what was going on, you would have seen *a lot* less of Yolanda, I can tell you that. I mean, Warrick was six years older than you, Raina. If he'd been a different type of guy—a pervert—he could've tried to take advantage of you. But lucky for you, he barely knew you existed."

"Lucky me," Raina murmured broodingly.

Her sister looked up at her, her gaze softening. "Do you want to know when I realized that your feelings for Warrick went deeper than a childhood crush?" she asked quietly.

Raina hesitated, then nodded reluctantly.

"It was when you decided to remain friends with Yolanda, even after you realized she was just using you. And don't look at me like that. We've been over this before, Raina, and I know how painful it was for you to finally accept the truth about your friendship with Yolanda. You helped her with her schoolwork so she wouldn't fail all her classes. You bought things for her even though you barely had a part-time job yourself. You were the mediator whenever she started running off at the mouth to older girls at school, girls who would've stomped her behind if you hadn't stepped in. Hell, Raina, you even did her chores sometimes. You were the mature, responsible friend, the good girl who never got into any trouble. As long as Yolanda said she was with you, no one would ever think she was up to no good. And she knew that. How many times did you cover for her when she told her mother she was spending the night at our house, when in reality she was over at some boy's place? And how many times did you lie to her boyfriends just to help her keep her stories straight?"

Raina frowned. "Our friendship wasn't always as one-sided as what you're describing, Reese. Things didn't change between me and Yolanda until we got to high school, and everyone used to say that was perfectly normal. If you're suggesting that I put up with her nonsense just because I liked Warrick—"

"What I'm suggesting, baby sister, is that you put up with it because you *loved,* not liked, Warrick. And no matter how badly Yolanda treated you, you wanted to believe the best of her. Not because of who *she* was, but because of who *he* was. Because you had Warrick on a pedestal, you rationalized that anyone related to him had to have at least some of the qualities that made him so special to you. You gave Yolanda the benefit of the doubt even when she no longer deserved it. Even when she became an accomplice to an armed robbery, then expected you to cover for her just as you'd always done."

Raina swallowed hard, the painful memories rushing to the surface of her mind. During their senior year in high school, Yolanda and her boyfriend Tate had held up a convenience store and accidentally shot the clerk, leaving the man permanently paralyzed. Evidence collected at the crime scene had led the police to Yolanda and Tate within days. Although both had claimed their innocence, they were arrested and charged with the crime. While Tate had priors, which all but ensured his conviction, Yolanda had never been in trouble with the law before. During her trial, the prosecution had portrayed her as an impressionable young woman who'd succumbed to the pressure of trying to please her boyfriend. But the state's case against her had hinged on Raina's testimony.

As far as Yolanda was concerned, Raina, as her best friend, was supposed to uphold the story Yolanda had concocted. Raina was supposed to be her alibi.

But Yolanda *hadn't* attended the senior-class party with Raina, and Raina's conscience wouldn't allow her to perpetuate her best friend's lie, especially since an innocent man had nearly died. Once Yolanda realized that Raina intended to tell the truth, she'd told her family that Raina was lying because she was jealous of Yolanda's relationship with Tate. And they'd believed her.

When no other students from the party came forward to corroborate or refute Yolanda's story, it came down to Raina's word against her best friend's. The jury had decided that Raina—a straight-A student whose father was a pillar of the community—was more credible.

Damn it. She didn't want to think about this, not now. Not ever. She'd spent the last twelve years trying to outrun the past, trying to make herself forget. But ever since Warrick's return, she'd been repeatedly forced to go back to that dark, devastating period in her life.

"When you were testifying that day in court," Reese continued quietly, "it wasn't Yolanda you were looking at. It was Warrick. And when you whispered *I'm sorry,* I must have been the only one in that courtroom who knew you were apologizing to Warrick, not his sister."

Raina fell silent. Even if she'd wanted to speak, the constriction in her throat made it difficult.

"I don't want to see you hurt again," Reese said gently. "Warrick Mayne can hurt you in a way no one else can."

Raina's chest tightened. With a supreme effort, she raised her chin and plastered a brave smile on her face. "You don't have to worry about me, Reese. I let my hormones get the best of me today, but believe me, it won't happen again. I'm not in love with Warrick anymore. I'm over him. Really."

Reese gave her sister a long, measuring look, letting the words hang in the air between them, as thick and palpable as the scent of the casserole wafting from the oven.

After another moment Reese sighed and shook her head mournfully. "Poor Bradford."

Raina's smile faltered. "What do you mean?"

"Well, just when I thought I'd finally found the perfect guy for you, someone who could compete with the legend of Warrick, this—" Reese gestured in the direction of Raina's backside, "had to happen. *He* had to come back."

Raina choked out a laugh. "What happened between me and Warrick has no bearing on what may—or may not—happen between me and Bradford."

"No? Then how do you explain the fact that you haven't returned any of Bradford's calls today? He told me you guys had a great time at dinner last night, and he was hoping to set up another date with you, but you haven't called him back yet."

"I haven't had a chance," Raina said defensively. "In case you've forgotten, I have a business to run. I get a little swamped. I should think a busy pediatrician like Bradford would understand that."

Reese arched a brow. "Being swamped didn't stop you from leaving early to go check out Randall Mayne's toy collection. And it sure as hell didn't stop you from having your little afternoon tryst with Warrick."

Raina opened her mouth to protest, then snapped it shut. What could she say? Her sister was right, and she knew it. They *both* knew it.

Reese sighed. "Look, I know you work hard seven days a week," she said in a conciliatory tone. "You're more than entitled to cut out early anytime you want. I guess I'm just saying that if you don't like Bradford, just say so. You don't have to make excuses."

"I do like Bradford," Raina insisted. "He's a really nice guy, and we *did* have a great time last night."

Reese eyed her warily. "But?"

"Well..." Raina hedged, trying to think of a diplomatic way to phrase her objection to Bradford Torrance. The longer she stalled, the more impatient Reese became.

"Oh, for God's sake, Raina," she finally snapped. "Just say it."

"He's a cheapskate!" Raina blurted.

"What?"

Raina groaned. "I didn't want to tell you, Reesey, but I guess it bothered me more than I realized. Bradford didn't want to pay for dinner. Or, rather, he only wanted to pay for his half."

"You mean you went...*dutch?*" Reese sounded so scandalized that Raina burst out laughing.

Her sister was not amused. "Girl, please tell me you're joking."

Raina shook her head, gasping for breath. "I thought it was just me!"

"Definitely not."

Wiping tears of mirth from her eyes, Raina said, "Don't get me wrong. You know I'm as independent as the next woman. I understand that this is the twenty-first century, and I definitely make enough money to pay for my own dinner. But it's the principle of the thing. I mean, going dutch is something that should be discussed and agreed upon beforehand. I don't think a man should ever just assume that his companion is okay with it. *Not* on the first date, and certainly *not* when that man is a doctor!"

"I know that's right," Reese muttered, still visibly appalled. "I don't know what the hell Bradford was thinking."

Raina chuckled. "I honestly believe he didn't see anything wrong with it." She paused, mouth twitching. "He also didn't want to pay for valet parking, which would've been fine if it hadn't taken him nearly thirty minutes to get out of the damned parking garage."

"Oh, God." Reese shuddered, shaking her head in disbelief. "I'm gonna have to have a little talk with him."

"Please don't," Raina said vigorously. "I don't want him to be embarrassed. Really. He's a terrific guy, Reese, just like you always told me. It's not his fault that his, er, frugality, put a slight damper on our evening."

Reese looked hopeful. "So does that mean you'd go out with him again?"

Raina hesitated, then answered truthfully, "I'd consider it. Like I said, we had a great time, for the most part."

"Wonderful!"

"Why?" Suddenly Raina was suspicious. "Wait a minute. I just realized something. It's almost seven. Why isn't dinner ready yet? We always eat promptly at six-thirty so you can be in bed by nine. And, hey, did you wear that dress to the hosp…" Trailing off, her eyes narrowed on her sister's face. "What's going on, Reese?"

Reese assiduously avoided her gaze as she carried the salad to the refrigerator. "There's been a change of plans. We're eating at seven-thirty tonight. And, uh, we're having company."

"Who?"

"Since he couldn't get in touch with you today, I sort of took the liberty of inviting Bradford to join us for dinner."

"You did what!"

"Before you say anything else," her sister hastened to add, "I also invited someone else from the hospital. I didn't want him to think I was asking him out on a date, so I made it seem like more of a casual get-together with friends. You and Bradford are the buffers."

As comprehension dawned, Raina's eyes widened. "Oh my God. You invited *Dr. Carracci?*"

"Yep." Reese grinned mischievously. "Remember what I told you about the nurse's husband proposing to her after she made him gnocchi *di* ricotta?" At Raina's nod, Reese said, "Well, I'm not looking for a marriage proposal—been there, done that. But if all goes according to plan, before this day is over, you won't be the only one who had a little bumping and grinding action!"

Speechless, Raina gaped at her older sister. A moment later they both burst into laughter.

They were still giggling hysterically when the doorbell rang.

They froze, staring at each other.

"They're early!" Reese cried, stricken. "I haven't set the table or put the garlic bread in the oven yet."

As the two women erupted into a flurry of activity, Reese looked over at Raina and gasped. "Oh, no! Your jeans!"

Damn. Raina had nearly forgotten about Warrick's handprints. Greeting Bradford with another man's prints all over her rear end probably wasn't the best way to start a possible relationship.

Reese said, "Quick! Run upstairs and find something in my closet to put on."

Raina was halfway up the staircase when her sister, walking to the front door, said, "Oh, and Raina?"

Raina glanced over her shoulder.

Reese's lips were twitching with wry humor. "The next time you're going to see Warrick, do yourself a favor. *Don't wear white!*"

Chapter 8

Bright and early the next morning, Raina headed to the spa intending to make a dent in the mounting pile of paperwork on her desk. She had payroll to do, contracts and invoices to review, and a proposal to prepare for a client who wanted to host her bridal shower at the spa next month. She also needed to work on a marketing plan for an upcoming business venture she was excited about. While Raina currently enjoyed partnerships with several top-tier bath and beauty product lines, one of her future goals was to launch her own line of all-natural spa merchandise. To that end, she had recently assembled a product development and market research team that included several clinicians and alternative health practitioners she'd frequently consulted since opening Touch of Heaven. She hoped to have the first draft of the marketing plan completed by the end of summer.

As she drove to the spa that morning, Raina looked forward to immersing herself in work. She was happiest when she was tending to the needs of her business and interacting with customers. And now, more than ever, she needed to occupy her mind with something other than thoughts of Warrick and painful memories from the past.

But the moment she entered the building, she was brought up

short by the sight of two of her massage therapists and the receptionist huddled around the front desk talking. That alone didn't bother Raina. The spa wouldn't open for another hour, and she was used to seeing her staff congregated around the reception desk drinking coffee and gossiping about everything from their weekend plans to the latest celebrity scandals. But judging by the hushed, agitated tone of their voices that morning, what they were discussing had nothing to do with visiting a new nightclub or speculating about which actor had jilted his wife for another woman.

When Raina heard her own name, she felt a whisper of foreboding. Juggling her purse, briefcase and a large box of glazed doughnuts, she stepped farther into the lobby and called out, "Good morning, everyone."

Three pairs of eyes swung in her direction. Instead of the cheerful chorus of "Good morning, boss!" that usually greeted her—especially when she was bearing goodies—Raina encountered three tense, grim expressions.

Uh-oh.

"What's going on, guys?" she asked warily as she approached the desk.

Trey Sutton, a feisty, attractive, brown-skinned man in his late twenties who was the only male employed at the spa, spoke up first. "Have you read the *Ledger* this morning?" he demanded.

Raina frowned, thinking, *That tabloid rag that tries to pass itself off as a newspaper? The publication that thrives on sensationalism and takes the meaning of yellow journalism to a disgusting new level? The paper that employs the likes of Deniece Labelle?*

She refrained from saying those things, answering neutrally, "I don't read the *Houston Ledger*. I prefer the *Chronicle*."

Trey snorted, trading glances with the others. "Well, after today you definitely won't ever read the *Ledger* again."

Raina frowned, the sense of foreboding tightening in her stomach. "Why?"

"There's an article about the spa in today's issue," said Alisa Alvarez, a stocky, middle-aged Hispanic woman.

"And it's *not* very flattering." Hand planted on his narrow hip, Trey glared accusingly at Raina. "Honey, why didn't you tell us you'd been approached about selling the business? Don't you think that's something we should have heard from *you* instead of some sleazy reporter?"

Raina grimaced as she set the bakery box on the reception desk and opened it, gratified when Nikki and Alisa each snagged a glazed doughnut.

"I'm sorry about that," Raina said contritely. "I was going to tell you guys at our staff meeting on Friday. I wanted to let everyone know at the same time and answer any questions you might have. I'm sorry you had to find out this way. But let me just assure you up front that I have no intention whatsoever of selling the spa."

Trey grumbled, "Well, that's pretty much what the article says. But it's *how* it was said that pissed us off." Snapping open the newspaper, he began reading aloud.

> "The only obstacle to the construction of the sprawling new office complex that could easily become one of Houston's most recognizable landmarks is a day spa owned and operated by Raina St. James. Touch of Heaven Day Spa, obscurely located on the outskirts of Uptown Park, opened two years ago with modest fanfare. Since then, it has struggled to compete with better-established spas in the area. While it appears that St. James does not appreciate the many benefits of having Mayne Industries headquartered in Houston, others in the community feel differently. Several local business owners beleaguered by the sagging economy believe that Mayne Industries' expansion will not only have a positive impact on the city, but will create a windfall effect for their establishments by stimulating economic growth in the community. They expressed optimism that Raina St. James, a Houston native, would not put her own needs above the greater needs of the community. St. James could not be reached for comment."

By the time Trey had finished reading, Raina was seething with fury. "Let me see that," she snapped, snatching the newspaper out of Trey's hand.

She skimmed the page, searching for the article's byline. When her gaze landed on Deniece Labelle's name, another surge of rage swept through her. She should have known Warrick would sic his old girlfriend on her, shamelessly using her to do his dirty work. And no doubt Deniece, who had always hated Raina, had been only too willing to do Warrick's bidding. Raina could just imagine the two of them lying in bed together, plotting ways to humiliate her and force her out of business. Warrick had probably been laughing at Raina the entire time he was kissing her yesterday.

"Asshole," she hissed under her breath, her jaw clenched so hard her back teeth hurt. She felt like such a fool!

"Not only does that article make you sound selfish and insensitive, Raina," Trey complained bitterly, "but it makes the spa sound like some bootleg operation that serves no purpose in the community. I've got news for Miss Thang Reporter. We've done *a lot* of good things in this community!" He ticked them off on his long, elegant fingers. "We've provided complimentary massages and facials to women from local homeless shelters, we've offered free health screenings and wellness workshops, we've given free maternity massages to the pregnant wives of soldiers fighting in Iraq, we *always* donate our spa products—which ain't cheap!—and we participate in community fundraisers and charity events all the time. Not to mention that our prices are very reasonable, even though each and every one of us is talented enough to command much higher rates. There's a reason we're often booked three weeks in advance—because we're damned good! Furthermore," he fumed, pointing angrily at the wall behind the reception desk, where several plaques and certificates were displayed, "we sure as hell didn't get all those awards and accolades for being 'obscure' or mediocre!"

When he had finished speaking, Nikki and Alisa cheered and clapped loudly in approval. Even Raina smiled a little, her own temper cooling slightly in the face of such fierce loyalty.

"Thank you, Trey," she murmured. "I can't tell you enough how much I appreciate your support. That goes for all of you."

Trey impatiently waved off the gratitude. "Honey, you don't have to thank us! You've got a good thing going here, and I'll be damned if I let some no-talent hack who can't even cut it at a real newspaper try to run you out of business. Deniece Labelle didn't even *try* to appear objective in that one-sided piece of trash she called an article. After devoting several paragraphs to how *wonderful* Mayne

Industries is, how *wonderful* Warrick Mayne is and how *wonderful* the company will be for Houston, she couldn't find *one* good thing to say about Touch of Heaven. Talk about media bias!" He shook his head in patent disgust.

Scanning the lengthy article, Raina said grimly, "You won't get any argument from me about Deniece Labelle's appalling lack of journalistic integrity, but I'm afraid she may be right about one thing. The economy is still in a slump, unfortunately, and not every business in this area has been doing as well as we have. I've already gotten an earful from Tyler Ralston, one of the owners of Ralston Development. I know there are plenty of people like him who will want to see Mayne Industries relocate its headquarters to this area. Thanks to this article, I'm probably going to start coming under a lot of pressure to sell."

"It's already starting," Nikki said, looking apologetic. "When I came in this morning, there were already two voice-mail messages from people who had read the article and wanted to urge you to reconsider your decision not to sell. And, um, that was me paraphrasing. They weren't as polite as that."

Raina scowled. "Great," she muttered under her breath. Just what she needed: more threats. First from Warrick, then Tyler Ralston, and now perfect strangers were calling to harass her.

"They can't pressure you into selling!" Trey cried, outraged. "We have to do something about this." He snapped his fingers. "I know! Maybe we can get someone at the *Chronicle* to write some sort of rebuttal to this story. An article that gives *your* perspective, Raina, and lets people know how much the spa has done for the community. Don't you have contacts at the *Chronicle*?"

"Several," Raina said wryly. "But given the local media's ongoing love affair with Warrick Mayne, I'd probably be hard pressed to find any editor willing to print a negative word about him, even if they're a little peeved with him for letting another paper break the story about his company's expansion plans."

Trey sucked his teeth. "*They're* peeved with him? I'm livid! I always thought so highly of that brother. Hell, I defended him when some of my friends from L.A. were saying he did that little actress wrong. What was her name again?"

"Simone Persia Fox?" Nikki helpfully supplied.

"Yeah, her! They were saying how Warrick Mayne strung her along, had her ready to give up her acting career and move all the way to Philadelphia just to be with him. He made her think he was ready to settle down with her. And then he changed his mind, broke that child's heart and had her head all messed up. You see she ain't been in any movies ever since the breakup, and that was two years ago!"

Nikki snickered. "The reason she ain't doing any more movies is 'cause that chick can't act!"

Alisa chortled, nodding in agreement.

Trey made a face. "Maybe so, but I still defended that brother when my friends were badmouthing him, saying how he played poor Simone."

"You defended him because you think he's hot," Alisa reminded him.

Trey scowled at her. "Well, I don't care how hot he is, or how much money he has. He can't just show up out of the blue one day and expect people to hand over their properties to him, no questions asked. It doesn't work that way! Ain't that right, boss?"

"Hmm?" Raina had only been half listening to the spirited exchange between her employees. She'd heard all the sordid stories about Warrick's high-profile breakups over the years. She'd stopped caring a long time ago.

Or so she told herself.

"We need to get support from the community," she murmured, thinking aloud, steering the conversation back on track. "It's safe to assume Warrick's already got the media in his corner. Maybe we can get the support of some community leaders and activists who are known for championing the cause of small businesses."

"That's a great idea!" Trey, Nikki and Alisa chorused in unison.

Raina chuckled. "Then it's unanimous. That's what we'll do."

"Do you have anyone in mind?" Trey asked hopefully, relishing the idea of a fight.

Raina pursed her lips, then nodded briskly. "Actually, I do. City Councilman Bonner. He's an old friend of the family. He always told me to give him a call if I ever need any favors."

Trey grinned. "Well, honey, you'd better get on that phone and start calling in those favors!"

"Better yet," Raina said decisively, "I'll pay him a visit."

* * *

When Raina arrived at Dwight Bonner's plush downtown law firm an hour later, his secretary informed her that the councilman was in his office with a visitor.

"I'll wait," Raina told the woman.

She sat in one of the visitor chairs, crossed her legs and grabbed a magazine to flip through while she waited.

After fifteen minutes a door opened, and the rumble of male laughter spilled into the corridor.

Raina froze.

She recognized one of those voices. A deep, dark timbre she would have known anywhere.

Her heart sank.

Warrick. He'd gotten to Councilman Bonner before she could. *Damn it!*

As the voices drew nearer, she thought about bolting. But it was too late.

Warrick and Dwight Bonner appeared in the reception area, laughing and talking like a pair of old friends. Raina ducked her head, pretending to become absorbed in the magazine, hoping and praying Warrick would leave without noticing her.

"It was great to see you again, Warrick," the councilman was saying. "I'll have my secretary get in touch with Mabel to set up a tee time next week."

Golf? Raina thought in exasperation. *They're playing golf together?*

"Sounds good," Warrick drawled, a smile in his voice. "I'm afraid my golf game isn't up to par yet, so you'll have to go easy on me."

"Yeah, like you'd go easy on me if we were on the basketball court."

The two men chuckled good-naturedly.

"Mr. Bonner, you have a visitor," the secretary announced, looking across the reception area at Raina. "I'm sorry, I didn't get your name, Miss—"

"St. James," Raina supplied, setting aside the magazine and rising. Deliberately ignoring Warrick—no easy feat, admittedly—she focused her attention on the short, gray-haired man standing beside him. "Hello, Councilman Bonner."

When Dwight Bonner turned and looked at Raina, his eyes widened in surprise and his smile wavered. He looked guiltier than a minister caught stealing money from an offering plate. Raina would have laughed if there were anything remotely amusing about the situation.

"Why, hello, Raina!" the councilman said, recovering his composure. He strode toward her, clasping both her hands and kissing her upturned cheek. "You know it's always a pleasure to see you."

Except when you're consorting with the enemy!

Shoving aside the uncharitable thought, Raina summoned a smile of genuine warmth. "I apologize for not calling first—"

"Nonsense! I've known you since you were a little girl. You don't have to call before stopping by for a visit." Glancing over his shoulder, Bonner cleared his throat discreetly. "And, ah, speaking of someone else who has known you since you were little. Of course you and Warrick remember each other."

He stepped aside, leaving Raina no choice but to acknowledge Warrick. He was already watching her, a knowing glint in his dark eyes, a ghost of a smile on his lips.

"Hello, Raina," he murmured.

"Mr. Mayne," Raina said in a voice frosty enough to freeze water. She raked him with a scathing glance, looking him over as if he were covered in dung instead of the finest Italian silk.

Then, before he could react, she cut her eyes away, coldly dismissing him as she smiled at Dwight Bonner. "I was wondering if I could have a few minutes of your time," she said smoothly.

"Of course, of course. Let me just say goodbye to Warrick."

As Bonner turned and shook Warrick's hand, his eyes communicated a silent apology that got under Raina's skin. She didn't know whether Bonner was apologizing for her rudeness to Warrick, or the fact that he felt obligated to give her an audience. Neither bode well for the outcome of her meeting with the councilman.

Before leaving, Warrick nodded coolly at Raina. "Be seeing you around," he murmured, his words both a promise and a threat.

Raina gave him a bored look, stopping just short of yawning before turning her back on him and walking away with Councilman Bonner.

Twenty minutes later, Raina emerged from the law firm with the bitter taste of defeat in her mouth.

Just as she'd feared, Dwight Bonner would be of no help to her in her mission to retain her property. Even if she'd had any hope of receiving his support after seeing how chummy he and Warrick were, that hope had been dashed the moment she'd stepped into the councilman's office and had seen, prominently displayed on the wall behind his desk, a framed poster of twenty-one-year-old Warrick suspended in midair as he took the game-winning shot that had helped his team clinch the NCAA championship. It was clear that Bonner was a longtime fan of Warrick's, and as such, he wouldn't stand in the way of Warrick's construction project.

To his credit, Bonner had backed up his decision with what he called "hard, cold facts." He'd given Raina the same talking points she'd already heard from Tyler Ralston, the same talking points recited in that morning's *Ledger* article: a Houston-based Mayne Industries would stimulate economic growth and development, create more jobs and help recruit major corporations. Additionally, the company's minority internship program would provide scholarships and valuable training opportunities to local college students. Councilman Bonner—unlike Tyler Ralston and Deniece Labelle—had stopped short of telling Raina that her spa couldn't begin to compete with the level of benefits that Warrick's firm would bring to the community.

In a gentle, fatherly tone, he instead had cautioned her against waging a long, bitter battle with Warrick, a battle he believed she would ultimately lose.

There was little more Raina could say after that. So she'd left.

As she strode across the parking lot, she rummaged in her handbag for her car keys and thought of how disappointed Trey, Nikki and Alisa would be when she returned to the spa and told them how the meeting with Councilman Bonner had gone.

"Raina."

She glanced up, startled to find Warrick leaning casually against the driver's side of his Bentley luxury car, which was parked on the same row as her car, but on the opposite end. He appeared to be waiting for her, his arms folded across his chest, his eyes concealed behind a pair of mirrored sunglasses.

A fresh wave of anger swept through Raina. Deliberately ignoring him, she continued across the parking lot toward her car, hoping he'd take the hint and get lost.

That was asking too much.

By the time she reached her car, Warrick had easily caught up to her with those long, ground-eating strides of his.

"We need to talk," he said.

"No, we don't," Raina snapped, retrieving her keys from her handbag. "We have nothing to say to each other."

"I disagree."

"Ask me if I care!"

"Damn it, Raina. I know you didn't get where you are in business by letting your emotions cloud your judgment."

Raina whirled on him, trembling with fury. "Don't you dare lecture me! I poured blood, sweat and tears into making my business the success that it is. I'll be *damned* if I'll let you waltz in here and take it away from me!"

"I'm not trying to take anything away from you," Warrick growled, impatiently removing his sunglasses, those dark, piercing eyes drilling into hers. "If you would just listen to my business proposal—"

"I don't need to!" Raina shouted. "I've heard more than enough from the people you put up to doing your dirty work. Tyler Ralston was bad enough, Warrick, but siccing your old girlfriend on me was just downright despicable, even for you."

Warrick scowled. "What the hell are you talking about?"

"Oh, please! Don't stand there and pretend you don't know about the smear job that was published this morning by that filthy rag Deniece works for." Raina's lips twisted into a contemptuous sneer. "It must have felt like old times again, Deniece interviewing you for the *Ledger* the way she used to interview you after games for the school paper. I'm sure the two of you had a wonderful time working on the article together, then celebrating afterward with a nice little roll between the sheets. Just like old times, huh, Warrick?"

There was a mocking gleam in his eyes. "What part are you objecting to, Raina?" he drawled sardonically. "The article Deniece wrote, or the way I repaid her afterward?"

Narrowing her eyes, Raina said with withering scorn, "Just when I think you can't sink any lower, you prove me wrong. I guess you can take the boy out of the gutter, but… Well, you get the point."

Warrick smiled, cold and narrow. "That's funny," he said silkily. "I didn't hear you complaining when this gutter boy had his mouth and hands all over you yesterday."

Raina flinched, heat stinging her face. "Go to hell, Warrick," she shot back. "And take that no-class bitch with you."

Shoving a pair of sunglasses onto her face, Raina ducked inside her car and slammed the door. As she sped out of the parking lot, still trembling with outrage, she couldn't help feeling as though she had won a small battle, but would ultimately lose the war.

Chapter 9

Lowering one shoulder, Warrick charged past his uncle and slammed the basketball through the hoop. The metal rim vibrated with the force of the dunk, drawing groans and raucous male laughter around the basketball court.

"Hey, War, why don't you take it easy on the old man?" Xavier Mayne, watching from the sidelines, called out to his brother.

"Yeah, man," chimed in Zeke Mayne. "We're trying to teach these young folks at the community center—which *you* founded, by the way—to respect their elders, not *abuse* them!"

Ignoring his younger brothers' half-serious protests, Warrick retrieved the rebound and said to his uncle, "Sixteen to eight. Had enough yet?"

Randall chuckled. "Nah, I'm just getting warmed up. Best of three."

Warrick shook his head. "Your funeral."

He dribbled the ball in place, waiting as his uncle removed his soaked T-shirt and tossed it off the court. His chest, like Warrick's, glistened with sweat in the summer heat, which was already blistering at eleven-thirty in the morning.

"See, son," Randall said, grinning, "I'm actually doing you a favor."

Warrick snorted, returning to the three-point line. "How're you doing *me* a favor?"

"I'm letting you burn off some steam and take out your frustrations on me."

Warrick scowled. "Who says I'm frustrated?"

Randall's grin widened. "Aren't you?"

"No." Jaw tightly clenched, Warrick advanced on the net, deciding to forgo the easy basket in exchange for rough physical contact. Randall grunted with the effort of blocking the basketball and took an elbow shot to the ribs. Refusing to give way, he stretched his arm above his nephew's head and successfully blocked the shot, then fought for the rebound and scored, drawing a round of applause and cheers from the onlookers.

"Don't forget who taught you how to play this game in the first place," Randall boasted, grinning at Warrick.

"Yeah, yeah, yeah," Warrick muttered. "Stop talking, start playing."

"Why? Because you don't wanna talk about what's been bugging you all morning, ever since you showed up here in a foul mood?"

"I wasn't in a foul mood," Warrick bit off, even as his temper spiked at the memory of his earlier argument with Raina. Her parting words, dripping with icy contempt, reverberated through his brain, taunting and tormenting him. *I guess you can take the boy out of the gutter…*

Warrick didn't know what infuriated him more. The fact that Raina still thought he was somehow inferior to her, or the fact that it still bothered him, after all these years and after all the wealth he had accumulated. What was it about Raina St. James that made him give a damn what she thought?

It shouldn't have bothered him that she'd automatically assumed he'd put Deniece up to writing that article, when in reality, he hadn't known a damn thing about it until Raina had brought it to his attention. Why had he been initially tempted to defend himself? He'd already warned Raina that he didn't play nice, and he'd already vowed to himself that he would show her no mercy when it came to getting what he wanted. Hell, he'd been handling her with kid gloves up to this point. Why should it matter whether she believed he'd conspired with Deniece on an article that maligned her business?

It shouldn't have mattered.

Except it did, damn it.

After the confrontation with Raina at Councilman Bonner's office, Warrick had called Deniece and bluntly demanded to know how she'd learned about his company's expansion plans.

"Baby, you know I can't reveal my sources," Deniece had protested. "That would be unethical. Besides, it's not as if *you* were going to tell me. I can't believe you intended to keep something that big a secret from me!"

Impervious to her wounded tone, Warrick had explained with forced patience, "I didn't want to go public with the story until the sale was finalized. Everyone involved has had to sign a confidentiality agreement. I didn't want to put you in the difficult position of having to choose between your job as a reporter and our friendship."

"I wish you'd told me that before," Deniece had said petulantly. "You know I would have chosen you over my job in a heartbeat! You know how much you've always meant to me, Warrick."

When he'd said nothing, she'd continued imploringly, "Please don't be mad at me, baby. I was only trying to help. And it worked! You won't *believe* how many phone calls and e-mails I've already received from readers who are excited about your company relocating its headquarters to Houston. I've heard from several people who plan to apply for a job at Mayne Industries as soon as the new office complex is open for business. I've even heard from mothers who hope their sons and daughters will get internships with you. *Everyone* is so excited, baby."

"And what about your managing editor?" Warrick had drawled sarcastically. "How excited is he that *you* got the scoop and broke the story before your competitors?"

Deniece had said nothing.

"That's what I thought." His tone had hardened. "Don't use me to advance your career or to settle personal vendettas, Niecy. Trust me, you don't want to play that game with me."

"I was only trying to help," Deniece had said in a small voice, sounding thoroughly chastened. "I thought this was what you'd want. I heard that Raina is playing hardball about selling her property. Based on the way people are already responding to my article, she won't be able to hold out much longer."

"Why don't you let me worry about Raina?" Warrick had suggested, in a milder tone than before. "Believe me, when it comes to competitors playing hardball, I've encountered a lot worse than Raina St. James."

"I know you can handle her. You wouldn't be where you are if you couldn't handle difficult people. Anyway, enough about Little Miss Thang. We've wasted more than enough time talking about her. What're you doing tonight, baby?"

"Hanging out with Xavier and Zeke."

"Oh." Deniece had sounded disappointed. "I was hoping we could get together this evening. I was going to make you dinner, then let you have me for dessert." She had laughed, low and sultry.

Warrick had felt a pang of guilt, remembering what his uncle had told him yesterday about Deniece's parents blaming Warrick for their daughter not being married. *Don't start something you can't finish,* Randall had warned.

When Warrick hadn't respond to her provocative invitation, Deniece had heaved a pouty sigh. "All right. I suppose I can give you a rain check so you can hang out with the fellas tonight. But while you're out partying on the town and meeting all kinds of women—'cause I know that's what you boys do—let me just leave you with some food for thought. I bought a new negligee yesterday, and just to give you an idea of how skimpy it is, I nearly threw it away with the receipt because I almost didn't see it. Oh, and did I mention it's edible?"

Warrick couldn't help chuckling softly. "I'm sure that thought will cross my mind once or twice while I'm out tonight."

"Well, if you change your mind about dinner," Deniece had purred seductively, "me—and the negligee—will be waiting."

Warrick had hung up the phone smiling. But his good humor hadn't lasted, and by the time he'd reached his temporary office downtown, his thoughts were once again dominated by Raina. He had sat through an hour-long videoconference with a team of his engineers, who'd eagerly updated him on the status of the vaporization project he'd commissioned. Warrick had jotted down notes, nodded at the appropriate intervals and asked all the right questions, but afterward he could hardly remember a word that had been said.

Thanks to Deniece's article, he'd been besieged with interview requests from reporters at various newspapers and television stations. Warrick had returned some of the phone calls, then handed off the rest to his media relations director and tried to catch up on some paperwork. But when he found himself unable to concentrate, he'd finally given up and told his secretary he was leaving early. Mabel had raised a surprised brow and asked him if he was feeling okay, clearly wondering if there was something in the Houston air that had made her notorious workaholic of a boss cut out early two days in a row.

Warrick had assured his worried secretary that he was fine and had headed out, silently cursing Raina for tampering with his business. As if it weren't bad enough that she was standing in the way of his construction project. Now she had to wreak havoc on his mental productivity as well?

He was still in a surly mood by the time he'd arrived at the Shawn Mayne Community Center, named in honor of his cousin, who was killed in a drive-by shooting when they were fourteen.

Stepping inside the large building—a building Warrick believed his cousin would have approved of—should have soothed Warrick's temper. But it hadn't.

He was so absorbed in his thoughts that he was caught off guard when his uncle suddenly charged past him and went for the easy layup. More applause erupted around the basketball court.

"*That's* how you school him, Uncle Randall!" Xavier Mayne laughingly called out.

Warrick turned and glared at his brother, who had served as executive director of the community center since it had opened five years ago. "Don't you have some paperwork to do?" he growled.

Xavier just laughed harder and traded a high five with Zeke, who, as the center's athletic director, coordinated all sports and recreation programs and coached the center's youth basketball league during the summers. The brothers, two years apart and in their early thirties, were not quite as tall as Warrick, nor were they as dark-skinned, having their mother's caramel complexion. But they shared their older brother's deep-set dark eyes and good looks, as well as his competitive nature.

"Xay, Zeke." When his brothers glanced over at him, Warrick said, "Y'all are up next. Twenty-one. I'll even spot you ten points."

Zeke grinned cockily. "It's on, man! And we don't need your ten points."

Xavier, for once, didn't look as confident.

Randall chuckled. "Don't take out your frustration on your brothers," he said to Warrick. "It's not their fault some woman's got you tied up in knots."

Warrick scowled. Lunging forward, he swiped the ball from his uncle and jumped up to make a basket. There was a smattering of applause from the young boys gathered around the court, whose loyalties were divided between their two heroes: Warrick, the former college basketball star and founder of the community center, and Randall, the easygoing retired cop who regularly volunteered at the center and gave the kids rides in his cool classic cars.

Randall, for his part, was not impressed by Warrick's steal and resulting score. He had other things on his mind, judging by the knowing look on his face. "You didn't deny what I just said, boy. So it *is* a woman."

Warrick frowned. "Are we having shrink time or playing ball?"

Randall grinned. "I need a time-out," he said abruptly, heading off the court.

Warrick hesitated, then reluctantly followed. He passed the basketball to a young boy as he and several other kids ran onto the court, joined by Zeke.

After shadowboxing with Warrick for a moment, Xavier announced that he was going back inside to do some "real work" since his bossy employer—Warrick—had decided to drop by unexpectedly.

Warrick followed Randall over to the bench where they'd left their towels and bottled water. Each man had always made a practice of keeping a change of clothes in a gym bag stored in the trunk of his car, always prepared for an impromptu pickup game.

They reclined on the bench and fell silent for several minutes as they drank from their water bottles and watched Zeke coaching the young players on the basketball court.

Warrick was proud of his younger brothers. After flirting with danger for a few years, Xavier and Zeke had finally resisted the lure of the streets and decided to make something of themselves. Both had attended college, worked hard, and landed good jobs, never expecting any handouts from their successful older brother. Both had been instrumental in the founding of the community center, rightfully earning the high-profile positions they held today.

Without warning, Randall asked Warrick, "What's going on between you and Raina?"

Warrick was so startled by the question that he choked on his water.

Chuckling, Randall reached over and pounded him on the back. "Didn't mean to catch you off guard there, son."

Warrick glared balefully at him. "The hell you didn't," he rasped.

"All right. Maybe I did." Randall grinned. "Answer the question, anyway."

Warrick took another sip of water, ostensibly to soothe his burning throat. What he was really doing was buying time.

Randall waited patiently, a knowing gleam in his eyes.

Finally Warrick muttered, "What makes you think something's going on between me and Raina?"

His uncle laughed. "I may be getting old, War, but I sure as hell ain't blind. I saw the way the two of you were looking at each other yesterday, like you couldn't wait for me to leave so you could jump each other's bones. Hell, why do you think I finally obliged you?"

Warrick stared at him, thunderstruck. "Why didn't you mention any of this yesterday? I was with you the entire evening!"

Randall chuckled. "Sometimes I like to play dumb and wait to see how long it takes you to 'fess up, like I did when you were younger and you thought I didn't know you'd done something you weren't supposed to."

"So what you're saying," Warrick drawled, "is that I shouldn't have kissed Raina?"

"So you *did* kiss her, huh? I suspected as much, the way she went running out of there like a bat outta hell."

Warrick scowled, pretending to take umbrage. "Some women happen to think I'm a good kisser," he grumbled.

Randall smiled. "You know what I meant. I knew by the way Raina took off when I returned to the garage that something serious had happened between the two of you. And I was right."

Warrick stretched out his long legs, his body stirring at the memory of the steamy encounter he and Raina had shared, which now seemed so long ago, like something he'd only dreamed. As it turned out, he'd been dreaming *a lot* about Raina lately. More than he cared to admit—even to himself.

"I can't say I'm surprised about you and Raina," Randall said.

Warrick frowned. "There *is* no me and Raina. We kissed. Doesn't mean we're eloping tomorrow." He paused, then couldn't resist asking, "But why aren't you surprised?"

"Well, she's a very beautiful woman," his uncle said pragmatically. "And one thing you've always appreciated, War, is a beautiful woman."

"That she is," Warrick murmured, remembering the way Raina had looked that morning in a black pencil skirt that molded her lush curves, her long, toned legs accentuated by a pair of four-inch stiletto heels. The combination of the skirt and heels had made Warrick want to drag her into the nearest vacant office, yank her skirt over her thighs and take her against the door. Hard and deep, fast and furious.

He shifted slightly on the bench, no longer surprised by the way his groin tightened at the mere thought of Raina.

Raina, who'd been ten years old the first time he ever laid eyes on her.

Raina, whom he'd never seen as anything more than his kid sister's best friend.

Glancing over at his uncle, Warrick said very casually, "You know, Deniece told me something interesting the other night over dinner. She said Raina had a crush on me when we were growing up." He paused, gauging his uncle's reaction. "Do you think that was true?"

Randall looked at him sideways, his eyes shrewd and assessing. "Now, what would you do with that kind of information?" he demanded.

Warrick frowned. "What do you mean?"

"Why do you suddenly care whether or not Raina had a crush on you?"

"I don't know. I was just curious."

"Just curious, huh?" Shaking his head, Randall took a swig of water.

Warrick's frown deepened. "Forget I asked," he muttered irritably. "It wasn't important."

"It was important enough for you to ask."

Warrick met his uncle's knowing gaze.

Thankfully, his cell phone chose that exact moment to ring.

Warrick dug it out of the pocket of his sweat shorts and checked the display screen. The caller was a woman he'd met back in Philadelphia two weeks ago. A beautiful, ambitious attorney at a large downtown law firm. They'd met for drinks a few times, but their busy schedules hadn't permitted much more. She'd been calling Warrick nearly every day since he'd arrived in Houston, leaving naughty voice-mail messages that made him chuckle. He was seriously thinking about flying her down to Houston for the weekend. Why not? They were long overdue for a real date, and he wouldn't be back in Philly anytime soon.

Returning the BlackBerry handheld to his pocket, Warrick made a mental note to call the sexy lawyer before he went out with his brothers that evening.

Amused, Randall shook his head at him. "I know what *that* was about."

Warrick chuckled, not even bothering to deny it. His uncle knew him better than anyone else.

Silence lapsed between the two men as they resumed watching the action on the court. Zeke—who, like Warrick, had also played college basketball—was helping a tall, lanky boy work on his jump shot. Warrick, who could already see that the kid had serious potential, made a mental note to talk to his brother later about arranging for the boy to attend Tracy McGrady's summer basketball camp in July. Because the NBA player was a personal friend of Warrick's, Mayne Industries already enjoyed a partnership with the Houston Rockets that awarded deserving students in the Houston area tickets to Rockets basketball games.

One of the reasons Warrick had founded the Shawn Mayne Community Center was to give at-risk youth from the Third Ward a safe haven from the streets—something he and his siblings had never had when they were growing up. The sprawling facility featured two indoor gymnasiums, a fitness center, a dance studio, a racquetball court, two outdoor basketball courts, two tennis courts, an aquatic swimming pool, a baseball field, a large playground and a modern cafeteria that served free breakfast and lunch to the children. But the center's mission was not only to provide clean, spacious facilities and nutritious meals, as well as a plethora of recreational and educational activities. It was there to provide the kids with opportunities they would not otherwise have. Growing up in the Third Ward, Warrick had played basketball against boys who were far more talented than he was, but their potential had never been realized due to a lack of opportunities. Warrick had always vowed that if he ever made it out of the projects, he would never forget those he had left behind.

"About Raina," Randall said suddenly, breaking into Warrick's thoughts.

Warrick looked at him. Something in his uncle's tone warned him a lecture was coming.

He wasn't disappointed.

"I know I was teasing earlier about leaving you and Raina alone in the garage yesterday," Randall said, "but all joking aside, War, I don't want you to hurt that girl. God knows she's been through enough with this family."

Resentment stirred within Warrick. It had been more than twelve years since Yolanda Mayne had been incarcerated. Would Randall ever stop taking Raina's side? What would it take to make him see the truth?

Deciding to overlook his uncle's last comment—at least for now—Warrick said in a deliberately mild voice, "What makes you so sure I would hurt Raina?"

Randall cut him a don't-insult-my-intelligence look. "Apart from the fact that you still blame her for what happened to your sister, which we won't get into at this time, I know for a fact that you're not ready to settle down yet. And any woman who becomes involved with you hoping differently is going to end up getting hurt."

Warrick didn't deny it. He couldn't.

Instead he drawled sardonically, "And you think Raina would hope—want—to settle down with me?"

Randall frowned. "She's not like those shallow models you date—"

Warrick bristled. "Wait a minute!" he protested. "I don't only date models. I date all kinds of women, from all walks of life, and they're not all shallow."

"No?" Randall's voice was heavy with skepticism.

"No," Warrick bit off. "The woman who just called me? She's a partner at a law firm. Smart, funny, likes to read. Definitely not shallow."

Randall quirked a brow. "How's her appetite?"

"I don't know," Warrick said, exasperated. "We haven't gone out to dinner yet. But I can tell she's really down to earth. I don't think she'd sit at a restaurant picking at her food—"

"Salad, you mean."

Warrick opened his mouth, then promptly lost his train of thought and burst out laughing. He couldn't help it. His uncle knew too damned much about him, including Warrick's ongoing quest to find a woman who enjoyed a good meal as much as he did.

As his laughter subsided, Randall said, smiling, "All right, so maybe all of your girlfriends haven't been shallow. But I can guarantee you that none of them have the qualities that make Raina St. James so special."

"How do *you* know?" Warrick challenged.

"Because if one had," Randall said with calm, implacable resolve, "you would already be married by now."

Warrick fell silent. What could he say? He didn't know Raina well enough to judge whether or not she was marrying material, nor did he ever expect that to change. But he was intrigued, in spite of himself, by what Randall had said. Intrigued, and a little shaken. Because if anyone knew what Warrick would want in a prospective wife, his uncle did.

"Raina's a good woman," Randall said quietly, a note of unmistakable pride in his voice. "She's the kind of woman who stands up for what she believes in, even if it costs her friends. She's the kind of woman who makes time for her family. The kind of sister who makes a point of having dinner with her sibling every week, the kind of daughter who calls or visits her parents every day and who still enjoys trips to the hardware store with her old man. God knows she's been more like a daughter to *me* than your cousin Lauren, who allowed her mother to poison her mind with lies about me." He shook his head, his mouth twisting bitterly.

Warrick remained silent, knowing how much his uncle's estrangement from his daughter still hurt and angered him. Lauren Mayne, a twenty-five-year-old aspiring actress living in Los Angeles with her mother, had made it painfully clear to her father that she wanted nothing to do with him. Since her parents' acrimonious divorce when she was five, Lauren had spurned all of Randall's attempts to have a relationship with her. Phone calls were rarely returned, birthday cards were often sent back unopened, gifts were accepted but seldom acknowledged and invitations to visit for the holidays were politely declined. Although Randall still blamed his vindictive ex-wife for turning their daughter against him, he also knew that Lauren, now an adult, could choose to meet him halfway if she really wanted to. Her refusal to do so spoke volumes.

But while Lauren had no use for her father, she apparently didn't feel the same way about her cousin Warrick. When he earned his first million dollars, Lauren was one of the relatives who had crawled out of the woodwork to ask him for money. The first time she'd asked for a loan so that she could attend an elite acting school, promising to pay him back as soon as she "made it big." When Warrick flatly suggested she contact her father—knowing she never would—Lauren had thrown a tantrum and hung up on him. The next time Warrick heard from her, she'd called to beg him to introduce her to an actress he was dating, in the hopes that the woman would introduce Lauren to her agent as well as some Hollywood bigwigs. This time Warrick had not minced words, telling his cousin to go straight to hell and to lose his damned number.

He'd never told his uncle about the phone calls. Warrick saw no reason to confirm Randall's worst fear, which was that his only child had turned out to be nothing more than a spoiled brat who used people for her own selfish gain.

"Yeah, Raina's nothing like Lauren," Randall continued reflectively. "She's got a good head on her shoulders, and a good heart. So don't you go breaking it," he warned, jabbing a finger at Warrick.

Warrick laughed, holding up his hands in mock surrender. "Relax, pops. I'm not interested in Raina like that. And to be honest with you," he added cynically, remembering with renewed anger what Raina had said to him that morning, "I don't think she'd let me get close enough to hurt her, anyway."

"Don't be too sure about that. She still—" Randall broke off abruptly and glanced away.

Warrick frowned, eyeing him curiously. "She still what?"

Randall idly watched as Zeke and his young players left the basketball court and filed into the building, presumably for lunch, before he answered, "She still feels bad about what happened with Yolanda and the rest of the family. Raina's a natural-born peacemaker. I can see her letting down her guard with you in an effort to reach some sort of compromise."

"That would be most helpful," Warrick muttered under his breath.

Randall glanced sharply at him, his lips thinning with displeasure. "Which reminds me. Don't think for one second that I didn't read that article in the *Ledger* this morning. Now, I'd like to think I had as much a hand in raising you as your mother did, so I know good and damned well I didn't raise you to become some ruthless corporate shark who preys on others to get what he wants. I don't care how the *Wall Street Journal* chooses to explain your success. That's not the man you are. So I'm going to give you the benefit of the doubt and assume you had nothing to do with that article—and I use the term loosely—written by your old girlfriend. And since this is the first major business decision you've ever kept from me, for reasons I won't speculate about, I'm also going to assume that you don't have an ulterior motive for choosing the site of Raina's day spa for your new office complex."

"I didn't choose it," Warrick said through gritted teeth. "My area research team did. And I happen to agree with their assessment of that site as the best location for our new headquarters. I make no apologies for that."

"I'm not asking you to," Randall retorted.

"Sure as hell sounded like it," Warrick grumbled.

"Then you need to get your hearing checked, because that's not what I was saying. But since *you* brought up the word, if you feel compelled to apologize, then that should tell you something without me ever having to say a word."

Warrick opened his mouth, then snapped it shut. There was no point in arguing semantics with his uncle. When it came to Raina, there was no getting through to Randall.

Instead of trying, he stood and hitched his chin toward the empty basketball court. "You still owe me another game, old man."

Randall gave him a knowing look. "Still need to blow off some steam?"

"I'm just getting warmed up," Warrick muttered.

Chapter 10

Raina was miserable.

Nothing seemed to be going right in her life.

Her beloved spa was facing the very real threat of a hostile takeover. She'd received a ton of phone calls from people urging her to sell her land to Mayne Industries, and she'd heard pretty much the same thing from every business and community leader she'd contacted for support.

Her employees were worried about job security. That afternoon, Raina had caught one of her massage therapists surfing the Internet for openings at other spas. Trey was sulking and grumbling under his breath about the tragic demise of small businesses in America. Tina looked like she didn't know whether to give Raina a hug, or ask her about the internship for her brother. Thankfully, she did neither.

Before Raina left for the evening, a forlorn Nikki informed her that she'd noticed a decrease in the volume of walk-in appointments that day. At any other time this news wouldn't have generated too much concern, as the massage therapists were usually booked solid in advance and could barely accommodate customers who didn't have reservations. But on a day like today, any news that even *hinted* at profit loss was like sounding a death knell.

Raina was furious with Warrick for waltzing back into her life after twelve years and turning her world upside down in a matter of three days.

So it was downright inconceivable that she could find herself feeling guilty—*guilty!*—about what she'd said to him during their argument that morning. Every time she replayed the words in her mind, a fresh wave of shame engulfed her.

I guess you can take the boy out of the gutter, but... Well, you get the point.

What in the world had possessed her to say something so malicious, so unforgivably condescending, to Warrick? No matter how angry or frustrated she was, there was no justification for the way she'd callously ridiculed the man's background. Warrick could no more control growing up in the projects than she could control being born female. His strength and resilience, his unrelenting determination to overcome the obstacles in his life, were some of the many things Raina had always loved and respected about him. She'd never looked down on him or his family. *Ever.* If anything, she'd admired their closeness, their strong ties to the neighborhood and their ability to turn any occasion into a festive, joyous event where everyone, family and strangers alike, felt welcome.

Never in a million years could Raina have imagined using Warrick's humble upbringing against him. She'd come off sounding like the stuck-up bitch Yolanda Mayne had once called her during a heated argument, for which she'd immediately apologized when she saw the wounded disbelief on her friend's face.

But for months afterward, Raina had wondered if any of Yolanda's siblings—namely Warrick—also believed that she was a snob, one who thought she was better than they were because her father was a doctor and her family lived in a nicer neighborhood.

Judging by the bone-chilling smile Warrick had given her that morning, he clearly hadn't been surprised to hear such contemptible words come out of her mouth. Something in his eyes had told Raina that instead of shocking or even offending him, she'd only reinforced a perception he had about her. A horrible perception.

And for some reason, that made her feel exponentially worse.

Not even her sister's tirade against Warrick could assuage Raina's guilty conscience.

"I can't believe he'd have the audacity to come back here after all these years and try to put you out of business!" Reese ranted when she called Raina that evening on her way home. "Does he have no shame? Haven't he and his family put you through enough?"

"Apparently not," Raina murmured dryly.

"How can you be so calm about this?" Reese shrieked. "You should be furious!"

"Believe me, I am. But I've had a few days to deal with it and get over the initial shock."

"And that's another thing. I can't believe you didn't tell me what was going on, Raina! I had to find out from one of my patients who read the article in the *Ledger*. And don't even get me started on that trifling hussy Deniece. She's always been jealous of you."

Raina snorted. "I don't know why. *She* had Warrick."

"And she can keep him! He's nothing but a low-down snake in the grass. As far as I'm concerned, those two deserve each other. Now we know why he kissed you yesterday, Raina. He was trying to seduce you into giving him what he wanted."

"Obviously," Raina muttered, silently castigating herself for being gullible enough to believe that Warrick, like her, had been swept away by passion.

Reese said angrily, "Now will you believe me when I tell you that Warrick Mayne can only hurt you?"

Raina blew out a deep, shaky breath that burned in her lungs. "Yes."

Hearing the note of resignation in her voice, Reese's tone gentled. "You sound like you could use a hug. And a pint of mint chocolate chip Blue Bell ice cream. I can be at your loft in an hour."

Raina chuckled softly. "Not that the offer doesn't sound tempting—the hug and the ice cream—but I already have plans tonight. You'll be happy to know that Bradford invited me over to his house for dinner, and I accepted."

"Good for you! Bradford is such a nice guy, Raina. Everyone at the hospital really likes him, and you should see the way he is with his patients. Those kids adore him! And I know he feels totally embarrassed about that little stunt he pulled after dinner on Monday night."

"I know," Raina said wryly. "Those were the first words out

of his mouth when he called me today. He apologized profusely and said he made the mistake of thinking I might be one of those ultraindependent women who prefers to go half on everything, like the last woman he dated. I wasted no time setting him straight. But I see *you'd* already done that, even though I asked you not to."

Reese chuckled. "Like I said, Bradford is a nice guy. I couldn't just sit back and let such a simple misunderstanding come between you two. And, hey, since he's cooking dinner for you tonight, at least neither of you has to worry about splitting a bill."

For the first time that day, Raina laughed.

"Anyway," Reese drawled, "I'm glad Bradford is keeping you company tonight, otherwise I would have had to cancel my date."

"You have a date?"

"Don't sound so surprised," Reese said indignantly.

Raina grinned. "Oh, hush. You know very well what I meant. Who are you going out with?"

"Take one guess."

Raina's eyes widened. *"Dr. Carracci?"*

"Yes!"

The two sisters squealed like they'd done as children on Christmas day.

"I knew it!" Raina exclaimed, grinning broadly. "I saw the way he was watching you over dinner last night. He couldn't take his eyes off you, Reesey. How could you have doubted that he's attracted to you?"

"I don't know," Reese said with a muffled groan. "He's just so damned good-looking—"

"No argument there," Raina agreed, thinking of the hunky Italian surgeon with the dark bedroom eyes and sexy accent.

"—and I didn't know whether or not he dates black women," Reese continued. "*I've* certainly never dated outside my race."

"There's a first time for everything," Raina said unequivocally. She cut in front of another car that was moving too slow. "So how did this date come about?"

Reese laughed. "He had me paged, if you can believe it. He was in surgery, but he wanted to make sure he caught me before I left for the day. Girl, when he came out of the O.R. and saw me standing there, he gave me this smile that just melted my insides. And then he asked me out to dinner." She sighed. "It was *so* romantic."

Raina smiled. "Sure sounds like it. Where's he taking you for dinner?"

Reese giggled. Smart, sensible, older and wiser Reese actually *giggled.* "I don't know. He's being so mysterious. He just told me to be ready by eight. When I asked him how I should dress, he said anything I chose would be perfect, because I always look beautiful no matter what." Another dreamy sigh.

Raina grinned. "Listen to you. Who are you and what have you done with my big sister?"

Reese chuckled. "I know. I'm pathetic. And— Oh, crap! I'm running late."

"Where are you?"

"Still at the hospital tying up some loose ends. I have to hurry home and change!"

"Maybe not," Raina drawled humorously. "Dr. Carracci thinks you look beautiful in anything, even the lab coat you're probably wearing right now."

Reese giggled. Again! "I gotta run, girl. You and Bradford have a wonderful time tonight. I want to hear all about it tomorrow."

"I was going to say the same thing to you. And don't stay up too late past your bedtime."

Reese laughed. "What bedtime?" Sobering after a moment, she said gently, "Raina?"

"Hmm?"

"Everything's going to be all right. I promise you that."

Raina managed a tremulous smile. "Thanks, Reesey."

As she got off the phone, she knew she didn't share her sister's optimism. Her life was falling apart before her very eyes, and there seemed to be nothing she could do about it.

Raina frowned, rethinking that sentiment. While she might not be able to control the words and actions of others, she could definitely control her own.

Before she could talk herself out of it, she pulled up the cell phone number she'd programmed into her handheld after contacting Randall Mayne yesterday. She pressed the button, then waited with mounting tension.

One ring. Two. Three—

"Warrick Mayne."

Raina's heart jackknifed. Her throat locked up for several moments.

"Hello?"

"Warrick, this is Raina," she finally blurted.

There was a heavy pause.

"Raina." His voice was about as warm and inviting as an Alaskan glacier.

Taking a deep breath to shore up her courage, Raina forged ahead, "Before you ask, no, I'm not calling to tell you I've changed my mind about your offer. I haven't, and I still think you're a heartless jerk for trying to pressure me into selling. That said, I owe you an apology. What I said to you this morning in the parking lot was inexcusable. I was angry and I lashed out, but I wanted you to know that I've never felt that way about you or your family. You may not believe me, but it's the truth, and I wanted you to know that."

Warrick was silent for so long that Raina wondered whether he'd hung up on her. But a quick glance at her caller display screen confirmed that he was still on the line.

When he finally spoke, his voice was bitingly mocking. "What's the matter, Raina? Can't stand the idea of someone actually thinking you might be a snob?"

Raina bristled. "You can think whatever you want. I don't give a damn."

"Obviously you do, or we wouldn't be having this little conversation."

Her temper flared. He was right, and they both knew it. "Go to hell, Warrick," she snarled.

He chuckled softly. "You told me that already. And yet, I'm still here."

"Surprise, surprise. Not even Satan will take you."

"Looks that way. Make a right at the next street and pull over," he said abruptly.

"Wha—?" Raina's gaze flew to the rearview mirror. She gasped, shocked to discover that Warrick's Bentley was right behind her, smoothly pacing her. How long had he been there? "Are you *following* me?"

"Yeah, Raina," he drawled sarcastically. "Like I really have nothing better to do than follow you around the damned city. Pull over."

"*What?* Why?"

"Because my phone battery's dying and I'd like to continue this conversation."

Raina didn't believe him, but she slowed down anyway and hooked a right at the next turn. It was a deserted, dead-end street marked by a No Thru Traffic sign. Warrick must have known that. He knew the city like the back of his hand.

She drove nearly to the end of the street and parked at the curb. As Warrick pulled in behind her, she climbed out of her car, spoiling for a fight.

Warrick stepped out of his vehicle and strode purposefully toward Raina, his dark, piercing gaze locked on hers. He was in shirtsleeves, his silk tie tugged loose and his shirttail hanging loosely over his pants. It went through her mind how reckless he looked, how dangerously male. How utterly *sexy.*

He came to a stop before her, towering over her, his broad shoulders blocking out the afternoon sunlight. Raina swallowed, her heart hammering wildly. Resisting the sudden urge to shrink back against her car, she held her ground and glared up at him.

"What do you—"

He cupped her face in his big hands, lowered his head and crushed his mouth to hers, cutting off the rest of her question.

Raina gasped.

When her hands jerked up to his chest in protest, he scooped an arm around her waist and drew her firmly closer. A melting warmth rushed through her. She resisted only a moment longer before gliding her arms around his neck and kissing him back with equal fervor, making him groan huskily in approval.

She let out a low moan of pleasure as he parted her lips with his tongue and delved inside, ravishing her mouth, staking his claim. Passion and need and a sharp, splintering ache swelled in her loins.

It didn't matter that they were standing on a public street. It didn't even matter that they were bitter enemies. All that mattered was this moment and the explosive feelings Warrick aroused in her.

As they kissed deeply and feverishly, the late afternoon spun away. From somewhere up the street Raina dimly registered the sounds of downtown traffic. Cars passed by. Music blared through open windows. Horns honked. But all of that seemed far away and disconnected from reality. What *was* real was Warrick's mouth on hers, his tongue tangling sensually with hers, the warm male scent of his body filling her nostrils and her lungs. And, oh yes, he tasted incredible. Hot and sweet, like he'd just eaten a melted chocolate bar. She pressed herself into him, feeling every sinewy muscle of his body, mindlessly grinding her hips against the thick bulge of his erection, greedy for more.

Warrick swore, low and savage, and lifted her off the ground.

When Raina suddenly found her back against the car, sanity returned. As though a bucket of ice water had been thrown in her face, her eyes flew open and her body went rigid with shock.

What the hell was she doing? Had she lost her mind? She was about to have sex with Warrick Mayne in the middle of the street! Wrong man, wrong place!

Raina tore her mouth from his—one of the hardest things she'd ever had to do in her life!—and buried her face in his broad chest, gasping for air. Warrick slowly lowered her to the ground, but he didn't release her. His heart thudded rapidly against her cheek.

Still struggling to catch her breath, Raina slid her arms from around his neck, braced her flattened palms against his chest and tried to shove him away. She would have had about as much luck moving a brick wall. Warrick barely budged.

Nuzzling her throat, he dragged his warm mouth to her ear and whispered, "Don't fight this."

Raina shivered in spite of herself. She didn't know whether he was referring to their powerful attraction, or the inevitability of his acquisition of her land. Neither was what she wanted to hear.

She shoved at him again, harder, and this time he reluctantly stepped back. His eyes were heavy-lidded and black as midnight, glittering with barely restrained lust.

Raina reached down, discreetly tugging at the hem of her form-fitting skirt. Warrick's dark gaze followed the movement and lingered, burning into her as if he could see right through the material.

She frowned. "Warrick."

His eyes lifted to hers, then slowly roamed across her face as if he were seeing her for the very first time. When his hot gaze settled on her lips, her belly quivered.

"You have the most incredible mouth," he said huskily. "I could kiss you all day and night."

Her knees went weak. "*Warrick—*"

"I have a proposition for you," he murmured.

Raina arched a censorious brow at him.

He chuckled, a rough, innately masculine sound. "Not that kind of proposition." He paused. "Unless, that is—"

"No."

His mouth curved in a lazy grin. "I didn't think so."

Again he gazed down at her, looking as if he had suddenly lost his train of thought. Raina would have reminded him, but when he stared at her like that, she could hardly remember her own name. When he reached out and trailed a finger lightly down her cheek, she almost forgot to breathe.

"What did you want to discuss with me yesterday?" he asked softly.

"What?" Raina wondered if she looked as dazed as she felt.

"In the garage. You said you got my number from my uncle because you wanted to discuss something with me. What was it?"

She swallowed with difficulty, wishing he would move back some more. She couldn't think, couldn't function when he was this close to her.

What was this power he had over her?

"It wasn't important," she mumbled, offering a silent apology to Tina's brother.

Warrick shook his head slowly. "I don't believe you."

Raina bristled. "That's *your* problem," she retorted, gratified that her voice didn't tremble. Bolstered by the small victory, she glanced pointedly at her watch and said, "It's getting late, Warrick. I really need—"

His expression darkened. "Why is it that every time I see you, you're rushing off for a hot date?"

Raina let out a strangled laugh. "That is *not* true! And even if it were, how is that any of your business?"

Instead of answering, Warrick reached out and brushed his thumb across her lips, making her pulse quicken. Raina knew she should slap his hand away and tell him to stop touching her, but she couldn't. If she were honest with herself, she would admit that she enjoyed being touched by him. Held by him. Kissed by him. Against her better judgment, and despite the bad blood between them, her body knew what it wanted, and what it wanted was Warrick.

Forgive me, Reese.

"So here's what I'm thinking," Warrick murmured, his dark gaze riveted on her mouth, as potent as his touch. "We can spend the next several days and weeks fighting this thing out, sullying each other's reputations, trying to sway the court of public opinion in our favor. Or…" Slowly his eyes lifted to hers. "We can agree to a compromise."

Raina gave him a wary look. "What sort of compromise?"

"Give me one week to convince you to sell. Let me court you the way I would any other prospective business client."

"The way you courted Ralston Development?" Raina said sardonically. "The elaborate presentation, dinner, drinks?"

Warrick hesitated, his eyes narrowing. "You spoke to Tyler Ralston?"

Raina gave a dry, humorless chuckle. "I wouldn't quite put it that way, since *he* did most of the talking. But, of course, you already knew that."

She looked at him, daring him to deny that he'd asked Tyler Ralston to do his dirty work. When he said nothing, she felt vindicated. And oddly disappointed.

Reese's words drifted through her mind. *Now will you believe me when I tell you that Warrick Mayne can only hurt you?*

Watching the play of emotions flitting across her face, Warrick said softly, "This isn't personal, Raina. It's just business."

"Oh, really?" Raina challenged. "So you're telling me you didn't feel the slightest bit of satisfaction when you found out that the site your research team chose for your company's new headquarters happened to be the site of my day spa?"

He looked at her, a muscle twitching in his jaw.

She waited, one brow arched expectantly.

After another moment he nodded curtly. "You're right. I won't deny it. But believe me, if the team had found a better location, I would've gladly moved on. But they didn't, so here we are."

"Here we are," Raina echoed.

Warrick gave her a knowing look. "If I were any other buyer, would you be giving me such a hard time?"

"Yes," she answered without hesitation, "because I'm not interested in selling."

"How can you know that if you haven't even heard my proposal?"

"I don't need to! I already know how much the spa means to me, and if you would just take the time to find out why, you would understand my reasons for turning down your offer."

Even as the angry words left Raina's mouth, a plan began to formulate in her mind. If she could somehow make Warrick see the true value of her business, then maybe, just maybe, he would withdraw his offer and find another location for his new office complex.

"One week, Raina," Warrick said, his gaze intent on her face. "Give me one week to court you, to wine and dine you and give you the VIP treatment. Let me do what I do whenever I've got my sights on a major contract, or I want to lure a client away from a competitor. I know that doesn't sound right to you, but one thing I've learned in this business is that no matter how good your products and services are, what people remember the most is how they were treated. And in the case of prospective clients, they have to be treated like royalty from the start. You know that. Your customers wouldn't keep coming back to the spa and referring their family and friends if you didn't treat them right."

"Of course not," Raina said with a dry chuckle. "I'm in the service industry. My business revolves around pampering customers."

"Then let me pamper *you,*" Warrick said softly. "You have something I want, Raina. Give me a chance to show you why you should give it to me."

Raina's stomach bottomed out. The look in his eyes made her wonder whether he was still talking about a business transaction, or something else entirely. But then again, that deep, dark voice of his could make the most innocent suggestion sound indecent. And downright irresistible.

"One week," she murmured thoughtfully.

Warrick nodded. "Give yourself one week to entertain my business proposal. Seven days to be courted."

Raina lifted her chin, her eyes narrowed in challenge. "And then what? What happens at the end of the week if my answer is still no?"

Warrick held her gaze for a long moment. "Then I walk away."

"Really?" It was the last thing she'd expected to hear. "You'd walk away? Just like that?"

He nodded slowly. "I wouldn't want to, but I would. I'd ask my research team to go back to the drawing board, and hopefully they'd eventually find a comparable location."

"Why can't you just do that now?" Raina demanded, exasperated.

He looked her in the eye. "Because I don't believe there *is* a comparable location."

Raina said nothing.

"So do we have a deal?" Warrick asked.

Raina hesitated. "On one condition."

One thick black brow sketched upward.

Again she hesitated, biting her bottom lip.

"Name your condition, Raina," Warrick murmured. "Speak now or forever hold your peace."

Odd that he should quote a refrain from a wedding ceremony, when Raina had spent much of her childhood daydreaming about marrying him.

Shoving aside the unsettling memory, she said, "One of my massage therapists has a younger brother who's an engineering major. He's a big fan of yours and would love to do an internship at your company. I know the application deadline has already passed for this year, but I was wondering if you could pass along his resume to your internship coordinator for future—"

Warrick's eyes narrowed on her face. "Is that what you wanted to discuss with me yesterday?"

Raina nodded, and waited for him to mock her for having the nerve to approach him for a favor when she refused to sell her property to him.

But instead he said, "What's his name?"

Surprised, she answered, "Alphonse Deveaux. He's from Saint Croix."

"Is that where he goes to school?"

Raina nodded. "If that's a problem—"

Warrick frowned. "Why would that be a problem? I have engineers working out of refineries all over the Caribbean. Send me Alphonse's résumé first thing tomorrow. After I've had a chance to review it, I'll give him a call."

Raina's eyes widened. "You will? *You'll* call him personally?"

His mouth twitched. "Is that a problem?"

"Of course not! I—I just wasn't expecting you to. I mean, you're the president and CEO and I know you're really busy, so I just figured it would be good enough if you forwarded his resume to the appropriate person and—"

Warrick shook his head, chuckling softly. "That's the difference between you and me, Raina. I've never been afraid to ask for what I want. If the situation were reversed, I would have demanded that *you* not only call Alphonse personally, but that you fly him out to Philadelphia to take a tour of the facilities and to spend a week shadowing one of the company's top engineers."

Raina stared at him. "You...you wouldn't really do that for him, would you?"

"Are you asking me to?"

Her mouth curved in a slow grin. "I'm *demanding* it."

"Then consider it done."

Raina laughed, surprised and delighted. "Alphonse is going to be thrilled! And so is Tina."

"Who's Tina?"

"Alphonse's sister."

"Oh." Warrick smiled. "So do we have a deal?"

Raina nodded, thrusting her hand forward. "Deal."

"Good."

He clasped her hand in his, and their gazes locked as currents of electricity passed between them, igniting Raina's blood, making her flesh tingle.

"One more thing," Warrick murmured, not releasing her.

"Yes?" she whispered.

"I dictate the terms of this...courtship. That means you don't refuse anything I give you, and you don't argue about anywhere I want to take you. Within reason, of course. Understood?"

"All right," Raina said evenly. "But you should know up front that I've never cared for expensive gifts, and while those are undoubtedly appreciated by the high-maintenance models and actresses you date, such gifts would have the opposite effect on me. In other words, Warrick, if I think you're going overboard in trying to bribe me, you might be very disappointed at the end of the week." She smiled sweetly. "Understood?"

Warrick looked at her, his eyes glimmering with amusement and a trace of grudging respect. "Loud and clear," he agreed softly.

"Good." Raina gave her hand a discreet tug, and after another moment he reluctantly released her.

"I can pick you up at eight," he said.

Raina arched a brow at him. "For what?"

"Dinner."

"Tonight?"

"Of course."

Raina shook her head. "Not tonight. I already have plans. Besides, the day's almost over. Let's just start our, ah, courtship tomorrow."

Warrick frowned. "I'd rather start it right away. With dinner this evening."

"Like I said," Raina repeated succinctly, "I already have plans. We can have dinner tomorrow."

"Tonight."

"No, Warrick." She gave him a level gaze. "*Tomorrow.*"

Warrick clenched and unclenched his jaw, looking as if he were trying to determine how far he should push the issue. This was obviously new territory for him. Devastatingly handsome, virile beyond measure, rich and powerful, he'd probably never met a woman who didn't come running at the crook of his finger.

Well, he's in for a rude awakening, Raina thought with satisfaction.

"Warrick?"

He nodded tersely. "Fine. Tomorrow."

Suppressing a triumphant smile, Raina said, "Let me give you my card so you'll know how to reach me."

She opened her car door and leaned across the driver's seat to retrieve a business card from her handbag. "I'm usually at the office all day, from nine until seven, but you can always reach me on my—"

As she straightened from the car and turned, she caught Warrick staring at her butt with a look that could only be described as *ravenous*. Really, there was no other word for it. She half expected him to lick his lips, he was so riveted.

Inwardly she smiled. "Here you go," she murmured, passing him the card.

"Thanks." Warrick hesitated, then held it up to his nose. "It smells good."

Raina laughed softly. "Oh, that was Tina's idea. All of our business cards are scented with one of the various massage oils we use at the spa. It's a great marketing tool. We mail promotional items to local fitness clubs, and you won't believe how many men show up at the spa to make reservations for their wives or girlfriends—or themselves—simply because they liked the way the card smelled."

Warrick smiled lazily. "I can believe it." He passed the card under his nose again, then tucked it inside his pants pocket.

Raina sighed. "Well, I'd better get going so I won't be late for my date. I still need to go home and get ready."

Warrick held the door open for her as she lowered herself into her car. First one leg, and then the other, deliberately letting her skirt ride up far enough to reveal the curve of her bare thigh.

When she glanced up, she saw that Warrick was once again a captive audience, his hooded, dark gaze latched onto her legs.

Men are so predictable, Raina chuckled to herself.

She reached for the door handle, but Warrick held fast. Swallowing a smile, Raina discreetly cleared her throat. He blinked, as if emerging from a trance.

"Thank you," Raina murmured as he closed the door for her. As she turned the key in the ignition, he gestured for her to roll down the window.

"What's up?" she said, smiling up at him, trying not to think about how unbelievably sexy he looked with his shirt untucked, his long legs braced apart, his hands thrust casually into his pockets.

"Don't forget to send the résumé," he reminded her.

"I won't. Tina would kill me if I did."

The corner of his mouth twitched, but he looked distracted. The next words out of his mouth made her realize why.

"How long you been seeing that guy?"

"Bradford?"

"Is that his name?"

Raina nodded. "Actually, I haven't been seeing him that long. Monday night was our first date."

"Looks like you two really hit it off, then."

"We did. I have to thank my sister. She introduced us to each other. She and Bradford work at the same hospital."

"Yeah? So he's a doctor like your old man, huh?"

Raina grinned. "Well, you know what they say. Daughters always want to marry men like their fathers."

"Damn, so it's like that? You're already talking about marrying this guy?"

Raina laughed coyly. "Of course not." Some perverse impulse made her add, "But I can definitely tell you he's the best blind date I've ever had."

Warrick's jaw tightened. "Yeah, well, you might want to let him know you're going to be tied up for the next week," he said brusquely.

"Oh, I'm sure Bradford will understand if we can't get together once or twice over the next few days," Raina said breezily.

"Wrong."

She paused, arching a brow at Warrick. "You intend to take me out for dinner *every* night this week?" She managed to inject enough displeasure into her voice to make Warrick scowl.

"If that's what I decide, yeah," he bit off. "So don't go making any plans with loverboy."

Raina gave him a long, measured look, then shrugged dismissively. "We'll play it by ear."

"Raina." His tone was hard, warning her that there would be hell to pay if she argued.

She huffed out a resigned breath. "All right. If you insist."

"I insist." With a curt nod, Warrick pivoted on his heel and strode toward his car.

Raina leaned out the window and called innocently, "Aren't you going to tell me to have a good time this evening?"

He growled something low and obscene that made Raina buzz up the window, then throw back her head and howl with laughter.

She was still laughing as she drove home, allowing herself to bask in the revelation that Warrick, for reasons unknown, had actually been jealous of her relationship with another man.

Chapter 11

At eleven-thirty the next morning, Raina had just hung up the phone with a vendor when Tina Deveaux came bursting into her office, squealing with excitement.

Raina stared at her. "What's going—"

The rest of her question was smothered in Tina's bosom, as the massage therapist had rushed around the desk and thrown her arms tightly around Raina.

"I just got off the phone with my brother," Tina exclaimed. "He said that Warrick Mayne called him this morning and offered him an internship at his company."

"That's wonderful, Tina," Raina said, her voice muffled against the woman's chest. "I'm so glad to hear that. But could you, uh, ease up a little? I can't...*breathe.*"

"What did you say? Oh!" Tina released her and stepped back, laughing boisterously. "I'm sorry, boss lady. I didn't mean to suffocate you. I got carried away!"

Raina grinned. "So I see."

Tina laughed. "You should have heard Alphonse. He was screaming into the phone, and then he started speaking patois so fast I could hardly understand him!"

Raina chuckled. "That's because you've been away from home too long."

Tina grinned. "No, believe me, *no one* would have been able to understand what my brother was saying. Not until he slowed down and took a deep breath." Her dark eyes twinkled with merriment as she sat down in the visitor chair. "When he finally calmed down, he told me that Warrick had called to tell him he'd received his résumé. At first Alphonse thought it was a prank! See, when I asked him to e-mail his résumé to me the other day, I decided not to tell him the reason, because I didn't want to get his hopes up for nothing. I just told him I wanted to see how much he'd added to his résumé since the last time I saw it. So the *last* thing he was expecting was to hear from Warrick Mayne this morning! He thought it was one of his crazy friends playing a joke on him, so he—"

Raina stared at her in horror. "Oh, no. Please tell me he didn't tell Warrick to kiss his ass or something!"

Tina laughed. "No, thank God! After a minute Alphonse recognized Warrick's voice from a television interview he saw last year. That man has a very distinct voice, you know."

That's an understatement, Raina thought wryly.

"Anyway, Warrick told Alphonse he was impressed by his résumé and started asking him some questions, like he was interviewing him. Alphonse said they were tough questions, too. The kind where you really have to think on your feet. He said he was nervous, but at the end of the conversation, Warrick offered him an internship for next summer! He explained to Alphonse that the program had already started this year, so he didn't want him missing anything important. But that's not all, Raina. Warrick is flying Alphonse to Philadelphia in *two weeks* to visit Mayne Industries! Can you believe it?" She let out another high-pitched squeal.

Raina laughed. "That's great, Tina. Your brother must be thrilled."

"Oh, but that's not all. Warrick is flying me, Julien and my mother up there to meet Alphonse when he arrives! My mother couldn't believe it when I just called and told her. She was so excited, she started crying and praising God."

Raina smiled softly, her heart swelling with gratitude that Warrick had delivered on his promise, and then some. "That's wonderful, Tina," she said warmly. "I'm really happy for Alphonse, and for you and your mother. I know you haven't seen Alphonse in a few years, so this will be like a family reunion for all of you."

Tina nodded vigorously, beaming with unadulterated joy. "Alphonse hasn't seen Julien since he was a baby. I can't even begin to tell you how grateful I am to Warrick Mayne for making this possible. And *you!* How can I ever repay you for telling him about my brother."

Raina waved off her gratitude, smiling. "Girl, you don't have to repay me. It was the *least* I could do. You've been a godsend to me ever since you started working here, and I mean that."

Tina laughed, embarrassed as she dabbed tears from the corners of her eyes. "Oh, stop it. You're going to make me cry, and Lord knows I've done enough of that this morning. I started boohooing when my brother called me, and then my mother just got me going all over again."

Raina chuckled, swallowing past a lump that had formed in her own throat.

"But seriously though, Raina," Tina said, shaking her head at her in amazement. "How in the world did you get Warrick Mayne to do all this, especially since you said you were so mean to him when he came here on Monday?"

Raina hedged, "Well, I, um, just—"

Mercifully, she was spared from answering when Nikki suddenly appeared in the doorway, grinning from ear to ear. She was carrying two beautifully gift-wrapped silver boxes tied together with a white satin ribbon and finished with an elaborate bow.

"This just came for you," she said to Raina in an excited rush as she crossed to the desk. "I asked one of the girls to cover the phone for me while I brought it to you. I just *had* to see what it was and who sent it to you."

Raina had a sneaking suspicion about the sender's identity, but she kept the thought to herself. As she carefully untied the ribbon and unwrapped the first present, Tina and Nikki leaned forward intently, almost breathless with anticipation.

When they saw the Carolina Herrera designer emblem on the clothing box, their eyes widened.

Raina frowned. *I thought I told him I didn't want any expensive—* Suddenly she gasped.

"What is it?" Nikki asked eagerly.

Slowly, almost gingerly, Raina reached inside the box and lifted out a silk halter dress with a jeweled collar and fitted bodice.

"Ooh," Tina and Nikki breathed in unison. "That is absolutely gorgeous!"

"It is," Raina murmured, turning the dress around so that she could admire it from every angle. Everything about it, from its sleek couture design to the lovely moss-green color, was exquisite.

"Oh my God!" Nikki suddenly exclaimed. "I saw that dress the last time I was at the Galleria. My best friend and I always browse around the Carolina Herrera store, even though we can never afford anything in there. When we saw that dress, our jaws dropped to the floor. We couldn't stop admiring it. But it cost, like, six thousand dollars!"

Tina gasped, staring at the dress with a new level of appreciation.

"Who sent this to you, Raina?" Nikki demanded excitedly. "Is there a card?"

Raina looked, and sure enough, a small white envelope was lying on the bottom of the box. She opened it and silently read the message:

Golden Girl:
You may not believe this, but I've always thought you looked good in this color. We have tickets to the orchestra tomorrow night. I'd be honored if you would wear this for me.
—WM

Stunned, Raina reread the card twice, unable to believe what Warrick had written. She didn't know what shocked her more: the fact that he remembered what he'd called her that afternoon at the beach eighteen years ago, or the fact that he'd ever looked at her long enough to not only notice what color she was wearing, but to form a preference.

When she finally glanced up, Tina and Nikki were staring at her, mouths agape.

"What?" Raina said.

Tina shook her head slowly, looking both astonished and fascinated. "I've never seen you smile like that before, Raina."

"And you're blushing!" Nikki added.

Raina clapped a hand to her cheek, muttering, "I am not," even as an embarrassed flush heated her face.

Tina and Nikki exchanged incredulous grins.

In an effort to distract them, Raina quickly began opening the other present. This time the box bore the logo of Bebe, another upscale women's boutique located at the Galleria.

When Raina saw what was inside the box, she covered her mouth with her hand and began laughing.

"What is it?" Nikki asked curiously.

When Raina held up a pair of white designer jeans, the receptionist looked a little disappointed. "That's nice, but you already have a pair like that. Didn't you just wear them on Tuesday?"

Raina nodded, grinning. "It's a long story."

The enclosed card read:

> I figured I owed you a new pair after our encounter the other day. I'll never look at the T-Bird the same way again.

That makes two of us, Raina thought, chuckling to herself.

"There she goes, blushing again," Nikki remarked to Tina.

Tina grinned slyly at Raina. "Are you going to tell us who sent you these gifts, or are you going to keep us in suspense?"

"Yeah, Raina, give up the goods. Who's your sugar daddy?"

Raina smiled, carefully refolding the jeans. "If you must know—and it seems you must—the gifts are from Warrick."

"Warrick Mayne?" Tina and Nikki exclaimed.

"Yes, and before you go getting the wrong idea, he's *not* my sugar daddy. As you both know he wants to buy this property, so this is his way of…courting me."

Nikki grinned. "Well, if these are the kind of gifts he's going to be sending, I say let him court you all he wants!"

"Amen to that!" Tina laughingly agreed.

After the two women left the office, Raina reached for her cell phone and dialed Warrick's number. He answered on the second ring, the rich, masculine timbre of his voice pouring heat into her ear.

"I thought we had an agreement," Raina said without preamble. "No expensive gifts."

Warrick chuckled softly. "Good morning to you, too."

She fought the tug of a smile. "Don't change the subject. We had an agreement. Now, I realize we may have different definitions of *expensive*, but come on, Warrick. A six-thousand-dollar dress?"

"Do you like it?"

"I love it," Raina answered truthfully. "It's beautiful."

"Then that's all that matters. I can't wait to see you in it," he said huskily.

Raina warmed with pleasure. Closing her eyes, she silently prayed for the strength to resist this man, who was too damned tempting for his—*her*—own good.

"Thank you for the dress," she said. "It was an unexpected surprise. So were the jeans. But I could have just sent you the dry-cleaning bill."

Warrick laughed, a low, sexy rumble that made her cross her legs. "I tried to warn you about the handprints," he drawled, "but you didn't give me a chance."

"Oh, God," Raina groaned, struck by a new realization. "Did your uncle see them?"

"Probably. But he didn't say anything. Not about that, anyway. Hope I didn't get you into too much trouble with your sister."

"You did, actually."

Warrick chuckled. "At least you weren't meeting your boyfriend for dinner. By the way, how was your date last night?"

"Wonderful," Raina said. It wasn't an outright lie. The meal had been delicious, Bradford's home was lovely and he was the perfect gentleman. They'd had a pleasant conversation over dinner, and at the end of the evening when Bradford had walked her to her car and kissed her goodnight, that, too, had been pleasant. She only wished she hadn't spent the entire time trying—and failing miserably—to keep Warrick off her mind.

"Did you tell him you won't be available for a week?" Warrick murmured.

"It didn't come up." Absently she ran her hand over the exquisite silk dress. "I want to thank you for calling Alphonse Deveaux this morning. His sister just left my office, and you should have seen how ecstatic she was, Warrick. You can't begin to imagine how much your generosity means to their family. I owe you a debt of gratitude."

"No, you don't," Warrick said softly. "I'm always on the lookout for fresh talent, and I was very impressed with Alphonse. If he turns out to be as gifted an engineer as I think he will be, I'm going to owe you a finder's fee."

Raina smiled. "If that happens, we can just call it even."

"Sounds good. So where'd you go on your date last night?"

"Aren't *you* nosy?"

"I've never claimed otherwise."

"Well, if you must know," Raina said loftily, "Bradford cooked dinner for me at his house."

"How cozy."

"It was. Very."

"Hmm. Is he a good cook?"

"He's a great cook. Anything else you want to know?"

"Nothing you'd be willing to answer."

"You're right. So don't even bother asking." *The nerve of the man, wanting to know whether she'd spent the night with Bradford! How was that any of his business?*

"So, you're taking me to the symphony tomorrow night?" she asked, deliberately changing the subject.

"Yeah, but technically it's called the orchestra." Warrick paused. "The Philadelphia Orchestra."

Raina frowned in confusion. "I don't understand."

"We're going to Philadelphia."

"Philadelphia?"

Warrick chuckled dryly. "You make it sound like it's on another planet."

"Why would we fly all the way there to attend the *orchestra* when we have a perfectly good *symphony* right here in Houston?"

"That's not the reason we're going to Philly," Warrick said mildly. "I want to give you a tour of Mayne Industries and introduce you to some of the staff members. I think you can make a more informed decision about my business proposal if you have a better idea of what we do and the type of projects we're working on."

"Why can't you just tell me?" Raina countered, exasperated. "Give me one of your bells-and-whistles presentations. Or better yet, I can read all about what you do on your company's Web site."

"It's not quite the same as touring the facilities and speaking directly to my engineers."

"That wasn't necessary for Tyler Ralston or his brother," Raina pointed out.

"That was different. They were already receptive to the sale." Warrick paused meaningfully. "You aren't."

Raina faltered a moment. "Well, be that as it may, I can't just drop everything and go flying halfway across the country with you!"

"I thought you might say that, so I took the liberty of having my secretary call yours to check your schedule. As it turns out, you don't have any appointments or meetings scheduled until next week, after the Fourth of July holiday."

Raina scowled, incensed by his high-handedness. "When did your secretary call mine?" she demanded. Nikki had just left her office, for heaven's sake.

"Just now, while we were on the phone. Mabel just sent me a message confirming that your schedule is clear." A note of wry amusement entered his voice. "Any other objections I can shoot down for you?"

Raina gnashed her teeth, silently fuming. "How long would we be gone?"

"We'll return on Sunday."

Four days! Raina thought, stricken. *Four days alone with Warrick? I can hardly spend* five minutes *around him without wanting to jump his damned bones. How on earth am I going to survive four whole days?*

"I—I can't, Warrick," she stammered.

"You can," he countered silkily, "and you will. Need I remind you of the terms of our agreement? You're not allowed to argue about where I want to take you. Remember that?"

Raina closed her eyes and shook her head at the ceiling, knowing she had run out of excuses. Warrick was right. Against her better judgment, she'd struck a deal with him and had agreed to his terms. He had already kept his word by personally contacting Tina's brother and offering an internship; he'd even gone above and beyond Raina's expectations by generously volunteering to fly Alphonse *and* his family to Philadelphia. The least Raina could do was keep her end of the bargain.

"Raina," Warrick prompted softly. "I'm waiting."

She sighed her acceptance. "All right. Fine. When are we leaving?"

"My pilot's fueling up the jet right now. We should be ready to go by two."

"Two!" Raina sputtered in protest. "But it's already noon. That doesn't give me much time to finish what I'm doing here, then go home and pack."

"Then I suggest you hurry," Warrick murmured, "because I'm picking you up at one-thirty."

"*One-thirty!* Now you wait just a minute—"

"The longer you sit there arguing with me," Warrick drawled, "the more time you waste."

Raina screeched her frustration into the phone, then hung up on his resonant, rumbling laughter.

A moment later she dropped her head onto the desk and groaned, thinking, *What the hell have I gotten myself into?*

The woman is driving me crazy.

There was no other way to describe what was happening to Warrick, what had been happening to him ever since he laid eyes on Raina for the first time in twelve years. No matter how hard he tried—and he'd tried his damnedest—he just couldn't get her out of his mind.

Case in point: last night at the club, where he and his brothers were attending the glitzy birthday party of a hip-hop mogul they'd known since childhood. There he was in the posh VIP lounge, surrounded by beautiful, scantily-clad women more than willing to warm his bed that night, and all Warrick could think about was the way Raina had looked getting into her car. He'd received lap dances that didn't turn him on the way watching Raina climb behind the wheel of that car—one long, shapely leg at a time—had done. For the rest of the evening he'd been tortured by that tantalizing image, along with images of her in the arms of Bradley, or Brandon, or whatever the hell his name was.

Warrick didn't know what irritated him more: the fact that Raina could kiss him so passionately one minute and rush off to meet another man the very next, or the fact that she seemed genuinely enamored of her new boyfriend. None of that should have bothered Warrick. As Raina had already told him more than once, what she did in her private life was none of his damned business. Yet he couldn't help wondering whether she had spent the night with the doctor, touching and kissing him, giving herself to him as hungrily as she had kissed Warrick.

By the time he'd woken up that morning—alone, despite the many propositions he'd received the night before—Warrick had devised a plan for getting Raina away from her boyfriend, and alone to himself, for a few days. And the beauty of his plan was that it required very little deception on his part. It made perfect sense for Raina to accompany him to Philadelphia to take a tour of Mayne Industries and to see firsthand what his engineers were working on. Who better to make his case than the hardworking men and women who were the backbone of his company? Not even Raina had been able to refute his logic, though not for lack of trying. She was the feistiest, most stubborn woman Warrick had ever known. He wasn't accustomed to dealing with headstrong females who opposed him at every turn. Without an ounce of conceit, he could honestly say he had yet to meet a woman who hadn't given him *what* he wanted, *when* he wanted it. Even the shrewdest, most formidable female executives he'd encountered in the business world couldn't resist him when he decided to lay on the charm.

But Raina St. James was the exception.

Even now, seated across from him in the spacious interior of his private jet, she defiantly ignored him. She'd spoken very little since they'd boarded the plane more than two hours ago. Amused, Warrick had watched as she glanced around the luxurious cabin, with its custom leather seating and rich mahogany paneling, and tried very hard not to look impressed.

Once the plane had taken off, and they were served cocktails and hors d'oeuvres, Raina had pulled out her laptop and gone to work. Warrick knew she was ticked off at him for the way he'd manipulated her into traveling with him, and she was now punishing him with her silence.

Chuckling to himself, he'd left her alone and retreated to the back of the cabin to make some business calls. At one point he'd heard Raina's cell phone ring. From her end of the conversation, he'd gleaned that Reese St. James was giving her sister an earful about leaving town with Warrick. He'd shamelessly eavesdropped on the brief exchange, which ended with Raina snapping, "I know what I'm doing."

Is that so? Warrick had wondered, intrigued.

When he'd returned to his seat, Raina had put away her laptop and was gazing out the window. Although she gave no indication that she was aware of his presence, Warrick knew better.

Deciding he'd endured the silent treatment long enough, he sprawled in the chair opposite hers and deliberately stretched out his long, denim-clad legs, his posture one of supreme relaxation.

Because he knew it bothered Raina, he slowly and deliberately allowed his gaze to travel the length of her. She had twisted her long, dark mane atop her head and secured it with Chinese hair sticks, a simple style that made her look even more exotic than usual. The V of her pink summer sweater drew his eye to the enticing valley between those soft, full breasts he longed to taste and explore. She wore a pair of low-rise jeans—dark this time—that clung to the ripe curves of her body. Toenails painted a soft shade of pink peeked from wedge sandals.

Warrick gazed at her, marveling that no matter how she was dressed, she always managed to look unbelievably sexy. Seeing her in this casual ensemble did more for him than being surrounded by an entourage of gorgeous women wearing scraps of clothing that left little to the imagination.

His gaze traveled back up to Raina's face, admiring the lovely, sensual contours of her profile, lingering on those lush, dewy lips. Man, she was beautiful. How had he never noticed before?

But you must have, at some point, his conscience prodded. *Somewhere along the way you noticed that she looks amazing in the color green. When did that happen?*

Warrick frowned, thinking of how surprising the revelation had been to him that morning. The moment he'd seen the Carolina Herrera dress, he'd instinctively known that it would look stunning on Raina. And that was when he'd realized that on some profound, subconscious level, he must have always known that she would one day blossom into a breathtaking beauty.

As Warrick stared at her, she drew a shaky breath that let him know she wasn't as unaffected by his presence as she wanted him to believe.

Hiding a knowing smile, Warrick crossed his booted feet at the ankles and let out a loud, exaggerated sigh.

No reaction.

Undeterred, Warrick began whistling the theme song to the show *Good Times*, which, for some inexplicable reason, used to send Raina and his sister into a fit of hysterical giggles.

The corners of Raina's mouth twitched, as if she wanted desperately to smile but wouldn't give him the satisfaction.

Chuckling softly and shaking his head, Warrick drawled, "The more things change, the more they stay the same."

Finally she looked at him, those dark, bewitching eyes glimmering with suppressed mirth. "What do you mean?"

"What does this scenario remind you of?" At her blank look, Warrick explained, "When I used to drive you home, you wouldn't speak to me, remember? You'd stare out the window and answer me in monosyllables until I finally gave up trying to make conversation with you and turned on the radio." He smiled, adding wryly, "I couldn't decide whether you were painfully shy, you hated my guts or you thought I had really bad breath."

Raina laughed softly. "None of the above."

"Really? Then why was it like pulling teeth just to get you to talk to me?"

"I don't know." She shrugged, an unnamed emotion flickering across her face and disappearing so swiftly he could have imagined it. "That was years ago. Who knows what was going through my mind at the time?"

But Warrick didn't believe her. Cocking his head to one side, he studied her through narrowed eyes. Assiduously avoiding his speculative gaze, Raina turned back to the window. But she couldn't hide from him entirely, and with a mixture of curiosity and fascination, Warrick realized that she was blushing.

More intrigued than ever, he probed, "You honestly don't remember?"

"No," she said quickly. A little *too* quickly.

Glancing at him, she added offhandedly, "Besides, what difference does it make? You can't possibly expect me to believe you cared whether or not your little sister's best friend spoke to you."

Warrick held her gaze. "Maybe I did."

Raina snorted out an incredulous laugh. "Yeah, right!"

"Why would that be so hard to believe?"

She gave him a look. "Warrick, you hardly ever spoke to me. Half the time you didn't even know I was there. The only time you acknowledged my presence was when you were taking me home, and that was only because you were being polite, and you knew you couldn't very well ignore the only passenger in your car."

Warrick stared at her. She had spoken matter-of-factly, but there was something in her voice, something indefinable that tugged at him and made him want to apologize, to somehow make amends. Which was ridiculous. He had nothing to apologize for. He'd never been unkind to Raina.

Until she'd given him a reason to be.

"Anyway," she said, her gaze returning to the window, "that's ancient history."

"Yeah," Warrick murmured, thinking about Yolanda, wondering how his sister would feel if she could see him and Raina now, on their way to Philadelphia to spend the next four days together. What would Yolanda say if she knew that Warrick had allowed his powerful attraction to Raina to override his hatred of her? What would Yolanda think if she knew that whenever Warrick was around Raina, his libido enabled him to forget what she had done to his sister, to his entire family?

But he didn't have to wonder. He already knew that Yolanda would feel angry and betrayed, and her feelings would be perfectly justified. Yet, knowing this had not lessened Warrick's desire for Raina. He wanted her with an intensity, a ferocity that would have shocked her senseless if she'd had even the slightest inkling. He wanted her hot and wet for him, quivering and panting beneath him, begging him to make love to her. He wanted to bury himself deep inside her, as deep as she could take him, and he wanted to hear her scream his name as she lost control.

And then maybe, once he'd had her, he would be able to purge her from his system, like a craving that had been satisfied. That was the way it had always worked for him. Once he slept with a woman, the mystery was gone, the thrill of the chase was over. Few women, no matter how beautiful or alluring, sustained his interest long enough to entice him into an actual relationship.

But if by chance Raina proved to be the exception to the rule, God help him.

Chapter 12

Warrick lived on the outskirts of Philadelphia in an exclusive suburb of Cherry Hill, New Jersey. As the Rolls Royce limousine transporting Warrick and Raina traveled along a secluded road flanked by towering pine trees, Raina found herself gazing out the window with a mounting sense of anxiety mingled with anticipation. She hadn't wanted to accompany Warrick on this trip, but now that she was here, she couldn't deny an overwhelming curiosity to see his home.

As the road gradually steepened in elevation she unconsciously leaned forward, pressing closer to the window. Warrick, on the phone with a client, was too preoccupied to notice how riveted she was.

The limousine rolled through a decorative metal gate and continued on a winding road that gently sloped uphill. They passed a lush expanse of manicured green lawn, then suddenly the trees broke, and Raina's eyes widened as a sprawling stone and stucco mansion came into view.

She must have gasped or made some other strangled noise, because suddenly Warrick's dark gaze was upon her, the shadow of a smile playing at the edges of his mouth.

The Rolls followed the curving path of the stone driveway before gliding to a stop in front of the main house. The driver, a red-haired man in his late twenties with a heavy South Jersey accent and an infectious smile, came around to open the door for Raina.

"Welcome to Casa Mayne, Miss St. James," he said with a gallant bow. "My name is Lanny. Pleased to be at your service."

"Thank you, Lanny," Raina murmured distractedly as she stepped from the limo, never taking her eyes off the imposing house.

Nestled by tall shade trees and meticulously pruned shrubbery, the mansion boasted an Italianate architecture, with sweeping windows, balconied terraces, stone columns and double stairways that ascended to the main entrance under a baroque covered porch. A vibrant profusion of summer foliage bloomed everywhere Raina looked, softly perfuming the air. She felt as if she were arriving at a picturesque country villa somewhere in Italy.

"Oh, Warrick," she breathed, unable to help herself as he appeared beside her. "This is…*magnificent*."

Warrick tipped his head modestly. "Thank you, Raina."

As Lanny retrieved their luggage, an older black gentleman in a neatly pressed dark suit emerged from the mansion and descended the stairs with an air of dignified elegance. The butler, Raina presumed. A place this size had to have a butler, as well as an entire fleet of household servants.

"Mr. Mayne," the man greeted Warrick as he and Raina reached the bottom of the stairway. "Good to have you back."

"Thanks, Mr. Gibbons. It's good to be back." Warrick turned to Raina at his side. "Mr. Gibbons, I'd like you to meet Raina St. James, from Houston. Raina, this is Cyrus Gibbons, who keeps this place running like a well-oiled machine."

Raina smiled warmly. "It's a pleasure to meet you, Mr. Gibbons."

"The pleasure is mine, Miss St. James," he said with an elegant bow. "I trust you had a restful trip?"

"Very," Raina answered.

Warrick chuckled dryly, his amused gaze meeting hers. "She worked the entire time so she wouldn't have to talk to me."

An embarrassed flush heated Raina's face. "I did not!" she protested, though she knew it was partially true. Was she *that* transparent, or did Warrick just know her that well?

Cyrus Gibbons smiled indulgently. "You must be losing your touch, Mr. Mayne."

"Apparently so," Warrick murmured, gesturing for Raina to precede him up the stairs.

The inside of the house was just as breathtaking as the outside. A soaring vaulted ceiling and double curving stairways punctuated the sheer magnificence of the massive skylighted foyer, which was decorated with glossy mahogany tables, gilded mirrors and towering topiaries. Gleaming wood floors contrasted beautifully with marble and stone, and intricately carved crown moldings arrested the eye.

As Raina took in her surroundings, she had to remember to keep her jaw off the floor.

"You know Ms. Evamay isn't going to be happy with you," the butler was saying to Warrick. "If she'd known you were coming home today, she would have wanted to be here to greet you and fuss over you."

Warrick grinned, a dazzlingly boyish grin. "That's why I didn't tell her. She needs to spend as much time as possible with her grandchildren."

Gibbons looked dubious. "Yes, but if she finds out you were here a day earlier than expected and you didn't let her know, *I'll* never hear the end of it."

Warrick chuckled, sifting through a stack of mail the butler had handed him. "I'll call her tomorrow. I need to make sure she's bringing her grandchildren to the Fourth of July party on Saturday, anyway."

At the mention of a party, Raina turned from admiring a gilt-framed oil-on-canvas painting to arch an inquisitive brow at Warrick. He hadn't mentioned anything to her about a party.

"We always throw a big Fourth of July celebration here at the house," he explained. "My employees and their families look forward to it every year. And in case you're wondering, Evamay Watts is the lady of the manor, so to speak. Nothing happens around here without her permission or input. Ain't that right, Mr. Gibbons?"

The butler heaved a resigned sigh. "Unfortunately."

Warrick laughed, clapping him warmly on the shoulder. "You know you miss her whenever she's gone."

The man smiled, taking the teasing in stride.

As Lanny returned from carrying the luggage upstairs, Mr. Gibbons said to Raina, "Your room is all ready for you, Miss St.

James. Maybe after you've had a chance to unpack and get settled in, you'd like a tour of the mansion."

Raina smiled. "I'd like that very much."

"I have to return an important call," Warrick told her, briefly touching her arm. "Mr. Gibbons will show you to your room."

Raina nodded, ignoring the way her skin tingled from his simple touch.

Forcing herself not to watch him go, she followed the butler up the wide, curving staircase and down an endless expanse of corridor. They passed one enormous room after another, each one sumptuously appointed with a collection of Italian and American art and antiques, plush Oriental carpets, custom drapery and rich fabrics in neutral tones with splashes of bold color throughout. Although the lavish furnishings had clearly cost a fortune, there was nothing gaudy or ostentatious about them. Everything was tasteful and artfully arranged, no doubt courtesy of a very expensive interior designer.

"How many bedrooms are there?" Raina asked, her voice filled with fascinated curiosity.

"There are twelve bedrooms and fifteen bathrooms—" Mr. Gibbons smiled at her audible intake of breath before continuing, "Every bedroom has its own private bath and balcony. In addition to the living room and family room, there's a solarium, a library, a gourmet kitchen, a formal dining room, a music room, an exercise room, a billiard room, a home theater and a ballroom that has seen its fair share of soirees. We also have a few gazebos on the property, an indoor and outdoor pool, a tennis court, a courtyard with a fountain, a wine cellar, a ten-car garage and an indoor basketball court where Mr. Mayne can usually be found if he's not sequestered in his study, or tinkering with one of his cars. He collects them, like his uncle, you know."

Raina smiled. She might have guessed. Warrick and Randall Mayne were two peas in a pod; they couldn't be more alike than if they were father and son.

"The master suite is on the west wing," Mr. Gibbons continued his proud recitation of the mansion's impressive features. "It has its own private elevator and—"

"Which wing are we on?" Raina interrupted.

"The east."

Raina breathed a sigh of relief that she would not be sleeping anywhere near Warrick. Although, even in a house this size, the mere knowledge that they were under the same roof would probably keep her awake and on edge for hours.

At length Mr. Gibbons led her into a huge but cozy bedroom suite decorated to look like something out of a classic French chateau, featuring sumptuous drapery, cherry antiques, a four-poster Louis XVI bed and a gorgeous marble fireplace. The luxurious adjoining bathroom was done in travertine marble, and beyond the tall French doors, a private balcony boasted a stunning view of the beautifully manicured gardens below.

Raina took a slow turn around the room, admiring everything in sight.

Watching her, Mr. Gibbons smiled quietly. "I trust you've found the accommodations to your satisfaction?"

Raina laughed. "Oh, yes, most definitely."

"Excellent." As he began bowing gracefully out of the room, he said, "Dinner will be served at eight. Make yourself at home, and please let me know if there's anything you need."

"Thank you, Mr. Gibbons."

Once the door had closed behind him, Raina wandered over to the huge, inviting bed. It was drowned in silk sheets in the richest hues of cream, burgundy and chocolate. Unable to resist, she dove onto the bed and rolled around, luxuriating in the heavenly texture of silk against her skin.

So this is how the other half lives, she mused. *The superwealthy. Must be nice!*

Raina liked to think she didn't have a materialistic bone in her body, but even *she* could appreciate the breathtaking grandeur of Warrick's secluded estate. She'd read articles, of course, about the "architectural masterpiece" he'd purchased and refurbished five years ago, but nothing could have prepared her for the real deal. Warrick had definitely come a long way from the dilapidated, drug-infested projects of the Third Ward, a thought that caused her chest to swell with pride and satisfaction. Because no matter what he and his family thought of her, Raina had never begrudged Warrick his success. She knew he'd worked hard to get where he was, never taking a single thing for granted. He deserved to enjoy the fruit of his labor.

Just not at the expense of mine, Raina mused, suddenly reminded of the reason for her presence in his home.

Over the next several days, Warrick was going to do everything in his power to try to convince her to sell her property to him. She had to be on guard, prepared to withstand any tactic he employed to weaken her resistance.

Because if she allowed him to successfully break down her defenses, her spa was not the only thing she stood to lose.

Two hours later, freshly showered and dressed in a leopard-print silk halter and pale linen slacks, Raina sat down to dinner with Warrick in the formal dining room. Accentuated with beautiful crown molding, Roman columns, a soaring marble fireplace and an elaborate crystal chandelier, the room was every bit as grand as the rest of the mansion.

But for the first time that evening, Raina was not riveted by the opulence of her surroundings. Something else had ensnared her attention. Or, rather, *someone* else.

Sitting across from her at the long mahogany table that seated thirty, Warrick was stunningly, brutally handsome in dark gabardine trousers and a black dress shirt open to the strong column of his throat. With little or no effort he exuded raw animal magnetism, a potent masculinity that Raina found utterly irresistible.

The chandelier was dimmed low and a pair of candles were lit on the table, lending an intimate quality to the cavernous dining room. Raina watched, transfixed, as candlelight danced across the hard angles and planes of Warrick's face, the ruggedness of his features softened only by the lush sensuality of his lips. As he raised his wineglass and took a languid sip of Merlot, Raina stared at his long, lean fingers, imagining those hands roaming over her body and stroking her fevered flesh as she shuddered through an orgasm.

When his dark, glittering gaze met hers across the table, she quickly glanced away, half-afraid he would read her mind. She stared up at the domed tray ceiling, studying the fancy trim work and molding with exaggerated absorption.

"This is quite a house you have," she remarked, striving for a normal tone. "The detailing in every room is exquisite."

"Thanks," Warrick murmured, sounding distinctly amused, "but you've already said that three times since we sat down."

Raina blushed. "Have I?"

"Yes. You have." He set down his glass, those midnight eyes probing hers. "Are you nervous, Raina?"

The husky timbre of his voice made her think of their naked, sweaty limbs tangled together as they thrashed around on the silk sheets in her bedroom.

She forced out a breathless laugh. "Of course I'm not nervous! I just get, uh, chatty when I'm hungry."

"Are you hungry?"

You have no idea!

Aloud she said, "It's been a few hours since we had those hors d'oeuvres on the plane. And I didn't get a chance to eat lunch before we left because *someone* was rushing me."

Warrick chuckled ruefully. "I guess I *have* been starving you today, huh?"

Raina grinned. "Just a little."

"Well, don't worry. My chef has something really special planned this evening. Ah, here he is now."

Raina glanced up, then did a double take at the sight of the stocky Italian man with a smooth, bald head and warm blue eyes that crinkled at the corners when he smiled, as he was doing now.

Raina stared at him in surprised recognition. "Oh my God! Aren't you Sonny Bellini?"

He laughed, carrying two large plates over to the table. "Last I checked my birth certificate."

"I've seen you on the Food Network cooking channel!" Raina exclaimed. "My sister is a huge fan of yours! She loves to cook, and I think she's even tried all of your recipes. She's not going to believe this. What're you doing here?"

Warrick chuckled dryly. "Sonny was my personal chef before he got his big break and left me for the bright lights of Tinseltown."

Sonny laughed, wagging his head at Raina. "Don't listen to him. *He's* the one who used his Hollywood connections to get me signed on with a big talent agency. *I* was perfectly content being his personal chef. The pay was phenomenal and he throws the best damn parties of anyone I know. But *he* insisted that I should be hosting my own cooking show, and when this man sets his sights on something, there's no stopping him."

Raina smiled weakly, hoping those words would not prove prophetic in her own dealings with Warrick.

Warrick drawled, "Every so often Sonny takes pity on me and comes back to cook for me."

The chef winked conspiratorially at Raina. "I want to torture him with reminders of what he's missing."

Raina grinned. "Well, speaking of that, my sister's going to torture *me* if she finds out that I met you and didn't at least get your autograph. I don't suppose you brought any extra copies of your bestselling cookbook with you."

"I have a few in the library," Warrick smoothly interjected. "I'll make sure you get an autographed copy before Sonny leaves. Which won't be until Sunday, because he has graciously agreed to cater my Fourth of July party this weekend."

"Really?" Raina asked.

"Yep," Sonny said, nodding and smiling at her. "My staff and I are looking forward to it. Like I said, this man knows how to throw one helluva party. Anyway, I'll leave the two of you to your dinner. Enjoy your meal."

Raina had been so enthralled by the unexpected appearance of the celebrity chef that she hadn't noticed what he'd served them until he'd left the room. When she glanced down at the table, her heart sank at the appallingly meager portion of food on her plate.

Warrick, who had picked up his fork to begin eating, noticed her dismayed expression and calmly inquired, "Is something wrong with your meal?"

"Um, yeah." Raina glanced over her shoulder to make sure Sonny was out of earshot, then whispered worriedly, "Where's the rest of it?"

"*Excuse* me?"

Raina stared at Warrick's face, surprised to realize that he obviously saw nothing wrong with what they had been served. She bit her lip, then shook her head. "Never mind."

"No," he clipped, "*what* did you say?"

"Nothing. Forget it." Raina reached for her fork, then couldn't resist mumbling under her breath, "I guess it's safe to assume you're not spending all of your money on *food*."

Warrick frowned. Slowly, deliberately, he set down his fork, pushed away from the table and stood. Raina watched, with mounting chagrin, as he walked over to the tall bay windows that overlooked the gardens and shoved his hands deep into his pockets.

Oh, great, Raina thought. Now she'd gone and offended him. Who knew he would be so sensitive? It wasn't *his* fault his former chef had served them such measly portions of food. And she had a right to be disappointed; she'd hardly eaten anything all day! Still, she felt guilty for sounding like such an ingrate.

She blew out a ragged breath. "Warrick, I'm—" she broke off abruptly, staring in disbelief as his broad shoulders began to shake. Wait a minute. Was he—?

Suddenly Warrick threw back his head and roared with laughter.

Raina's mouth dropped open. She gaped at him, comprehension slowly dawning. "You mean… You're not really—"

The rest of her query was drowned out by another shout of deep, masculine laughter. Warrick turned, shaking his head at her, tears of mirth glimmering in his dark eyes. "You should have seen your face, Raina. Your expression was priceless!"

Raina sputtered uselessly, then glared accusingly at him. "You had me worried that I'd offended you!"

Grinning, he strode over to her, leaned down and planted a quick kiss on her forehead. "Priceless."

Raina didn't know what got to her more: the affectionate kiss, the boyish prank, the engaging warmth of his smile or the unabashed merriment in his eyes. Her insides melted faster than a snowball on a summer afternoon in Houston, and she began to laugh.

On cue Sonny reentered the dining room carrying two steaming plates, a wide grin on his face. Raina laughed harder.

"How's that?" the chef asked teasingly as he set down the plate in front of her.

Raina took one look at the appetizing spread before her—balsamic chicken with mango-glazed shrimp and herbed potatoes—and nodded approvingly. "Now *that's* more like it!"

Sonny and Warrick traded pleased, conspiratorial grins before the chef departed with a cheerful, *"Buon appetito!"*

Raina, still chuckling, shook her head reproachfully at Warrick. "You got me so good."

He grinned. "I know. The look on your face when you saw that first plate said it all. For a minute there I was afraid you were going to stab me with your fork."

Raina laughed. "Would've served you right! That was a cruel joke to play on me, Warrick, especially after I had just told you how hungry I was. And pray tell, was it also part of the prank to tease me with tidbits of food earlier on the plane?"

Warrick nodded, watching as she cut into her chicken. "I wanted you to be good and hungry by dinnertime so you'd have no excuse not to eat your food."

Raina gave him a bemused look. "Why on earth would you think you'd need to starve me in order to get me to eat?"

He smiled enigmatically. "I have my reasons."

"Well, trust me, one thing I've never had a problem enjoying is a good meal." To prove her point, Raina ate a bite of chicken and closed her eyes on a deep, appreciative sigh. "Mmm, that is *sooo* good."

"Yeah? You like it?"

She nodded vigorously. "It's tender, juicy and *very* flavorful. But don't take my word for it. Try it yourself."

Warrick sampled a forkful and nodded. "That *is* good. But, then, I don't think Sonny has ever made anything I *didn't* like."

Raina grinned. "Bet you kick yourself all the time for letting him go."

Warrick chuckled. "Every so often," he admitted. "But then I remind myself that Sonny's culinary gift was meant to be shared with the world, and it would have been selfish of me to deprive him of bigger and better opportunities."

"How very noble of you," Raina said with a teasing smile.

Warrick winked at her. "Anyway, it all worked out for the best. I have a new personal chef that I'm very pleased with. He's away for the holiday weekend, but take my word for it when I tell you how talented he is. As he should be. He received his culinary training under a good friend of mine."

"Oh? Who?"

"Michael Wolf."

Raina stared at him, fork halfway to her mouth. "You know *Michael Wolf?*"

Warrick smiled at her awestruck tone. "He used to be an engineer before he went into the restaurant business and became a celebrity chef. We both belonged to the National Society of Professional Engineers. When I first launched Mayne Industries, I approached Michael about going into business with me, but by then he was already thinking about pursuing his lifelong dream of owning a restaurant. Needless to say, I was very happy for him when he called me a few years later to invite me to the grand opening of Wolf's Soul in Atlanta."

"And now he has, like, five locations!" Raina enthused.

"Seven," Warrick corrected.

"Oh my God! My sister *loves* Michael Wolf. I seriously think she would get on her knees and propose to him if she ever met him. I'm not kidding!" Raina added at Warrick's soft chuckle. "Reese has every cookbook he's ever written and religiously records his show. She keeps hoping that he'll open a restaurant in Houston." She paused, looking hopefully at Warrick. "You wouldn't happen to have any insight into his future expansion plans, would you?"

Warrick grinned, shaking his head. "Sorry to disappoint you but, no. I don't."

"But you're friends with him," Raina pressed, undeterred. "You could always call him and find out, then put a plug in his ear about how great the Houston market would be for a restaurant like Wolf's Soul."

"I could," Warrick agreed, reaching for his wine and taking an idle sip. As he slowly lowered the glass, his amused gaze met hers. "Are you asking me to?"

Remembering the way they'd negotiated Alphonse's internship, Raina said boldly, "I'm not asking you to. I'm *demanding* it."

Warrick laughed. "Bravo, Miss St. James," he said, his eyes filled with warm admiration. "You learn fast."

Raina grinned broadly, inordinately pleased with herself.

As they resumed eating, Warrick said conversationally, "So, Raina, tell me about yourself."

It was a strange request coming from a man she'd known since she was ten years old. She faltered for a moment, unsure of how to respond.

Noting her reaction, Warrick said quietly, "You can know a person more than half your life, and never really know them at all."

Amen to that, Raina mused bitterly, thinking of the way Yolanda Mayne had betrayed her trust and turned her entire family against her. In their eyes Raina was the villain, the one who'd seemingly changed overnight and violated *their* trust, leaving them to wonder if they'd ever truly known her.

Raina searched Warrick's face, trying to decipher the meaning behind his own words. But his expression was unreadable.

She took a sip of wine, then asked carefully, "What do you want to know?"

"Whatever you want to tell me. For starters, what do you enjoy doing in your spare time?"

Raina hesitated, knowing that whatever she told him would sound incredibly dull in comparison to the jet-setting lifestyle he led—traveling around the world aboard his private jet, hosting fabulous house parties, mingling with celebrities and corporate tycoons, dating glamorous women, attending glitzy award shows and movie premieres. Just that morning she'd heard on the radio that he was among the glitterati who'd converged on the town last night to attend the birthday bash of a popular hip-hop artist, who, incidentally, had also dedicated his first hit single, "Boyz from Da Ward," to Warrick.

Nothing she shared with Warrick could possibly interest or impress him.

Why do you care? an inner voice demanded. *Your life is no less fulfilling or important than his just because you don't travel in the same social circles. You have nothing to prove to him!*

Warrick was watching her with a mixture of exasperation and amusement. "Is it just me," he said, "or do you always take this long to answer a simple question?"

"I like to go salsa dancing," Raina blurted.

A spark of interest lit his eyes. "Salsa dancing?"

She nodded, smiling. "A few years ago Reese talked—no, *bullied*—me into taking salsa lessons with her. At first I felt really silly and clumsy, like I had two left feet. I've always considered myself a pretty good dancer, but salsa requires a different level of skill and coordination. Reese was a natural, of course, being a cheerleader in high school and college. *I,* on the other hand, needed some help. Thankfully, our instructor was very patient and understanding, not to mention a hottie," she added with a naughty grin.

Warrick shook his head, mouth twitching. "I'm sure he didn't mind putting in some extra time after class to, ah, give you more personalized attention."

Raina's grin widened. "No, he didn't seem to mind at all. Anyway," she continued when Warrick's black brows furrowed together, "once I got over my self-consciousness, I really began to enjoy salsa dancing. It's fun, energizing and very liberating."

"Liberating, huh?"

Raina nodded quickly, warming to her subject. "Whenever I go salsa dancing, I really lose myself in the music and the movements. All my worries melt away, and I find myself becoming..."

"Uninhibited?" Warrick supplied.

"Yes! That's a perfect word. I feel totally uninhibited. Don't laugh, but it's like the music reaches inside my heart and grabs hold of my hips, and I just go wherever the rhythm takes me. It's amazing. Mesmerizing. I feel powerful and sensual and—" she broke off abruptly, her face flushing as she realized, too late, that she'd just revealed rather intimate details about herself.

Stifling an embarrassed laugh, she reached for her glass and took a hasty gulp of merlot.

Warrick remained silent, staring at her with an expression she didn't know how to interpret. He probably thought she was crazy, getting all worked up over something as simple as salsa dancing.

Suddenly eager to change the subject, Raina said, "I also enjoy reading biographies. I always find them fascinating, just to know where people came from, what they had to overcome to achieve their success." She smiled whimsically. "Maybe one of these days I'll be reading *your* biography."

Warrick smiled faintly. "And maybe I'll read yours."

Raina laughed. "You never know!"

He drank his wine, watching her with a quiet, focused intensity that made her feel a little breathless. "What else do you enjoy, Raina?"

She ate a bite of shrimp and chewed thoughtfully. "I like to unwind at home with a good movie or a good book—usually a mystery or a historical romance."

Warrick smiled a little. "Are you a hopeless romantic, Raina?"

She chuckled wryly. "Guilty as charged," she admitted, thinking of the paperback novels she'd snuck out of her mother's closet and eagerly devoured as a young girl. Those damned romance novels had fueled more than enough tortured fantasies about Warrick to last her a lifetime.

"I'm afraid I don't have any romances in the library," he said smilingly, "but I'd be more than happy to add some to my reading collection so you'd feel right at home the next time you're here."

Raina's lips parted in surprise. She was so startled—and ridiculously touched—by the unlikely offer that she didn't bother to remind Warrick that this would be her first and only visit to the mansion. But as she gazed at him, an unnamed emotion flickered across his face, and he ducked his head over his plate and became absorbed in his meal.

They ate for a few minutes in silence.

After casting about for something else to add to her list of favorite pastimes, Raina said brightly, "I also like to attend plays and concerts. I really enjoy the Jazz in the Park series during the summers. Sometimes I like to go there by myself, spread out a blanket and just soak up the mellow music."

Warrick raised an amused brow. "Do you break out into dance?"

She laughed, nearly choking on a mouthful of wine. "Of course not. And don't you dare make fun of me just because I told you all that stuff about the salsa dancing."

"Oh, believe me, Raina," Warrick said in that dark, intoxicating voice that made her think of hot flesh and silk sheets again, "ridiculing you is the *last* thing on my mind when I imagine you salsa dancing."

Raina's belly quivered. She tore her gaze from his and stared into the ruby contents of her glass, willing her racing pulse to return to normal, even as she realized that there was no such thing as a normal pulse whenever Warrick was around.

"So what about the doctor?" he murmured.

Her eyes snapped to his face. "Who?"

Warrick chuckled, low and soft. "You've forgotten him already?"

"Of course not," Raina retorted. "I'm just used to referring to people by their *name,* not their profession. I wouldn't, for example, refer to you as the engineer or the CEO, nor would I expect to be referred to as—" she broke off at the glittering amusement in Warrick's eyes. "Oh, for heaven's sake. You know what I'm trying to say. He has a name. It's not 'the doctor,' or 'that chump,' or 'Loverboy,' or anything else you choose to call him. It's Bradford. Repeat after me. *Brad-ford,*" she enunciated as if she were instructing a child or someone who spoke a foreign language.

"Bradford," Warrick repeated dutifully, his eyes still twinkling with humor and mischief.

"Very good. Anyway..." Raina trailed off, frowning. "What was the question again?"

Warrick burst out laughing.

Raina bit the inside of her cheek to keep from joining him.

As his mirth subsided, Warrick idly traced the rim of his glass with a finger, gazing at her. "What I was going to ask is whether the doctor—I'm sorry, *Bradford*—shares a lot of your interests."

"Of course," Raina said quickly. Too quickly.

At Warrick's arched brow, she said more smoothly and convincingly, "He's a great guy. I wouldn't be seeing him if we didn't have a lot in common."

"Of course," Warrick murmured. He stared into his glass, deep in thought for a moment.

Raina was about to change the subject when he said softly and reflectively, "You and your sister are so close. Any man you eventually decide to marry is going to need Reese's stamp of approval just as much as your father's."

Raina chuckled. "That's definitely true. It's funny, because she's always trying to fix me up with different guys, even though *she* ends up dismissing all of them for one reason or another, saying they're not good enough for me." She sighed, then added without thinking, "At least she likes Bradford."

"Well, there you go," Warrick drawled. "Now all you have to do is introduce him to your father, and it won't be long before you're sending out invitations." He downed the rest of his drink, then reached for the bottle to refill his glass.

Raina watched him, wondering about the strange tension suddenly vibrating around him.

"More wine?" he offered, lifting the bottle.

She shook her head quickly. "I've probably had more than I should have. That's an excellent merlot. From your wine cellar, right?"

Warrick nodded. "Imported from one of the best vineyards in Tuscany. Have some more. I insist."

"All right," Raina acquiesced, because it *was* an amazing merlot. "But just half a glass, please. I think we both remember what happened the *last* time I had too much to drink."

"Ah, yes," Warrick murmured, mouth twitching as he poured more wine into her glass. "We certainly wouldn't want you to spend all night praying to the porcelain god."

Raina stuck out her tongue at him, and he laughed.

As Raina ate the last of her meal, she glanced up to find Warrick gazing at her with a look of mild fascination.

"What?" she asked self-consciously.

"You finished all of your food." He sounded surprised.

Raina chuckled. "I don't know why you didn't think I would. I told you I was hungry, and the meal was delicious. Besides, need I remind you that, even as a little girl, I had no problem demolishing your uncle's steaks at cookouts?"

Warrick grinned. "I remember. And he always gave you the biggest ones, too."

"I know." She sighed affectionately. "I adore that man."

Warrick rolled his eyes. "The feeling's mutual," he grumbled, and Raina laughed.

Chapter 13

After lingering over dessert—a decadent double-chocolate tart that was second to none—Raina and Warrick emerged from the dining room, smiling companionably at each other. Although Raina was beginning to feel the effects of the wine, she wasn't quite ready to retire for the night.

Or, rather, she wasn't ready to part company with Warrick.

Foolish girl, her conscience admonished. *When will you stop being a glutton for punishment?*

Shoving the thought aside, Raina asked Warrick, "What time are we heading out to your office in the morning?"

"Nine o'clock," he answered. "That should give us enough time to avoid rush-hour traffic."

As they walked, their footfalls sounded against the polished parquet floor and bounded up to the vaulted ceiling. Gazing around, Raina shook her head and muttered under her breath, "This isn't a mansion. It's a freakin' *castle.*"

Warrick chuckled.

"Seriously. An entire NBA basketball team could hole up here and you'd never even know it."

"Nah," Warrick drawled. "Believe it or not, I know this house like the back of my hand."

Raina shot him a disbelieving look. "You couldn't possibly."

He quirked a challenging brow at her. "Wanna bet?"

She laughed. "Warrick, if I hid anywhere in this house, it would take you a month to find me."

"Ten minutes."

"What?"

"It would take me ten minutes to find you. Probably less, because you wouldn't know where to hide."

"Ten minutes?" Raina scoffed. "No way!"

Warrick stopped midstride and turned to her, his eyes glinting with sudden mischief. "I'll prove it to you. Go ahead and hide somewhere, and I'll find you. If it takes me more than ten minutes, you can come out of your hiding place and gloat all you want. Go on. I'll close my eyes and count to one hundred while you hide."

Raina snorted out a laugh. "I'm not going to play hide-and-seek with you, Warrick! How old do you think—"

He closed his eyes. "One, two—"

With a muffled squeal Raina took off, racing down an endless stretch of corridor.

Warrick was right, of course. She didn't know where to hide; she barely knew where she was going, though Mr. Gibbons had graciously given her the grand tour before dinner. Raina had been so overwhelmed by the lavish furnishings and the vastness of the mansion that she'd hardly registered the layout, let alone potential hiding spots.

She passed the framed entryway to the living room and kept running, thinking that might be one of the first places Warrick would look for her. For that same reason she bypassed the library and family room. She knew a house like this had to have all sorts of hidden passageways and secret doors, but, unfortunately, she didn't have time to search for them.

From far behind her she thought she heard Warrick reach fifty. Stifling a breathless giggle, Raina paused and leaned against a wall, quickly tugging off her strappy sandals and mentally kicking herself for not having the foresight to remove them earlier. As she took off again in her bare feet, adrenaline sang through her veins, making her feel more exhilarated than she'd felt in years. Who knew that playing a simple childhood game with Warrick could be so thrilling?

Rounding a corner, she came to the music room and rushed through the arched doorway. She swept a hurried glance around, taking in the gleaming mahogany curves of a Steinway that dominated one corner of the room. On the opposite side was an assortment of antique instruments mounted in glass, none of which she could take cover behind.

Making a quick decision, Raina shoved her feet back into her sandals, then dashed around the grand piano and hid behind the heavy brocade drapes that adorned the tall French windows.

From somewhere down the corridor Warrick's strong, resonant voice drifted toward her, a soft taunt. "Ready or not, here I come."

Raina flattened her body against the wall, trying to make herself as invisible as possible. When she glanced down at her feet to check if they were showing, she was relieved to see that the curtain hung all the way to the floor.

After what seemed an eternity, she heard the soft tread of approaching footsteps. Her pulse quickened as Warrick paused in the doorway. She imagined his eyes scanning the room, his head cocked at an angle as he strained to listen for the slightest noise that would betray her position.

Raina squeezed her eyes tightly shut, as if by doing so she could somehow make herself disappear.

After several nerve-racking moments, Warrick called out conversationally, "Maybe you're right, Raina. Maybe this house *is* too big for me to find you."

Her breathing grew shallow. Her heart was racing so fast she felt light-headed, giddy with excitement and tension.

Warrick stepped into the room.

As he started toward the piano, Raina's heart hammered so violently against her rib cage she half wondered if he could hear it. She didn't move a muscle.

Warrick came to a stop at the piano. As Raina waited breathlessly, he plucked out a few idle notes that gave her pause. As she listened, the soft notes soon evolved into the smooth, beautifully harmonious chords of a classical sonata.

Her brows shot up. When had Warrick learned to play like that?

Her very next thought was, *What* can't *those talented fingers do?*

Before her imagination had a chance to wander, the music changed, the haunting concerto spilling into another song that struck Raina as vaguely familiar.

And then in a deep, smoky voice, Warrick crooned, "Just lookin' out of the window—"

Raina clapped her hand over her mouth to stifle the hysterical giggle that bubbled up in her throat, but it burst forth anyway.

Abruptly the music stopped.

Raina squealed as Warrick snatched back the curtain and said triumphantly, "Gotcha!"

Between howls of laughter, Raina managed to cry out protestingly, "No fair! You *tricked* me into giving away my position."

Warrick laughed, looking boyishly handsome and immensely pleased with himself. "I told you I'd find you, woman. And it only took—" He flicked a glance at his watch, "ten minutes. Just like I said."

Giggling helplessly, Raina punched him on the shoulder. "You play dirty, Warrick Mayne. Singing the theme song to *Good Times.* You knew that would get me!"

"Precisely." He grinned, his dark eyes glimmering with satisfaction. "It didn't work on the plane earlier, so I figured I'd try again. Anyway, I knew you were here the whole time."

"I know. You probably heard exactly where I was going. I didn't think to remove my shoes until it was too late. Otherwise—"

Warrick shook his head at her. "Just can't accept defeat, can you?"

"Nope," Raina retorted, wiping tears of laughter from the corners of her eyes. "It's not in my DNA."

"Hmm. I'll have to remember that," Warrick drawled, his amused gaze wandering across her face.

"By the way, when did you learn how to play the piano? Was that Mozart?"

"Chopin. I took piano lessons a few years ago." He shrugged. "I figured if I'm going to own a Steinway, I might as well learn how to play it."

"You play beautifully. I was very impressed." Raina gave him a teasing smile. "What other hidden talents do you possess?"

As soon as the lighthearted words left her mouth, she immediately realized it was the wrong thing to say.

Warrick's lazy grin faded.

And just like that, the air between them changed, crackling with the latent heat and sensuality that pulsed between them every time they were near each other.

Suddenly Raina couldn't draw enough air into her lungs. She was acutely aware of the sheer breadth of his shoulders, his clean, masculine scent, the warmth radiating from his body. Nervously she ran her tongue over her parched lips.

Another mistake.

Warrick lowered his eyes to her mouth, his thick black lashes sweeping down with the movement. The intensity of his hot, focused gaze made her pulse accelerate. An internal alarm warned her to leave, to get away from this dangerous man *right now,* but she couldn't move. Her feet remained rooted to the floor, her back pressed against the wall.

When Warrick shifted a fraction closer, her nipples hardened, and a throbbing ache flooded her loins.

What would it be like, she wondered, to have this gorgeous, virile man clasped between her legs, moving inside her with deep, penetrating thrusts that drove her to a mind-blowing orgasm?

When she found herself mentally calculating how long it would take them to reach her room—or the master suite, whichever was closest—she knew she was in trouble.

When he moved again, her hips arched off the wall of their own volition, instinctively seeking the heat of his body. His big, warm hands grasped her waist, gently pulling her against him, letting her feel his rigid arousal. The deep ache between her thighs intensified until she thought she would come right there, fully clothed. Just like before.

Warrick lowered his head, angling his mouth over hers. But instead of kissing her, he let their shallow breaths mingle, and somehow that was just as powerfully arousing as the brush of his soft lips would have been.

"I wonder," he murmured, the low, velvety timbre of his voice sending jolts of sensation shooting from her belly to her throbbing loins.

Raina was half out of her mind with the blind, desperate hunger that had overtaken her, but somehow she managed to frame a coherent response. "Wonder what?" she breathed.

Slowly, deliberately, Warrick brought his face closer to hers, so close that their mouths were separated by less than a hairsbreadth. Raina shivered uncontrollably, on the verge of begging him to kiss her.

"I wonder," he whispered huskily, "what the good doctor would say if he could see us now."

Raina stiffened, his words hitting her like a sharp blast of ice water, instantly cooling her ardor. Anger and humiliation swept through her.

Warrick stepped back and slowly lifted his gaze to hers, a terrible, mocking gleam in his eyes. "Not that I don't enjoy a little foreplay," he drawled insolently. "But I thought at least one of us should remember that you're practically engaged."

Glaring at him, Raina said the only thing she could: "Go to hell, Warrick."

He gave a low, mirthless laugh. "I'm already there, Raina. Believe me, I'm already there."

But Raina hardly heard his response above the boiling rage coursing through her blood, pounding in her ears.

Giving him one last scathing look, she stepped around him and strode out of the room with her shoulders squared and her head held high.

Once she was safely out of sight, however, she sagged against the nearest wall and closed her eyes against the hot, bitter sting of tears.

She was as furious with herself as she was with Warrick. How could she have forgotten, even for a moment, how ruthless and calculating he could be? How could she have let down her guard so easily with him after vowing not to let such a thing happen? No matter how charming and attentive he'd been tonight, no matter how fierce the attraction between them, the hard, cold truth was that Warrick hated her guts. The generous deeds, the expensive gifts, the thoughtful little notes, the endearing playfulness. It was all part of his grand scheme to get what he wanted from her. By his own admission, he was courting her the way he would any other prospective client. And *still* he couldn't resist humiliating her, punishing her in his own cruel little ways.

Reese's sage warning echoed through her mind. *Warrick Mayne can hurt you in a way no one else can.*

Raina drew a deep, shuddering breath that burned in her lungs. She'd allowed herself to get caught up in one of her foolish girlhood fantasies. The grand mansion with the enchanting gardens, combined with the romantic candlelight dinner with Warrick, had cast a spell over her. She'd almost tricked herself into believing she was starring in her own fairy tale. But she wasn't an ugly duckling turned swan princess, and Warrick was no Prince Charming.

They were enemies. Two adversaries squaring off on the dueling field, trying to see who could draw first blood, each determined to be the last one standing.

With a new resolve steeling her spine, Raina straightened from the wall. If Warrick thought she was going down without a fight, then he really *didn't* know her at all.

After Raina stormed out of the music room, Warrick swore under his breath, sank down heavily on the piano bench and dropped his head into his hands.

He'd expected to feel satisfied, profoundly vindicated after the way he'd humiliated Raina. Instead he felt angry and disgusted with himself for behaving like such a callous jerk. He'd wanted to punish her, but now as he reflected on the outcome of his action, he realized that *he* was the only one being punished. Because he still wanted her with a vengeance. But after the way he'd behaved, he'd be damned lucky if she let him anywhere near her again. And that, as far as he was concerned, was unthinkable.

Warrick lifted his head from his hands and looked across the room, staring sullenly at the empty doorway. She'd only been gone a few minutes and he already missed her. Damn. What the hell was going on here? What was happening to him?

Warrick had experienced more adventures in his thirty-six years on earth than most people experienced in a lifetime. He'd known the pure adrenaline rush of racing through the hills of Germany in a turbocharged Ferrari sports car built expressly for the autobahn. He'd experienced the exhilaration and triumph of scaling Mount Fuji, and diving out of an airplane at an altitude of thirty thousand feet. He'd traveled to breathtakingly exotic locales and had made love to countless beautiful women. But not one of those experiences had ever made him feel the way he'd felt tonight, engaged in something as simple, as *uneventful*, as having dinner with Raina St. James.

Throughout the evening, almost from the moment he and Raina

sat down at the dinner table, Warrick had experienced a range of emotions unlike anything he'd ever felt before. He'd been helplessly mesmerized when Raina talked about her salsa dancing. When he'd imagined her beautiful, supple body gyrating to the sensual music, lust had clawed at his insides.

The note of self-deprecation in her voice when she'd admitted to being a hopeless romantic had tugged at something deep within him, something he couldn't identify. And the way she'd enjoyed her food… Who knew that watching a woman eat could bring him so much pleasure and contentment?

And who knew that he'd get such a thrill out of chasing her through the halls as they'd played hide-and-seek? He'd felt like a kid again, buoyant and carefree in a way he'd rarely known in his embattled childhood. When he'd realized that Raina was hiding in the music room, he'd absurdly wondered if she knew that this was one of his favorite rooms in the house. He'd wanted to play something soulful and romantic for her. Corny as it sounded, he'd wanted to serenade her with a love song.

And when he'd had her cornered, and she'd licked those luscious lips and stared at him with those sultry eyes, he'd wanted to take her right against the wall. And she'd wanted him to, the smoldering passion in her gaze and her restless, undulating hips telling him so. But then he'd thought about Bradford, who was a doctor like Raina's father and who had already won over her sister. He thought about Bradford, who was supposedly a great cook and a great guy, who was free to love Raina with a clear conscience, unburdened by the past. Warrick thought about Bradford holding her, caressing her, kissing her—and something inside him had snapped.

He'd rejected Raina, coldly and unmercifully. But all he'd succeeded in doing was offending her, and depriving himself of what could have been the most incredible night of his life.

Damn it all to hell.

Seated at the piano, Warrick fingered the ivory keys and plucked out a few moody notes, thinking he might play for an hour or two, something that usually relaxed him after a long, stressful day. But tonight he was too frustrated, too edgy and miserable to concentrate on a composition or to take any pleasure in playing.

Cursing under his breath, Warrick slammed the hood over the keyboard with a loud, discordant *ping!* and stalked out of the room, knowing that sleep would elude him that night.

Chapter 14

During the drive into downtown Philadelphia the next morning, Warrick was silent, staring broodingly out the window at the passing scenery, which undoubtedly was as familiar to him as the bustling streets of Houston. For the life of her Raina couldn't fathom why *he* was in a foul mood. *She* was the one who'd been cruelly rebuffed and humiliated last night, and had hardly slept a wink as a result. If anyone should be silent and brooding this morning, it was her. Instead she'd gone out of her way to be pleasant and upbeat, determined to show Warrick that she could take whatever he was vindictive enough to dish out.

The limousine rolled through downtown traffic, gliding past historic landmarks and high-rise office buildings before reaching an imposing granite-and-glass skyscraper on Broad Street in the heart of the city's business district.

Lanny guided the limo into the underground parking garage and descended to the parking level reserved for the company's chief executives. He let Warrick and Raina out in front of a private elevator.

The uniformed security guard posted at the elevator tipped his head deferentially to Warrick. "Morning, Mr. Mayne. Welcome back. How was Houston?"

"Good," Warrick said with the first smile Raina had glimpsed all morning. "There's no place like home."

Once Warrick and Raina were alone in the elevator, the relaxed smile disappeared, and he became absorbed in perusing a folded-up copy of the *Wall Street Journal.* Undaunted by his remoteness, Raina chattered animatedly about previous trips to Philadelphia, describing her enchantment with the historic museums and fine restaurants until Warrick glanced at her with a mildly exasperated expression. "Are you always this cheerful in the morning?"

"Are you always this grumpy?" she fired back.

That seemed to disarm him. He hesitated, then chuckled softly. "No, I'm not. And you're right. This is your first visit to my company, and I'm being an ungracious host. I'm sorry."

Raina hesitated. "Apology accepted," she said, feeling slightly deflated. She'd enjoyed proving to him that she could be the bigger person, and now he'd taken even that away from her with his humble apology. Damn him.

The elevator arrived on the sixtieth floor with a discreet chime, the doors opening to reveal a large reception area paneled in rich mahogany and gleaming marble. An attractive brunette was seated behind a large reception desk topped with glass, the mahogany base bearing the distinctive insignia of Mayne Industries.

Raina and Warrick had barely stepped off the elevator before they were greeted with a warm chorus of "Good morning, Mr. Mayne! Welcome back, Mr. Mayne!" from employees passing by on their way to different offices and cubicles. Warrick nodded and returned their greetings, calling several people by name. Women gazed admiringly at him and offered demure smiles while eyeing Raina curiously. Even the receptionist couldn't stop beaming at Warrick as she relayed important messages and nodded briskly at the instructions he gave her. When he introduced Raina, the knowing gleam in the woman's eyes told Raina that the receptionist, like the majority of Warrick's employees, understood that Raina was the only obstacle to their company's expansion plans.

Warrick and Raina left the reception desk and started toward the office suites occupied by the senior executives. The rooms were situated along both sides of a long, thickly carpeted corridor adorned with contemporary paintings and plaques. Secretaries were seated outside the executive offices in spacious cubicles made of mahogany and glass.

As Warrick and Raina walked past, heads swiveled in their direction. Conversations halted. More greetings were called out to Warrick.

At the end of the corridor, set apart from the other offices and featuring its own private reception area, was Warrick's corner suite. Outside the office was a large, meticulously tidy desk that stood empty.

"That's where my secretary sits," Warrick explained. "She's currently in Houston with the rest of the transition team, overseeing the expansion project."

Raina thought it odd, and a little presumptuous, that he already had a transition team in place when nothing had been finalized, but she kept the thought to herself. Maybe that was the way things were done nowadays in corporate America.

Warrick unlocked the door and gestured her inside an enormous office that boasted a sleek, ultramodern steel-and-glass design. The suite was stylishly appointed with deeply cushioned leather chairs, Deco lighting, a rare collection of contemporary art and built-in bookshelves that were lined with every title imaginable for the professional engineer. But the most impressive thing about the very impressive office was the stunning, panoramic view of the downtown skyline.

Raina drifted toward the floor-to-ceiling windows, unable to resist the lure of that view. "Nice," she murmured, aware of how inadequate the word was.

Warrick chuckled. "Glad you approve."

He had barely set down his briefcase and sat behind the massive glass desk before his phone trilled. Raina listened with one ear as he spoke to one of his project managers at a refinery in California, calmly talking the man through a minor crisis involving a pipeline under construction.

At one point during the conversation Raina glanced over her shoulder to find Warrick reclining in his chair, his dark gaze fixed on her. It was the longest he had looked at her all morning.

As Raina stared back at him, unable to glance away, heat and tension crackled across the distance that separated them. With a supreme effort Raina finally dragged her gaze away and resumed staring out the window, more than a little shaken.

Minutes later Warrick ended his phone call just as a new voice said, "Heard you were here. Glad to see you made it back in one piece."

Raina turned from the window to identify the owner of the smooth, low voice. A tall, handsome, brown-skinned man in an impeccably tailored dark suit had wandered into the office, his hands thrust casually into his pockets.

"Thanks for holding down the fort in my absence," Warrick said to the newcomer in a lazy drawl.

Broad shoulders shrugged. "I figured I might as well earn my keep around here." As the man's amused gaze strayed across the room to where Raina stood at the window, his mouth suddenly curved in a wide grin. "Well, hello there. You must be Miss St. James."

"Yes." Raina smiled politely, starting forward with an outstretched hand. "It's nice to meet you, Mr.—?"

"Fuller," he provided, striding purposefully toward her. "Stephon Fuller, at your service."

He clasped her hand, his gold-flecked dark eyes roaming across her face with frank male appreciation. "It's a pleasure to finally meet you, Miss St. James."

"Thank you," Raina murmured, though she couldn't help wondering just what Warrick had told this man about her. "Please call me Raina."

"With pleasure."

Warrick had risen from his chair. "Stephon is our vice president and chief operating officer," he informed Raina.

Stephon shook his head slowly. "Why didn't you tell me the sisters in Houston are so beautiful?" he asked Warrick, who pointedly arched a brow at Raina's hand, still clasped in Stephon's.

With a soft chuckle Stephon released her, albeit reluctantly. "Is this your first trip to Philly, Raina?"

"No, I've been here several times. I went to school in New York, so it was fairly easy to hop on the train and head down to Philly anytime. I was just telling Warrick earlier how much I enjoy visiting the city."

"I'm glad you feel that way," Stephon said with a pleased smile. "I met Warrick at Texas A&M, but I'm originally from Philly. I can't tell you how many times I've patted myself on the back for talking him into accepting his first job here, which obviously worked out for me when he decided to stick around and start his own company."

Raina smiled. "I guess everything happens for a reason."

"Absolutely. Have you had a chance to hit the town yet, do any shopping or sightseeing?"

"Not yet. We got in a little late yesterday evening."

Stephon nodded. "Well, since it's a holiday weekend, we're closing at one. So maybe—"

"Raina and I already have a full day ahead of us," Warrick interjected brusquely.

Raina looked over at him in surprise. "We do?"

He scowled. "Of course."

"I mean, I know we have tickets to the orchestra tonight—"

"That's not until eight. You said you'd like to visit the art museum after we leave here, so that's what we're doing."

Raina didn't think he'd been paying attention to her in the elevator, but apparently she was wrong. Swallowing a smile, she said meekly, "All right."

Stephon, dividing a speculative glance between them, said to Warrick, "I know Leland was waiting for you to arrive so he could talk to you about the Lake Charles onshore project. If you don't have time to give Raina the tour—"

"I have time," Warrick bit off, his jaw clenched.

"Are you sure? I know Leland said it was really important—"

"Leland can wait," Warrick growled. Stalking around his desk, he gently but firmly cupped Raina's elbow and began escorting her from the office, instructing over his shoulder to a grinning Stephon, "Close the damned door on your way out."

Over the next three hours, Raina learned more about Mayne Industries than she could ever hope to retain.

Warrick gave her a complete tour of the modern facilities and introduced her to the many men and women who worked out of the company's civil, electrical, mechanical, structural, telecommunications and network infrastructure divisions. Raina was pleased by the diversity of his staff and undeniably impressed by the wealth of knowledge, talent and dedication each individual brought to the firm. After hearing about some of the innovative projects the various teams of engineers had successfully completed, Raina was no longer surprised by the numerous industry awards Mayne Industries had garnered over the years.

Prior to her visit that morning, her knowledge and understanding of the company's capabilities had been largely limited to its role in the oil-and-gas industry. And while that was an integral part of the business, the scope of the firm's services was so much broader than that. Among the new technologies being developed and tested by company researchers was an airless tire that could withstand extreme punishment. The objective was to boost the security of military vehicles and save the lives of countless soldiers whose convoys were routinely targeted with improvised explosive devices in combat zones. If successful, the airless-tire technology could eventually be applied to domestic-passenger vehicles sold in the United States, decreasing the incidence of rollover and tire-related deaths.

During the tour, Raina also met electrical engineering students who, as part of their summer internship, were creating robots that could one day be utilized to perform jobs that were too hazardous for humans to carry out. Gathered inside one of the company's state-of-the-art labs, Raina was given a demonstration of a prototype robot simulating such dangerous tasks as cleaning out boiler pipes and oil storage tanks, and carrying out land-mine detection. The remote-controlled robots were designed to navigate independently through a path without human supervision. As Raina watched the presentation, Warrick explained to her that Mayne Industries had recently teamed up with NASA to fine-tune the robots' technology, which was another benefit of relocating the company's headquarters to Houston—the proximity to the Johnson Space Center. It was the only direct reference to the expansion project he'd made all morning, and it was so subtle that Raina hardly noticed.

From the very beginning of the tour she had watched, reluctantly fascinated, as Warrick slid into the role of chief executive officer—a commanding figure who radiated confidence, charisma and authority with the natural ease of a born leader. When he strode into a room people sat up and took notice, responding not only to his status as head of the company, but to the strength and virility he exuded. But even in his expensively tailored suit and Italian loafers, bristling with command and raw energy, Warrick never came across as unapproachable. His warm regard for his employees was evident every time he inquired about a new baby, teased a father whose teenager had just obtained a driver's license or bantered easily about the upcoming football season and the Philadelphia Eagles' playoff chances. As Raina watched Warrick interact with his employees, it was clear to her that they not only respected and admired him, they genuinely liked him. And *that* impressed her nearly as much as all the awards they had received and the cutting-edge work they performed as a company.

She was immensely proud of Warrick for the thriving enterprise he had built, and the valuable services he provided to his clients and to the global community. But did that mean she was ready to sacrifice her own business so that he could build his desired new headquarters? Before touring Mayne Industries that morning and meeting its wonderful employees, Raina's answer would have been an unequivocal, resounding *no.* But now she wasn't so certain, and that scared her almost as much as the prospect of losing her heart once again to the company's dynamic, dangerously compelling leader.

Warrick couldn't take his eyes off Raina.

That evening, as they sat across from each other on the outdoor veranda of an exclusive downtown restaurant, all he could think about was how breathtakingly beautiful Raina looked in the Carolina Herrera dress he'd bought her.

The moment he first saw her, wafting down the stairs where he'd been patiently waiting for her at the bottom, the air had rushed out of his lungs, and his heart had lodged painfully in his throat. She was a vision in that dress. An absolute goddess. The silk hugged her sublime curves, and the soft green color beautifully complemented her golden-brown skin, just as Warrick had known it would. Her dark hair was swept into an elegant chignon that accentuated the slender, graceful column of her neck and made him want to kiss and caress her nape. And he didn't want to stop there. He really didn't want to stop there.

She'd smiled shyly and murmured an apology for taking so long, but Warrick had been so thunderstruck that he'd hardly heard a word she'd said. He must have stood there gaping like an idiot, because after another moment Mr. Gibbons had cleared his throat and discreetly nudged him.

An hour and a half later, Warrick was still mesmerized every time he looked at Raina.

The view from their table was perfect. Lush foliage surrounded the veranda. A gentle summer breeze carried the scents of hibiscus and jasmine, and the sky held the promise of a breathtaking sunset.

But Warrick only had eyes for Raina.

The sound of her soft, smoky laughter suddenly lured him out of his trance. "I just want you to know," she drawled in an amused voice, "that you're making me feel *very* self-conscious."

Warrick smiled a little. "I'm sorry. I don't mean to."

"Then stop staring at me like that," she suggested, those entrancing dark eyes twinkling with mirth.

"I can't help it," Warrick admitted huskily. "You're an incredibly beautiful woman, Raina."

She blushed prettily. "Thank you, Warrick. Now will you promise me that you won't say that again for at least the rest of the evening?"

He shook his head. "I can't make that kind of promise."

"Why not?"

"Because I'd probably break it within seconds of making it. You're beautiful. See what I mean? It just keeps slipping out."

Raina laughed, shaking her head in helpless exasperation.

Warrick smiled softly at her. He was glad she'd decided to forgive him for the unconscionable way he'd behaved last night. When he'd got up that morning—on the wrong side of the bed, because he'd tossed and turned all night—he'd fully expected to encounter a cold, resentful woman. To his surprise, Raina had been friendly and cheerful. *Too* damned friendly and cheerful. Which had only made him feel worse.

But she'd called him out on his foul mood, and just like that, the air had been cleared, allowing them to enjoy a relaxing afternoon at the Philadelphia Museum of Art, followed by a leisurely stroll along the Benjamin Franklin Parkway. Warrick had visited the art museum and walked along that scenic route countless times before, but he'd never enjoyed those experiences as thoroughly as he had today with Raina by his side. There was something about her, something about *being* with her, that made the simplest things seem profoundly special. Magical.

Like now.

Sitting at that cozy table with her, Warrick felt an indescribable sense of contentment wash over him. He could have stayed there with Raina all night, although she probably wouldn't appreciate missing the orchestra, which she'd looked forward to all day.

They finished their meals and ordered dessert, although they both laughingly agreed—after the waiter left—that nothing on the menu could be as good as the double-chocolate tart Sonny had served them last night.

Smiling across the table at Warrick, Raina said teasingly, "I bet you and Stephon used to compete over girls all the time back in college."

Warrick chuckled. "What makes you say that?"

"Just a hunch. Am I right?"

"You are," he admitted, smiling lazily. "But I'd like to think it was a healthy competition."

"Healthy, huh?"

"Yeah. We were so eager to outdo each other and impress the ladies that it kept us on our best behavior." When Raina arched a dubious brow at him, he grinned. "Well, not always. But it's the thought that counts."

"Of course."

"Hey, at least we respected each other's territory. If I knew Stephon was really into someone, I backed off, and vice versa. We never let any woman come between our friendship."

Although that had nearly changed today, Warrick mused darkly, remembering how murderous he'd felt that morning when Stephon had been on the verge of asking Raina out on a date. He'd wanted to haul Stephon across the room and toss him out the damned window, a violent urge that had surprised him. This whole jealousy thing was as new to Warrick as all the other emotions he'd been experiencing lately.

Raina smiled at him. "I really enjoyed taking the tour of your company this morning. You have some amazing people working for you."

"Thank you for saying that," Warrick murmured. "They *are* amazing. Every last one of them. I feel very fortunate."

"I'm sure they feel the same way. In fact, I know they do. When you got called away to the phone, a group of them told me how much they love working at Mayne Industries. Not only do you pay exceptionally well and offer generous benefits, they said, but the culture you've created is nothing like the cold corporate environments many of them had experienced at other jobs. One of them described Mayne Industries as a 'world-class company with a warm, family feel.'"

Warrick grinned, even as his chest swelled with pride and satisfaction. "Whoever told you that is getting a very nice raise."

Raina laughed.

"You made quite an impression yourself," Warrick said, adding sourly, "Especially on Stephon."

Grinning, Raina shook her head at him. "Why does that bother—"

"Hello, Warrick," a brittle feminine voice interrupted.

Warrick glanced up and inwardly groaned when he saw the statuesque, long-haired woman who had appeared at the table. Angela Harvey, the attorney he'd met a couple of weeks ago. Damn, he'd forgotten all about her.

"I *thought* that was your limo parked outside the restaurant," Angela said coolly, her red lips twisted accusingly. "I didn't even know you were back in town."

"It was a last-minute decision," Warrick said evenly. He glanced across the table at Raina, who was watching the exchange with a strained expression.

Warrick bit back a sigh of frustration. *Damn it. Just when everything seemed to be going so well between them.*

He rose from the table. "Angela, I'd like you to meet—"

"I'm not interested in meeting your newest little plaything!" Angela snapped, her dark eyes flashing with fury. She raked a contemptuous glance over Raina and sneered, "She looks kind of young, Warrick. Even for you."

Raina scowled. Before she could open her mouth to defend herself, Warrick shot her a warning look before returning his attention to Angela. A hushed silence had swept over the veranda. Out of the corner of his eye, he could see several people staring at them, alerted by Angela's sudden outburst.

Warrick clenched his jaw, his gaze boring into hers. Very deliberately, keeping his voice low and controlled, he said, "Look around you. What if one of your clients is here? Do you really want them to see you making a scene in public?"

Angela barked out a harsh laugh. "Don't try to pretend you're worried about *my* reputation," she jeered. "The only person you care about is yourself, Warrick Mayne!"

His expression hardened. "If you say so. Now if you'll excuse me, I'd like to finish my dinner in peace."

Her nostrils flared. As her eyes shot to the table and homed in on his freshly refilled wineglass, Warrick read the intent in her gaze. Before she could reach down and snatch the glass, he caught her wrist midair.

"Don't."

Angela stared into his rigid face, seeing the lethal warning in his eyes. With a strangled cry of frustration she yanked her wrist free, then spun on her heel and hurried away.

Warrick watched her go, his temper simmering. After taking a deep, calming breath, he smoothed down his silk tie and sat back down, ignoring the scandalized stares and whispers of the other diners. He didn't give a damn what strangers thought of him. But he *did* care what Raina thought, and judging by the way she was looking at him, it wasn't good.

"Sorry about that," he murmured.

Raina just shook her head. Warrick could tell by the thinly veiled disgust on her face that the spectacle she'd just witnessed hadn't shocked her. Instead it had only reinforced her opinion of him as a shameless womanizer, a reputation he'd gained over the years after a string of high-profile breakups.

Warrick swore viciously under his breath. "Raina—"

She threw up a hand. "Despite what she assumed, I'm not your girlfriend. You don't owe me any explanation."

Warrick snapped his mouth shut.

An awkward silence settled over the table. The relaxed camaraderie he and Raina had enjoyed before Angela's appearance was gone, perhaps for good this time. Warrick mourned the loss, even as his temper flared at the unjustness of it.

He shoved back his chair and stood. "Excuse me," he said tersely.

Raina stared at him as he turned and strode purposefully from the veranda.

Angela and two of her friends were standing in the elegant reception area, waiting to be seated. The two women appeared to be consoling Angela, whose head was bobbing angrily as she ranted about what had just happened. Only her friends saw Warrick barreling down on them, their eyes widening so dramatically that he would have laughed if there were anything remotely funny about the situation.

Angela was saying, "And he had the nerve—"

"Come with me," Warrick growled, seizing her wrist and dragging her down the tiled corridor to a private alcove around the corner from the restrooms.

Angela stared at him as if he'd lost his mind. "Are you—"

"What the *hell* was that little stunt you just pulled?" he demanded, cutting her off.

She folded her arms defiantly across her chest. "All right. Maybe I lost my head a little."

"Maybe?" Warrick thundered incredulously.

"I'm sorry!" she burst out. "I didn't know how else to react when I saw you sitting at the table with that *woman.* You're not even supposed to be in town!"

His eyes narrowed dangerously. "Did I miss something here? Since when do I have to check in with you before I come and go? When did I put a damned ring on your finger?"

Angela flinched, her face flushing with humiliation. "I never thought—"

"Sure as hell could have fooled me, the way you just performed back there!" He shook his head, staring at her as if he'd never seen her before. And maybe he hadn't. The vengeful, hysterical woman who'd just made a fool of herself on the veranda bore no resemblance whatsoever to the smart, witty, *confident* attorney Warrick had met a few weeks ago.

Angela said bitterly, "I've been calling you every day since you left, and you didn't even have the decency to respond to any of my messages. What was I supposed to think when I showed up here and saw you with another woman?"

Warrick stared at her, dumbfounded. "We've never even been on a real date, Angela. We've gone out for drinks a couple times, and that's it. Where do you get off acting like we had something more than that?"

Hurt flared in her eyes. "Because I thought we did. I thought we really had a connection, Warrick, but I guess I was wrong. All those tabloid stories I've read about you are obviously true, and that *child* out there is obviously your latest conquest!"

Warrick scowled. "First of all, she's not a child. She's thirty damned years old. And she's not my *conquest.*"

"Yeah, right," Angela scoffed, her lips twisting cynically. "I suppose you're also going to tell me she's just a friend, right? She's just an old, long-lost friend you've known since childhood, right?"

"Actually," Warrick snarled, "I've known her since I was sixteen. Does that count as childhood?"

Angela faltered, her eyes narrowing. "I don't believe you."

"Believe whatever the hell you want. And while you're at it, Angela, lose my damned number."

"Warrick, wait!" she cried out, grabbing his arm as he started away. "I'm sorry. I overreacted, okay? Believe me, I've never behaved that way before. When I wake up tomorrow morning and remember what I did tonight, I'm going to be mortified. All I can say in my defense is that I'm really feeling you, Warrick. I was looking forward to spending more time with you and getting to know you better."

Warrick stopped and turned, his jaw flexing as he gazed down at her. "Believe it or not, Angela, I wasn't trying to hurt you. I think you're a smart, accomplished woman, and any man would be lucky to have you. But it won't be me."

Her chin quivered. "I was playing hard to get!" she burst out desperately. "That's why we haven't been on a real date, Warrick. Not because I couldn't make time for you in my busy schedule, for God's sake. It's because I didn't want you to think I was too easy. I thought you wanted a challenge. A woman who wouldn't sleep with you right away, like all the others. But if you want—"

"I don't," Warrick said almost gently. "And it has nothing to do with you. Take care of yourself, Angela."

With that he turned and walked away, heading back to Raina, hoping that what had been an incredibly perfect evening could be salvaged, though somehow he knew better.

Chapter 15

Several hours later, Warrick stood at the window in his study nursing a cold beer and gazing out at the moonlit grounds of his estate. By the crack of dawn tomorrow, employees from a local rental company would arrive to begin setting up carnival rides and inflatable games, and Sonny and his catering staff would commandeer the kitchen, snarling at anyone who dared to enter. By midafternoon the south lawn would be overrun with hundreds of laughing, frolicking children with paint smeared over their faces and their fingers sticky from cotton candy as they raced from one amusement to another.

It was going to be a long day.

But the thoughts dominating Warrick's mind that night had nothing to do with tomorrow's Fourth of July party. Even if he'd been in charge of the preparations—which he wasn't—it wouldn't have mattered.

For the second night in a row, sleep had eluded him. And there was only one reason why.

Raina.

Just as he'd feared, the remainder of the evening had been a bust.

Although the orchestra had been pitch perfect and he and Raina had had the best seats in the house, nothing could have undone the damage caused by Angela Harvey's outburst at the restaurant. Raina had been withdrawn for the rest of the night, and when they'd returned to the house, she'd retreated to her room as if she couldn't get away from him fast enough.

If Warrick could have strangled Angela and gotten away with it, he would have.

Rousing himself from his grim musings, he turned and started back toward his desk, where he'd been designing schematics for a new pipeline project in Lake Charles, Louisiana.

When a movement across the room caught his eye, he glanced up.

And froze.

Raina stood in the doorway, and for the life of him he couldn't fathom why his heart thumped violently at the sight of her. He wished he could blame it on being startled by her sudden appearance, but he knew better. The woman had been wreaking havoc on his nervous system for the past five days. Why should this time be any different?

Lifting his beer to his mouth, he gave her a once-over. While he had only removed his suit jacket and tie in the hours since they'd been back, Raina had changed for bed, though Warrick couldn't tell what she wore beneath the long silk robe that was belted tightly at her waist, teasing his imagination. With her hair scooped into a loose ponytail and her face scrubbed clean of makeup, she looked fresh and wholesome, and as young as Angela had assumed she was.

As Raina stood across the room watching him with a silent, brooding expression, Warrick wondered how long she'd been there. More to the point, *why* was she there?

"Are you lost?" he murmured.

She shook her head. "I came downstairs to get a glass of water, and I saw your light on."

Warrick gazed at her. "Couldn't sleep?"

"No."

"Neither could I."

Their eyes held for a long moment.

"I'm testing a theory," Raina said softly.

"A theory?"

She nodded. "If I don't go to bed mad at you, then maybe I can actually get some sleep."

"I see." His mouth twitched. "And how do you intend to get over being mad at me?"

She shrugged. "I suppose by talking to you until I'm not mad anymore."

"Ah." Warrick swallowed a smile, ridiculously pleased by the simple proposition. "Makes sense."

Raina just looked at him.

Smothering a soft chuckle, he walked over to his desk and sat down. When he glanced up again she was still standing in the doorway.

He raised an amused brow at her. "Are you waiting for an invitation?"

"Are you extending one?"

"Yes, Raina," he said with exaggerated patience. "Please come in."

He watched as she wandered slowly into the room, glancing around casually. "You sure do like mahogany," she murmured.

"Is that a criticism?"

"No, just an observation. And a compliment. You have excellent taste."

She said it matter-of-factly, without inflection, as if she were a bored queen bestowing favor upon a loyal subject. If Warrick had still been standing, he would have bowed in grateful submission.

"What're you working on?" Raina asked, approaching his desk.

"Work stuff."

"I can see that. What kind of work stuff?"

When he told her about the Lake Charles project, she gave him a bemused smile. "But you're the CEO, with an army of engineers and project managers at your disposal. Why would you have such a hands-on role in the designing of a pipeline?"

Warrick smiled. "I like to keep my skills sharp." He paused. "Do you have a massage license, Raina?"

She shook her head. "I have my hands full enough running Touch of Heaven. When I first decided to open a spa, I knew that I couldn't become a full-time practitioner and still expect to have a profitable business. So I leave the client services to my experienced staff and focus on the business side of the house." She pursed her lips thoughtfully. "But I guess it's a little different for you. You were a licensed engineer before you became a CEO. Although you have complete confidence in your employees, it must be a little hard for you to relinquish control of projects you once enjoyed so much."

"You're right," Warrick smilingly admitted, both amazed and pleased by her perceptiveness. She'd summed up his feelings perfectly. It was a little disarming. Almost as disarming as her scent as she drew nearer. She must have showered before going to bed. The scent of soap on her skin teased his senses, as did the tantalizing curves of her body beneath the silk robe. When she propped a shapely hip against the large L-shaped desk, Warrick was surprised, and secretly thrilled, that she'd ventured so close to him. His nerve endings hummed with awareness.

"Is that the project?" Raina asked, nodding toward his computer monitor where he'd been working in AutoCAD, an advanced engineering software program.

"Yeah," Warrick answered.

Raina stared at the large screen, her brows furrowing at the complex, crisscrossing network of pipelines that he'd designed. Warrick inwardly smiled. She had no clue what she was viewing.

As if she'd read his mind, she shook her head dazedly and murmured, "I can't even begin to comprehend what I'm looking at."

He laughed. "I figured as much."

Her lips curved in a sheepish grin. "Don't make fun of me. You went to school for this. You eat, sleep, and breathe this stuff."

Lately the only thing he'd eaten, slept and breathed was Raina, but Warrick saw no reason to mention this. Instead he gave her a teasing smile. "Would you like me to explain the schematics?"

"Yes, please."

But as he slid his chair toward the monitor and leaned forward, something on the shelf behind him caught Raina's eye.

She let out a startled cry that made him glance sharply at her. "What?"

"The snow globe!"

Warrick followed the direction of her shocked gaze. Puzzled by her reaction, he reached out and picked up the small snow globe with a wooden base. Inside was a clever little scene depicting a sandy beach nestled smack dab in the middle of downtown Houston. The words "Nothing is Impossible" were inscribed on a banner that drifted lazily across the skyline. When Warrick shook the globe, tiny white flakes swirled around the glass dome so that it appeared to be snowing on a summer afternoon in Houston, hence the inscription, "Nothing is Impossible."

Smiling, Warrick turned back to Raina. "I received this as a gift for—"

"Your college graduation," she whispered. "I know."

"It's amazing," Warrick said, his smile softening as he gently shook the globe again and watched the resulting snowstorm. "I'd never seen one like it before. Someone gave it to me at my graduation party, but there wasn't a card or anything, and when I asked around, no one knew who—" Suddenly he stilled and lifted his eyes to Raina's face.

The way she was looking at him made his heart clutch in his chest. As comprehension dawned, he stared at her. "*You* gave this to me?"

She nodded slowly, her eyes soft and glowing. "When you delivered the valedictorian speech at your high-school graduation, you told your classmates that nothing is impossible. You exhorted them not to let anything or anyone stop them from achieving their dreams. It was a beautiful, awe-inspiring speech, Warrick, and when it was over, there wasn't a dry eye in the house. I've never seen a standing ovation that lasted so long. Even your brothers were moved." She gazed wonderingly at him. "Don't you remember?"

Warrick swallowed hard, wondering at the strange tightness in his throat. "I've given a lot of speeches since then," he joked lamely.

Raina smiled a little. "I never forgot it. I was at Galveston Beach with my family a few months before your college graduation, and when I saw that snow globe at one of those novelty shops, I thought it would be a perfect gift for you. You were going out into the real world, and I knew you'd let nothing stand in your way—" Her voice hitched, and she quickly glanced away.

Warrick returned the snow globe to the shelf, handling it almost reverently now, and rose from the chair.

"Raina?" He reached out and caught her chin, gently forcing her face toward his. He was surprised to see tears glistening in her dark eyes.

"Why are you crying?" he asked softly.

Embarrassed, she choked out a teary laugh. "It's so silly. The day of your graduation party, I got cold feet about giving you the snow globe, especially when I heard what other people were getting for you. Yolanda told me your mother was sending you on a trip to Jamaica, and your uncle bought you new furniture for your very first apartment because you'd accepted the job in Philly. I was embarrassed to give you such a simple, inexpensive gift, so I removed the card so you wouldn't know who it was from. You didn't open your presents until after the party, so I never knew what you thought of the snow globe, and Yolanda never said anything. All these years, I thought you didn't like it—"

"I loved it," Warrick said fervently. "I thought it was the most unique gift I'd ever received in my life. Believe me, Raina, if I'd known it was from you, I would have thanked you. So fourteen years later, I'm saying *thank you.*"

Raina gave him a tremulous smile. "Better late than never," she quipped. She searched his face. "Did you really like it?"

His heart constricted with an emotion so intense it made him ache. "If I didn't like it," he said huskily, "why would I have kept it all these years? Why would it still hold a special place of honor on my shelf after all this time? When I was trying to get my company off the ground, I used to look at that snow globe and remind myself that no matter how tough things seemed, nothing was impossible." He smiled tenderly. "Do you still doubt that I liked it?"

Raina shook her head, tears welling in her eyes. As Warrick gazed at her, a single tear escaped and rolled down her face.

That was his undoing.

He gently cradled her face in his hand and wiped the tear away with the pad of his thumb. Raina trembled, her lashes fluttering as he leaned down and brushed his mouth over hers. Her soft lips parted, sending a jolt of agonized longing through him. As he deepened the kiss, he knew that this time, nothing short of a natural disaster would keep him from making love to her.

The moment Warrick kissed her, Raina knew she was lost.

She couldn't have resisted him to save her life. She wanted this, wanted him more than anything else in the world. More than the very air she breathed.

As she curved her arms around his neck, Warrick pulled her against him until their bodies were fused together from shoulder to knees. Her nipples tightened against the iron slabs of his chest. Her aching loins throbbed against his rigid arousal. She rocked her hips fitfully against him, and he groaned deep in his throat.

He lifted her off the floor and into his arms. As she wrapped her legs around his waist, the silk folds of her robe parted. Warrick slid his hands beneath the raised hem of her nightshirt, kneading her thighs before reaching beneath her silk underwear to grasp her bare bottom. Raina gasped, his touch searing her skin, firing her blood. She ground her pelvis against him, and this time they both groaned.

He set her down on his desk, kissing her feverishly, thrusting his tongue deep inside her mouth. She moaned, erotic sensations tumbling through her, faster and faster. She could feel him everywhere—her breasts, her stomach, between her thighs. His taste was in her mouth. His scent was in her nostrils. His breathing, as rough and ragged as her own, resonated in her ears.

As he sucked her bottom lip, she tightened her thighs around him and gripped his hard-muscled back, feeling the heat of his skin beneath his shirt. She wanted him out of his clothes. Wanted to feel his naked, powerful body against hers. Wanted to feel him moving between her legs.

Cradling her face in his big hands, he kissed the length of her throat, nibbling and nipping as he went, making her shiver with need. All the while his hips moved against hers in a slow, measured rhythm that made her writhe desperately against him.

"Easy," he murmured. "Don't rush this."

Easy for him to say, Raina thought. *He* hadn't been waiting for this moment practically all his life. But hadn't she known, after their first kiss, that he would be this way, a skilled, patient lover who would take his time pleasuring and tormenting her?

She whimpered softly in protest as Warrick lifted his head from hers. Holding her gaze, he reached for the belt of her robe and slowly, deliberately, began untying it. Raina's heart thundered, anticipation coiling in her belly.

As he slid the robe from her shoulders, the friction of the silk, combined with the warm brush of his knuckles against her skin, made her shudder convulsively. She closed her eyes and swayed against him as he leaned down, placing an openmouthed kiss on her bare shoulder.

"You have such beautiful skin," he said huskily.

Raina quivered as he rained hot little kisses down her arm. He kissed her slowly, thoroughly, sparing no inch of skin his sensual onslaught. When his warm mouth reached the heaving valley between her breasts, her nipples hardened. Warrick rasped his thumbs over them, sensuously tracing their outline through her silk nightshirt. Desire coiled tighter in her stomach. Moisture pooled between her thighs.

Warrick brought his mouth back to hers and kissed her. A deep, carnal kiss that left her panting, hungry for more.

She opened her heavy-lidded eyes and watched as he sank to his knees before her. He gazed up at her, his midnight eyes blazing with fierce sensuality. Raina was mesmerized, completely under his spell. His for the taking.

His hands moved slowly up her legs, first grasping her ankles, then her calves, before sliding up her thighs to push her nightshirt out of the way. Without being asked Raina braced her hands on the desk and raised her hips, and he grasped her panties and slowly dragged them off her legs.

And then he just stared at her, his hungry, possessive gaze devouring the sight of her.

"Beautiful," he whispered reverently. "So damned *beautiful.*"

Raina shook all over, feeling as if she were having an out-of-body experience. There she was, perched on the edge of Warrick Mayne's desk, her legs spread open, completely exposed to him. But she felt no shame. All she felt was a powerful, consuming need to have him buried deep inside her.

He caressed her inner thighs, gently kneading her, leaving a trail of fire everywhere he touched. A woman could become a slave to those experienced hands. *She* already was.

Holding her gaze, he let one long, thick finger wander into the neat triangle of curls between her thighs. When his probing finger reached the slick entrance to her body, Raina moaned. She was burning from the inside out, already on the verge of climaxing.

He stroked the swollen, pulsing folds of her sex, rumbling appreciatively, "Mmm. You're so wet."

When he slid his finger inside her, Raina cried out, pleasure coursing through her. He pushed deeper, stoking the flames threatening to engulf her.

"*Warrick...*" she whimpered his name helplessly. She didn't know how much more she could take.

And then he pressed his hot mouth to her, and her hips jerked off the desk as she let out a keening wail.

His strong hands gripped her waist, holding her in place, giving her no reprieve. Her eyes closed and her head fell back as she felt his tongue move skillfully across her pulsing flesh. Her heart pounded furiously against her ribs.

He murmured her name, his voice hoarse with desire and primal need.

Keeping one hand around her hip, he pushed his finger back inside her, stroking her insides as he simultaneously suckled her engorged clitoris. It was the most powerfully erotic thing Raina had ever experienced. She moaned and rocked against him, feeling an orgasm building in her loins. Warrick stayed with her, his long finger penetrating her in controlled thrusts, his tongue tormenting and pleasuring her until a burst of ecstasy shimmered through her. She sobbed his name as her body convulsed, arching tightly against his mouth.

He didn't release her right away, licking at her wetness until she stopped trembling.

Dazedly she opened her eyes and met his smoldering gaze. The expression on his face was feral, primal.

To Raina's astonishment, she felt a fresh wave of arousal. Her body had had its first taste of what this man could do to her. Like an addict, it wanted more.

She was already tugging at Warrick's broad shoulders as he straightened from his kneeling position. Desperate for the feel of his bare flesh, she began unbuttoning his shirt, her fingers fumbling in her haste. *Why are there so many damned buttons!*

Cursing impatiently, she gave up the effort and yanked his shirt open, sending buttons flying and scattering across the floor.

"Sorry," she breathed.

Warrick laughed, dark and masculine. "Believe me, I've got plenty more."

Frantically Raina stripped off his shirt, then ran greedy hands over his hard-honed, bare chest. He was magnificent. Solid power and muscle, not an ounce of flab to be found. She delighted in the tremor that rippled through him at her touch.

Next she attacked his belt, hurriedly unzipping his pants and tugging down his dark briefs. She gasped as he sprang into her hand—long, thick and gloriously hard. Her womb contracted in eager anticipation. He was every bit the superb male specimen she'd imagined he would be.

He sucked in a harsh breath as her hand closed around his throbbing erection, stroking up and down the rigid length until he groaned, moisture beading the swollen tip. Raina wanted to taste him, wanted to wrap her mouth around him, but suddenly he caught her wrist and shook his head, his eyes glittering dangerously.

"Not now," he said, a low, savage growl.

Raina nodded, heady with the knowledge that she could arouse him as easily as he aroused her.

Warrick reached out, dragging her nightshirt over her head and tossing it aside. She trembled as his dark gaze swept over her naked body, staring at her breasts with a hungry reverence that took her breath away.

He hauled her into his arms, a deep shudder racking their bodies as they came together, chest to breasts, skin to skin. He seized her mouth with his, kissing her fiercely and possessively. When her nipples puckered against him, he drew back and gently cupped her breasts in his palms. The feel of his rough, masculine fingertips against her flesh made her shiver.

"Ahh, Raina," he groaned huskily. "Every inch of you is exquisite."

She felt a thrill of pleasure at his words.

Then he dipped his head and drew an erect nipple into his mouth, and a jolt of sensation ripped through her.

Warrick kicked off his pants, then cupped her bottom and lifted her tight against him, his erection probing the slick entrance to her body. Raina clamped her thighs around his hips.

Their gazes locked. He thrust into her, stretching her, and she cried out hoarsely. Warrick swore under his breath, closing his eyes as if he were in excruciating pain.

Raina knew the feeling. He felt so good inside her, so big and thick that the pleasure was almost unbearable. Their bodies fit perfectly, hand in glove. As her inner walls contracted around his penis, she knew she wouldn't last very long.

Legs braced wide, Warrick began thrusting into her. She held on to his shoulders, her fingertips digging into the hard pad of muscle and sinew. As he plunged in and out of her, she felt every swollen, incredible inch of him.

His mouth sought hers, their tongues tangling erotically.

His strokes deepened, sending her breasts bouncing up and down. Pressure built inside her.

Their breathing grew ragged, harsh. As sweat broke out on their bodies, Raina tightened her legs around his waist so she wouldn't slip from his embrace. He cupped her butt in his hands, his powerful body slapping against hers, pounding into her until she moaned uncontrollably.

She could feel her orgasm building, even more explosive than the first one.

Warrick drove into her, ruthless and demanding, fueled by the same urgent need that gripped her. She felt the tension mounting in his body, knew that he, too, was on the verge of release.

They erupted, the orgasm tearing through them at the same time.

Together they cried out, shuddering and whispering each other's names. As Raina's muscles clenched around his throbbing shaft, she felt the vibrations deep in her womb, like the aftershocks of an earthquake.

And as she and Warrick stared into each other's eyes, their bodies locked in a profound moment of ecstasy, Raina knew her life would never be the same again.

Chapter 16

With a soft, dreamy smile on her lips, Raina awakened in Warrick's bed the next morning. She felt boneless, thoroughly and deliciously sated, as memories of last night drifted lazily through her mind. After their passionate coupling in the study, Warrick had taken her upstairs to his bedroom, where they'd made love long into the night, making her glad she was on the pill.

Raina might have thought she'd dreamed the entire thing if it weren't for the masculine arm draped possessively across her waist, the solid warmth of the male body fitted snugly against hers.

She should have been mortified by the total lack of guilt she felt. But she wasn't. Because no matter how wrong it was, no matter the obstacles that lay between them, she'd thoroughly enjoyed making love to Warrick. And though she searched, she couldn't find it in her to regret what had been the most spectacular night of her life.

For several moments she didn't move, simply basking in the rightness of waking up in his arms, something she'd fantasized about long before she probably should have.

Sunlight filtered through the draperies across the enormous

bedroom suite, which featured rich, masculine furnishings and a terrace that provided a panoramic view of the sprawling estate.

As Warrick stirred behind her, Raina carefully lifted her head from the pillow and glanced over her shoulder at him. His eyes remained closed, his thick black lashes resting on his cheeks. Unable to help herself, she let her gaze roam over him, taking in the dark stubble that shadowed his jaw, the sensual curve of his mouth, the broad expanse of his shoulders. He was beautifully, brutally male. And last night, at least, he'd belonged only to her.

As if he'd sensed her appraisal, those dark, piercing eyes suddenly opened and fastened on her face.

They stared at each other for an endless moment.

"Good morning." Warrick's sleep-roughened voice spiked her pulse.

"Good morning." As Raina turned to face him, he kept his arm around her waist, as if to keep her from escaping. Which was the absolute last thing she wanted to do.

"Did you sleep well?"

"Mmm-hmm. The best I've slept in a long time, although it couldn't have been more than a few hours."

His mouth curved. "You can take a nap later, after the party."

The only thing Raina wanted to do after the party was make love to him again. In every room in the house, if possible.

"Are you hungry?"

"What?" Had he read her mind?

"I was thinking we could eat breakfast out on the terrace."

"Sure. That would be nice."

His eyes probed hers. "Are you having second thoughts about last night?"

Raina hesitated, then shook her head. "I wanted to be with you."

"And I wanted to be with you," he said with quiet intensity. "More than you can imagine."

Her knees trembled beneath the covers. Lowering her gaze, she admitted, "I don't know where to go from here. There's so much—"

Warrick leaned forward, his lips tenderly brushing hers. It wasn't a kiss meant to stir passion, but her belly quivered just the same.

"We'll take it one day at a time," he murmured.

She nodded slowly. "All right."

Suddenly there was a firm knock at the door. "I'm sorry to disturb you, sir," Mr. Gibbons said, his voice raised to be heard across the vast expanse of the room, "but I wanted you to know that you have company downstairs."

"Company?" Warrick frowned. "What time is it?"

"Noon, sir."

Warrick and Raina stared at each other and mouthed, *Noon?*

"The party doesn't start until four," Warrick called back to Mr. Gibbons. "Who's showing up so early?"

Even before the butler responded, Raina felt a premonition of doom, which was understandable after the fiasco at the restaurant yesterday. *Please*, she prayed, *don't let it be another one of Warrick's spurned lovers!*

It was even worse.

"It's your family, sir," Mr. Gibbons elaborated. "Your uncle, mother, sister and niece. They flew out here to surprise you."

The look on Warrick's face told Raina that he was surprised all right. Surprised—and braced for impending disaster.

"How could you bring that woman into this house?" Bertrice Mayne demanded furiously an hour later.

She had cornered Warrick in his study, where he'd been chatting with his older sister and bouncing his three-year-old niece on his knee. Seeing the deadly look on her mother's face, Yasmin Mayne had grabbed her daughter's hand and beat a hasty retreat just as Randall entered the room.

Ignoring his mother's question, Warrick rose from his desk and wandered over to the window, drawn by the sight of Raina. He watched as she walked across the sprawling lawn with his housekeeper, who had arrived early that morning to oversee preparations for the party. Evamay Watts had taken an instant liking to Raina, and as Warrick watched the two women consulting with the vendors that were setting up the party equipment, he wondered what it would be like to have Raina there on a permanent basis, as the mistress of his home.

A scenario that would have been unthinkable a week ago now seemed rather…intriguing.

When Raina tossed her head and laughed, Warrick's mind was filled with another image of her, head flung back, lips parted on a breathless cry as he thrust into her. As his body stirred, he remembered that he'd made love to her without protection, something he'd never done in his life. Over the years he'd had multiple sex partners, but he'd never, ever forgotten to use a condom. It was reckless and irresponsible, and a man in his position couldn't afford to take such stupid risks. But when it came to Raina, all bets were off. She made him lose control, like an animal heeding only its primal instincts to mate. After days of fantasizing about her, he'd been too ravenous to concern himself with using protection. And maybe a part of him had feared Raina would come to her senses if he stopped what they were doing to go hunt down a condom. He'd wanted her so bad he'd refused to give her a chance to reconsider sleeping with him.

Behind him, his mother's shrill voice interrupted his reverie. "Answer my question, Warrick!"

Before Warrick could respond, his uncle interjected impatiently, "Damn it, Birdie. Leave the boy alone. It's *his* house—he can invite whomever he wants."

"Not her! Not that *girl!*"

Even after all these years, Birdie Mayne refused to utter Raina's name, as if it were a vile blasphemy.

"That's not your decision to make," Randall growled.

"The hell it isn't!" Birdie raged. "He's my son—"

"And he's a grown man!"

As their bickering continued, Warrick glanced down at the floor and saw one of the buttons that had popped free of his shirt in Raina's frantic haste to undress him last night. Inwardly he smiled.

Everywhere he looked there were reminders of her. The shelf with the snow globe. The desk where they'd made love for the first time. Nothing would ever be the same again. *He* would never be the same again.

Randall was saying apologetically, "Believe me, War, if I'd known you were taking Raina home this weekend, we wouldn't have come. The last thing I want to do is intrude—"

"Intrude?" Birdie echoed incredulously. *"She's* the one who doesn't belong here. She's not his family—we are!"

Heaving a harsh sigh, Warrick turned from the window and faced his mother with all the enthusiasm of a condemned prisoner facing a firing squad.

Birdie sat in one of the visitor chairs across the room. Her long, slender legs were crossed, and one sandaled foot tapped angrily in the air. Her skin was the color of melted caramel and just as smooth. Her hair, as always, was impeccably groomed and cut in short, stylish layers that accentuated her fine-boned face. At fifty-five years old, she didn't look a day over forty. She'd had Warrick when she was nineteen, and had often seemed more like an older sister to him than a mother. She was stubborn and temperamental, and had a predilection for dramatic outbursts. She also had a sharp tongue that could cut a man off at the knees—as she'd demonstrated on numerous occasions.

Warrick considered himself fortunate that he'd rarely, if ever, been on the receiving end of his mother's notorious temper. She'd doted shamelessly on him, to the point where his siblings had often accused him of being her favorite.

Warrick loved his mother dearly, but that morning she was severely testing his patience. Right or wrong, he'd been enjoying Raina's company, and while he'd always welcomed visits from his family, this time was the exception. He'd wanted Raina all to himself for as long as possible, and he resented having to explain himself to his mother, resented the way she'd turned up her nose at Raina as if she were something Warrick had dragged in off the street. Raina had every right to be there, yet he knew she would go out of her way to avoid his family for the rest of the weekend.

"We were supposed to be visiting Yolanda this week," Birdie was ranting at him. "You promised we could go together as a family when Yasmin and I got back from our cruise yesterday. But I guess you forgot all about that when you decided to run off to be with that despicable child!"

Warrick closed his eyes briefly against a pang of guilt. He hadn't forgotten about visiting his sister, but admittedly it hadn't been high on his list of priorities that week. Everything, it seemed, had taken a backseat to Raina. Including his sanity.

"Now we'll have to wait until *next* week to see Yolanda," his mother complained bitterly.

"I'm sorry," Warrick murmured.

"You should be! How could you do this to your sister? You know how much she always looks forward to seeing you. If you still lived in Houston, she *never* would have told us not to visit her so often.

You've always been able to cheer her up. How could you choose that little liar over your own flesh and blood?"

"Ma—"

"Where's your loyalty to your family?"

Something snapped inside Warrick. "Don't you *ever* question my loyalty to this family!" he roared. "Everything I've ever done has been for you and my brothers and sisters. Everything! No one loves this family more than I do."

Birdie gasped, her eyes widening in shock.

Warrick had never uttered a disrespectful word to her, let alone raised his voice. But, damn it, she'd pushed him too far.

He glowered at her for a moment, then turned back to the window, fighting to rein in his temper.

"Everyone just needs to calm down," Randall said wearily. "We came here to spend time together as a family, not tear one another apart."

"*I'm* not the one who's tearing the family apart," Birdie snapped.

Warrick shot her a warning glare.

"Well, it's true!" she said defiantly. "When Yolanda finds out that you've been carrying on with that woman—"

"Her name is Raina," Warrick snarled, whirling from the window. "Whatever feelings you may have about her, at least have the courtesy to call her by her name. Let's not forget that there was a time you welcomed her into our home and treated her like one of your own daughters."

"And look how she repaid me," Birdie hissed. "By stabbing Yolanda in the back!"

"Maybe she regrets that!" Warrick fired back, surprised to hear the words leave his mouth.

Until that moment, he'd never considered the possibility that Raina might regret testifying in court against his sister. Raina had been a scared teenage girl, overwhelmed by the legal ramifications of what her best friend may have done. Maybe she'd spent the past twelve years blaming herself, punishing herself for not defending Yolanda. Maybe if Raina had to do it over again, she wouldn't have caved to pressure and testified against Yolanda. Instead of asserting that Yolanda hadn't been at the party, maybe Raina would have allowed for the possibility that she and Yolanda had simply missed each other.

Or maybe your sister lied to you.

As if she'd intercepted the traitorous thought, Birdie shook her head at Warrick, her lips curled in disgust. "I never thought I'd live to see the day that my own son would sell out his family for a piece of ass."

"That's enough!" Infuriated, Randall rounded on Birdie, his dark eyes blazing. "Damn it, woman, you just never know what to say out of your mouth, do you?"

"Of course, *you* would defend Raina!" Birdie exploded, leaping from her chair. "She's always had you wrapped around her little finger. And now, apparently, she's done the same thing to Warrick. I guess the apple doesn't fall far from the tree."

A stunned silence swept over the room.

Warrick stared at his mother, the blood draining from his head. "What are you talking about?"

"Yes, Birdie," Randall said, his voice as rigid as his body, "what *are* you talking about?"

She looked at each of them in turn, her eyes glinting with vicious satisfaction. "You heard what I said."

Warrick shook his head slowly. "I don't think I did."

"You're just like *him,*" she spat, pointing at Randall. "Just like your father!"

Warrick felt like he'd been leveled in the gut with a steel crane. The air whooshed out of his lungs, and he staggered back a step.

When his gaze swung to his uncle—*his father?*—he realized that Randall wasn't putting on an act; he was genuinely as flabbergasted as Warrick was.

In unison they turned and stared at Birdie with identical expressions of outraged disbelief.

Birdie stared back at them belligerently.

"Why now?" Randall demanded, taking a menacing step toward her. "Why did you wait so long to tell us? *Why?*"

"You mean you've never told Warrick about the time you slept with your brother's wife?" Birdie said mockingly. "You never told him how I came to see you that night, upset because your no-good brother was messing around on me and hanging out with drug dealers instead of getting a job? You mean you never told Warrick how, after you fed Yasmin and rocked her to sleep for me, you started consoling me, and one thing led to another—"

"Damn you!" Randall thundered, his face contorted with fury. "You know damned well I never told Warrick or anyone else about that night. We *both* agreed on that. And it only happened once."

Birdie smirked. "Once was all it took." She nodded toward Warrick. "There's your proof."

Randall gaped at her, looking like he didn't know whether to choke her or burst into hysterical tears. He stared at Warrick for a prolonged moment, then sank weakly into a chair and passed a trembling hand over his face. He looked so devastated that Warrick almost felt sorry for him.

He whirled on his mother, rage twisting his insides. "How could you have kept something like this from me? From *both* of us?"

She divided an incredulous look between him and Randall. "I can't believe the thought never crossed either of your minds. Look at the two of you. You're the spitting image of each other!"

Warrick and Randall glanced warily at each other, silently acknowledging the obvious.

"And as for the man you *thought* was your father," Birdie snarled at Warrick, "he wasn't worth a damn. When he wasn't strung out on crack, he was out looking for his next piece of ass. God only knows how many of his bastards are running around Houston. My only consolation is that you're the only child I *didn't* have with him!"

Warrick shook his head at her, staggered by her complete lack of remorse. "All this time," he whispered disbelievingly. "You lied to me. You lied to all of us!"

"What difference does it make?" Birdie cried. "I didn't keep you and Randall apart! The two of you couldn't *be* any closer. God knows you've had a better relationship with Randall than you ever had with that sorry excuse for a man I was married to. You two have *always* had each other."

"Not always," Randall said tersely, rising to his feet. "Let's not forget that I didn't enter Warrick's life until he was fourteen. *Fourteen,* Birdie! That's an awfully long time to keep a man away from his own son."

Birdie met his gaze unflinchingly. "It's not my fault you and your brother stopped speaking to each other. It was your choice to stay out of our lives for so long. *Your* choice, not mine."

"That's not the point!" Warrick interjected, enraged. "My God, Ma, can't you even acknowledge that you were dead wrong for keeping such a secret from us? *Can't you?*"

Her chin lifted in stubborn defiance. "I did what I thought was best, and I make no apologies for that."

Warrick's face hardened. "I'll never forgive you for this."

Birdie's eyes widened, filling with tears. "You don't mean that, baby. You know how much I love you—"

But Warrick was already striding furiously from the room.

"Warrick, wait!" his mother pleaded desperately. "Warrick—"

"Let him go, Birdie," Randall barked. "Goddamn you, woman! What have you done?"

On his way out of the study Warrick nearly collided with Raina, who'd been hovering near the doorway. Her stricken expression told him she'd heard enough of the conversation to be horrified on his behalf.

"I wasn't eavesdropping," she hastened to assure him. "One of the vendors wanted me to ask you—"

"Not now, Raina," Warrick growled.

Without a backward glance he stalked off.

Randall found Warrick sitting alone in the darkened home theater, staring broodingly at the blank movie screen.

"Mind if I turn on the lights?" Randall asked quietly.

Warrick said nothing.

Taking his silence as acquiescence, Randall adjusted the recessed lighting, then walked into the room and selected a seat on the first row, right in front of Warrick.

Neither spoke for several moments.

"I didn't know," Randall said in a low voice.

Warrick remained silent.

"Did you hear me? I said I didn't know."

"I heard you," Warrick said curtly.

"If I'd had the slightest inkling that the baby Birdie was carrying was mine—"

"Did you love her?"

Randall seemed startled by the question. After what seemed an eternity, he let out a deep, shuddering breath and nodded resignedly.

"I did. Once upon a time. Before I knew what she was really like." He paused. "No offense."

"None taken."

Randall said nothing.

As the awkward silence stretched between them, Warrick frowned. He didn't know how to deal with this new tension between them. He hoped it wasn't a sign of things to come.

Staring down at his folded hands in his lap, Randall began quietly, "Your mother and I grew up together in the Third Ward. Birdie was beautiful, the girl every fella wanted. But she always went for the dangerous types, like my brother Tariq. She thought I was boring because I wanted to go to college and become a police officer. She used to tease me all the time about how broke I was going to be, working as a lowly cop." He let out a mirthless chuckle. "Your mother has always liked the finer things in life."

A ghost of a smile touched Warrick's mouth. "I know." He had the credit card statements to show for it.

Randall sighed. "I thought she was too good for my brother, but Birdie insisted that they loved each other and could build a life together. She was only seventeen when she got pregnant with your sister. Tariq didn't want to marry her, but Birdie and her mother kept pressuring him until he finally gave in. On the night Yasmin was born, Tariq was nowhere to be found. He was out boozing and getting high with his friends."

Randall shook his head, the old anger tightening his voice as he continued, "Birdie was devastated. I was livid. I went to Tariq and confronted him, telling him he needed to be a man and handle his responsibilities. We got into a fist fight right there in the parking lot. A couple of his buddies came out to help him. One of them shoved a gun in my face and asked Tariq if he wanted him to blow my brains out. My brother said no, but he warned me that if I ever came near him or his wife again, he'd kill me himself."

Warrick shifted his gaze from the blank theater screen to the back of his uncle's—father's—head, wondering why he'd never heard this tale before.

"I wasn't afraid of getting shot by my brother," Randall said grimly. "He was too spineless to pull the trigger, anyway. But I was furious with Birdie for being so blind about Tariq, for allowing herself to settle for less than she deserved. I couldn't stand by and watch her throw her life away, so I left. I went away to college and only kept in touch with my mother. I knew I never wanted to return to the projects, so two years later when I was home for the summer, I got a full-time job and rented out an apartment in a better part of town. That's where I was living when Birdie came to see me that night, and, well, you know the rest."

"Indeed," Warrick murmured sardonically. "So that's how I was conceived. Out of an adulterous one-night stand. Good to know."

Randall twisted around in the seat to glare at him. "Don't make it sound like that. It wasn't some cheap one-night stand. I really loved your mother, and she needed a shoulder to cry on."

Warrick snorted. "You gave her a helluva lot more than your shoulder, didn't you?"

Randall's nostrils flared.

The two men stared each other down for a long, challenging moment.

Randall was the first to glance away. "Like I said, I didn't know."

Warrick clenched and unclenched his jaw, then blew out a ragged breath and glared at the ceiling. "I'm not blaming you," he said gruffly. "I know it wasn't your fault Ma kept the secret from you. I'm just trying to process everything. And I'm trying to figure out how we're going to make the transition from being uncle and nephew, to father and son."

"If it makes it any easier," Randall said very quietly, "I've always considered you the son I never had."

Warrick's throat constricted.

He thought of all the times he'd wished that Randall were his father. He lamented the fourteen years they'd lost, and reflected on how different his childhood would have been if he'd lived with Randall and had been raised as his son. His mother was definitely right about one thing: Randall had been more like a father to Warrick than Tariq Mayne ever had.

Swallowing a hard knot of emotion, Warrick leaned forward and gently squeezed Randall's shoulder.

Randall caught his hand, held it for a moment before releasing him.

This time when they lapsed into silence, the tension was gone.

Struck by a sudden thought, Warrick muttered, "Wait a minute. If you're my father, that means Lauren is my half sister."

"That's right." Randall turned in the seat to face him. "Is that going to be a problem?"

Remembering the way he'd told Lauren off the last time she'd called begging for a favor, Warrick smiled narrowly. "No problem at all."

Randall hesitated, then ventured carefully, "You didn't mean what you said about not forgiving your mother, did you?"

Warrick's jaw hardened. "I haven't decided."

"You have every right to be angry with her. What she did was deplorable, and there's no excuse for it. But she loves you, son. She was so upset after you left that I had to carry her upstairs to her room, because she could hardly walk. It would kill her if you stopped speaking to her, War."

Warrick said nothing. Given everything he'd just learned, he now viewed his relationship with his mother in a whole new light. She'd always treated him differently than his siblings, never bothering to disguise the fact that he *was* her favorite. But now Warrick couldn't help wondering if she loved him more simply because he *wasn't* Tariq's child—or because he was the son of a man she'd fallen in love with.

He searched Randall's face. "You really got over Ma?"

Randall blew out a deep breath, then nodded. "It wasn't easy, but I did."

Not for the first time, Warrick thought about what Deniece had told him about Raina's childhood crush. If she was right, and Raina *had* loved him at one time, how easy had it been for her to get over him?

As if reading his mind, Randall said quietly, "She's a good woman, son."

Warrick didn't even have to ask who his father was talking about. He closed his eyes. "I know."

A moment later he was up and striding toward the door.

"Where are you going?" Randall asked.

"To find Raina. Who else?"

Randall smiled knowingly. "Who else indeed."

Chapter 17

Raina smiled at Warrick as she took his hand and led him through the doors of Touch of Heaven.

They had arrived in Houston that morning and had spent the rest of the day in bed together, alternately making love and talking for hours. As expected, the topic that had dominated their conversation was the stunning revelation that Randall Mayne was Warrick's father. Raina had listened quietly as Warrick shared his feelings with her, telling her that ultimately, despite the way his mother had deceived him, he felt blessed to have Randall as his father. Raina's heart had melted at the admission. Seeing her tender expression, Warrick had dragged her into his arms and made love to her with a desperate urgency that left her trembling long after it was over.

After working up an appetite, they'd ventured out for dinner before ending up at Touch of Heaven. Since the spa was closed on Sundays, Raina had decided today was a perfect opportunity to give Warrick a tour.

As they moved through the reception area, he asked about the plaques on the wall, and she told him about the outstanding services her spa provided to its clients and to the community. She could tell, by the way Warrick's expression softened, that he was both impressed and proud of her.

She took him through the sauna and the different treatment rooms, explaining the function of each, smiling as he sniffed appreciatively at fragrant candles and massage oils.

When they had completed the tour, she turned to him with a bright smile. "Well, what do you think?"

"I think," Warrick said in a voice like sin, "that you have a very nice spa. And I think I'd like to receive one of those incredible massages you were describing."

Raina chuckled, even as her knees went weak. "I'd be more than happy to make you an appointment with one of my skilled massage therapists."

"But I'm here now," Warrick countered silkily. "No time like the present."

"But I'm not licensed."

"I'll take my chances."

So she capitulated, unable to resist him.

She turned on the soft, tranquil music and prepared the treatment room the way she'd been shown by her staff. And when Warrick returned from the changing room with a towel draped loosely around his waist, she gulped hard and averted her gaze, her voice husky as she instructed him to lie down on the table.

She poured massage oil into her palms and rubbed them together for warmth. The soothing scent filled the air as she lowered her hands to the mahogany expanse of wide shoulders and taut sinew. The moment she touched Warrick, her breath caught and her breasts tingled.

He let out a low, satisfied moan that curled between her legs like the sinuous flames from the candles lit around the room.

Recalling what she'd been taught, Raina moved her hands over him with sure, gentle motions, finding and kneading the pressure points until he melted beneath her touch. She massaged the corded muscles of his back, his firm buttocks, his long, powerful legs. She even massaged his feet until he groaned with pleasure.

Although they'd spent the day in bed together, exploring and pleasuring each other's bodies, Raina was as aroused as if she were seeing him for the very first time. His body was a revelation. The silky heat of his skin electrified her fingertips, and his deep, purring moans made her loins ache.

He turned over suddenly, the towel falling away to reveal the jutting length of his erection. "I need you," he said, his voice so low and husky the words were almost a growl.

Raina swallowed.

In the far recesses of her mind she remembered that this was her place of business, and as such it was inappropriate to do what they were about to do. But she didn't care. She wanted him, and she could no more deny him than she could deny her lungs of air.

Warrick watched her, his hooded eyes smoldering with desire as she slowly undressed, then stood naked before him. Emboldened by his hungry gaze, she poured massage oil into her hands and deliberately, sensually, smoothed it all over her body.

Warrick nearly came off the table, but she pushed him back down, her lips curving in a naughty little smile. His nostrils flared and his heart thudded against her palm as she rubbed oil all over his chest. His skin was so hot the liquid practically melted on contact.

She only got as far as his abdomen before he reached for her, his feral expression warning her that he would not wait any longer. She climbed onto the table, so eager for him she forgot to remove her high heels.

Her legs bracketed his hips as she straddled him. Leaning over him, she lavished his throat and chest with hot nips and licks while he cupped her aching breasts and sucked her erect nipples.

She skated her open mouth down the rigid length of his body before taking his engorged penis deep inside her mouth. Warrick groaned, closing his eyes as he began thrusting upward. She stroked him with her hand, laved and suckled him with her lips and tongue.

When he was on the brink of release, Raina pulled back and lifted her body over his. The heat of his shaft against her throbbing sex was unbearably arousing. She rubbed her clitoris against him, the erotic friction making them both shudder.

Their gazes locked as she took him in her hand and guided him into her body. Her breath hissed out of her as she slowly sank down on him. He was impossibly hard, so thick and swollen that he stretched her painfully, and she had to lean back on his thighs to take him deeper.

He began moving inside her with slow, fluid strokes, his fingers tweaking her clitoris like the keys of a piano. It was maddeningly arousing. As she met his deep thrusts, she could already feel the pressure of an orgasm building in her stomach and thighs. She wondered if she would ever get enough of making love to this man.

Soon the slow, seductive rhythm changed. As their movements grew frenzied, they breathed in harsh, rapid pants. Warrick grabbed Raina's butt and thrust harder and faster, bucking so violently beneath her she thought she'd fall off the table. She leaned forward and clamped her thighs around his waist, her inner muscles squeezing his penis in a viselike grip. Perspiration mingled with the oil that already slicked their skin.

Raina drew her knees up, her spiky heels digging into the table, her thighs spread wide as she rode the thick length of him. Warrick swore hoarsely, his eyes blazing with arousal at the savagely erotic position.

"Raina," he rasped over and over again. "Raina…"

As she gazed down into his face, Raina realized she had never felt closer, more connected to anyone than she did to Warrick. And it wasn't just the physical joining of their bodies that made her feel this way. She loved him, loved him with a ferocity that had not abated over the years. Whatever tomorrow might bring, she would always love him.

Tightening her thighs around his waist, she leaned down and seized his lips, pouring years of pent-up longing into the kiss. He returned it with equal fervor, whispering endearments so tender that tears rushed to her eyes.

Moments later they erupted in a shattering orgasm that sent waves of ecstasy crashing through Raina's womb. Warrick shouted her name, his voice raw and achingly reverent.

As her body convulsed Raina threw back her head, her throat vibrating with her secret confession and silent entreaty.

I love you. Please don't hurt me again.

Two days later, Raina realized she'd tempted fate by praying for such a thing.

The moment she arrived at the spa on Tuesday morning and saw a group of her employees gathered around the reception desk, she felt a sinking sense of déjà vu. Wasn't this the same scene she'd stumbled upon just a week ago?

"Our favorite reporter has struck again," Trey said disgustedly as he passed Raina a copy of the *Ledger*. When her gaze landed on the salacious headline, her heart lurched sickeningly, and the ground tilted beneath her feet.

Spa Owner Offers Sex In Lieu Of Sale

Raina made a strangled sound of disbelief.

"It gets worse," Trey fumed. "We've already had several cancellations this morning. One client bluntly admitted that she didn't want to be here if the police decided to raid the spa."

"And speaking of the authorities," Nikki added grimly, "the article suggested that the FBI intends to investigate allegations of prostitution at the spa."

"Prostitution!" Raina cried.

Trey scowled. "Read it yourself. It's all there in black and white."

With the newspaper gripped tightly in her hands, Raina sank weakly into the nearest chair in the reception area. To her horror, the article accused her of trading sexual favors with Warrick in order to retain her business. Citing unnamed sources, Deniece Labelle detailed Raina's affair with Warrick as a "lurid seduction" that began with a weekend tryst at his New Jersey estate, followed by a happy-ending massage at her spa. The article even went so far as to suggest that this was not the first time Raina, or her employees, had used sex to curry favor with county officials and local politicians.

By the time Raina finished reading the slanderous article, her blood was boiling with rage. Her employees stared at her as she lunged from the chair, keys in hand, and stormed out of the spa with one destination in mind.

Twenty minutes later, she marched past Warrick's shocked, protesting secretary and strode through the open doorway of his office. He was seated behind his desk and had just hung up the phone when Raina entered the room. He glanced up in surprise.

Behind Raina, his secretary sputtered indignantly, "Miss, you can't—"

Raina slammed the door on the woman's startled face and charged Warrick's desk, wishing she had something heavier than a folded newspaper to bludgeon him with.

He rose from his chair, frowning. "Raina—"

"Have you seen today's *Ledger?*" she demanded furiously.

"No, I've been in meetings all morning. What—"

She hurled the newspaper at him, and he caught it as it hit him squarely in the chest. "How could you do this to me?" she raged. "I trusted you!"

His frown deepened. "What are you talking about?"

"Like you don't know!"

Warrick glanced down at the paper. When he saw the headline, he stiffened visibly. Looking up at Raina, he said, "I didn't know anything about this."

"Liar!" Raina snarled. "I know damned well you put Deniece up to this. Just like the last time!"

"I didn't put her up to anything—this time or before."

"Do you really expect me to believe that?"

"Yes!"

"Then you must think I'm the world's biggest fool. And maybe I am. I trusted you, but I should have known better."

"Raina—"

"If you didn't know about the article, then please explain to me how Deniece found out about Sunday night. There were only two of us at the spa that night, Warrick, and *I* sure as hell didn't tell her!"

"Neither did I!"

"I don't believe you!"

Warrick stared at her incredulously. "How can you think I'd have anything to do with this?" he demanded, holding up the newspaper.

"Because you're a heartless, despicable ass!" Raina roared, trembling with fury. "And because you're willing to do anything to force me out of business. Why? Because you want to get back at me for what happened to Yolanda."

"That's not true!"

"Yes, it is. Ever since you came back home you've been doing your level best to turn the entire town against me." She sneered. "Well, congratulations. Mission accomplished. I hope you're satisfied."

"Damn it, Raina!" Warrick flung aside the newspaper as if it were covered in manure and rounded the desk. As he came toward her she backed away, throwing up her hands to ward him off.

He kept coming, reaching out for her. She evaded his grasp and spun toward the door, intending to leave before she did something foolish, like burst into tears.

But before she could escape he grabbed her, hauling her roughly against him. "I didn't tell Deniece anything about us," he whispered fiercely into her hair. "I don't know where she got her information—"

"Stop lying to me!" Raina cried, twisting out of his arms and stepping backward. She glared thunderously at him, her chest heaving with the effort to control her tattered breathing.

Warrick clenched his jaw. "Raina—"

"God, I'm such a fool! I played right into your hands when I agreed to your little 'courtship' proposal. Reese kept trying to warn me that you were up to no good, but I didn't listen."

His face hardened. "Your sister doesn't know a damned thing about me."

"Oh, yes, she does. She told me you were going to hurt me, and she was right."

He reached for her again. "*Raina*—"

"Don't touch me!" she shouted, jerking out of his grasp and stalking across the room, needing to put as much distance as possible between them. She was shaking so badly she thought she'd go into convulsions at any moment. The pain of his betrayal was staggering.

Warrick said evenly, "I can understand why you're so upset—"

Raina whirled on him. "You don't understand anything. If you did you wouldn't have done this to me. My God, Warrick, do you have *any* idea what it's been like for me to love a man who I know will never love me in return? That's right," she jeered at his stunned look. "I love you. God help me, I've loved you since I was ten years old!"

Warrick shook his head slowly. "I didn't know."

She barked a mirthless laugh. "Of course you didn't. You hardly knew I existed, let alone that I was carrying a pathetic torch for you."

"Raina—"

"It happened the very first time I met you, the day Yolanda invited me over for a sleepover. You and your friends were going out, but when you saw a little boy across the street sitting alone on his porch, you told your friends to wait in the car, then you walked over to the boy's house and sat next to him. Yolanda told me that his mother had recently died, so he'd been sent to live with his grandmother. I stood at the window watching as you talked to him, tied his shoes for him. Teased him until he started giggling." Raina shook her head, awash in bittersweet memories. "From that moment on you could do no wrong in my eyes. Everything you did made me love you more. Twenty years, Warrick. I've loved you for *twenty years.* Do you have any idea what that's been like?"

Warrick closed his eyes as if he were in agony. "Raina—"

"Do you know what hurt me the most during the trial? It wasn't the fact that everyone was calling me a liar and a traitor for testifying against Yolanda. It was the fact that *you* thought I was a liar and a traitor. It never once occurred to you that I was telling the truth."

"Who was I supposed to believe?" Warrick shouted. "Yolanda's my sister!"

"And she had everything to gain by lying about what happened that night. I had no reason to lie. If she'd really been at that party with me, I would have said so in court. My God, Warrick, do you really think I *wanted* to see my best friend go to prison?"

He clenched his jaw, his eyes flashing in warning. "Let's not rehash the past—"

"But the past has everything to do with why we're standing here today. You wanted revenge!"

"I don't! I did at first, but not anymore."

"What happened?" Raina sneered. "You grow a conscience?"

"Damn it, Raina. I fell in love with you!"

"Liar!" Raina roared, enraged by his cruel audacity. "You don't know the first thing about love. You use and discard women like trash, reducing them to hysterical parasites who make spectacles of themselves in public. You wouldn't know what love is if it walked up to you and bit you on the ass!"

"And I suppose Bradford does," Warrick challenged.

"I can guarantee he knows a helluva lot more about love than you do."

His lips twisted mockingly. "Then why isn't *he* the one who's been warming your bed every night for the past week?"

Raina recoiled as if he'd slapped her. "Damn you! Why couldn't you leave my spa alone? Haven't you taken enough from me? What more do you want? You have *everything!* Money, power, fame. The world at your feet, eating out of the palm of your hand. Everything!"

"And none of that means a damned thing if I can't have you!" Warrick exploded.

Raina raked him with a contemptuous look. "You can have my

property, Warrick Mayne, but you will *never* have me. I'd rather die than spend the rest of my life with someone like you."

Something like grief crossed his face before his expression hardened. "In that case," he said coldly, "have a nice life."

"I will if you stay the hell out of it!"

He scowled, then strode to the door and held it open for her.

Not sparing him another glance, Raina stormed out of the office. The door slammed behind her with shattering finality, officially putting an end to all her hopes and dreams.

As soon as Raina left, Warrick stalked across the room and snatched the newspaper off his desk. When he'd finished reading Deniece's article, he let out an enraged bellow that brought his secretary running, her eyes wide with panic.

"Is everything all—"

"No," Warrick snapped, marching across the room with a lethal expression that made her shrink against the door as he passed her.

"Where are you going, Mr. Mayne?"

"To handle some unfinished business. If I'm not back in an hour, call my damned lawyer."

"Your lawyer?" Mabel asked worriedly. "Why would you need your lawyer?"

"To bail me out of jail," Warrick snarled.

An hour later, he emerged from the downtown building that housed the offices of the *Houston Ledger*.

When he'd arrived, Deniece had taken one look at his face and begun stammering unintelligibly. As if fearing for her life, she'd run to her boss's office, which was where Warrick had been heading next.

In no uncertain terms, he'd informed Deniece and her managing editor that he would sue them *and* the newspaper if they didn't immediately retract the libelous article about Raina. But he hadn't stopped there. He'd promised them that if they ever printed another word about him or Raina, he would use his connections to launch an advertising boycott against the *Ledger* that would effectively put the newspaper out of business.

By the time he was through with them, the spineless managing editor had demanded Deniece's resignation. Warrick was too furious to feel an ounce of sympathy for Deniece, especially when she'd spitefully admitted to him that she'd written the article to get back at him for choosing Raina over her.

As Warrick left the building and climbed into his car, he didn't know what infuriated him more: the fact that Deniece had been camped outside Raina's spa on Sunday night so she could spy on them, or the fact that he'd underestimated just how malicious she could be.

Hell hath no fury like a woman scorned, he thought humorlessly.

Which only made him think about Raina.

He couldn't believe she'd accused him of conspiring with Deniece. How could she claim to love him when she thought he was capable of such underhanded cruelty?

Almost at once, guilt nagged at Warrick's conscience. Could he really blame Raina for the way she'd reacted? Considering that he and his family had ruthlessly disowned her years ago, she had no reason to give Warrick the benefit of the doubt concerning the newspaper article. From the very beginning he'd made it clear to her that he would do everything in his power to wrest her property from her.

But that was before you fell in love with her.

Warrick frowned, staring bleakly out the car window at the downtown skyline. It made him think about the snow globe Raina had given him. She'd loved him so much that she'd remembered his kindness to a neighbor's grandson, had remembered the words to a speech he'd given eighteen years ago. That kind of love was a rare, precious gift.

And he'd trampled all over it.

Warrick swore under his breath.

In spite of everything that had happened between them, in spite of the fact that he'd spent the past twelve years blaming Raina for his sister's imprisonment, he'd done the unthinkable and fallen in love with her. She was the first and only woman he'd ever considered marrying. He wanted to spend the rest of his life with her.

But he'd ruined any chance of that happening.

And some way, somehow, he'd have to learn to live without what could have been.

Chapter 18

Over the next four months, Raina learned the meaning of going through the motions. She ate, slept, and breathed like someone operating on autopilot. She even went through the motions of dissolving her business as if it were something she did every day, though, admittedly, she'd hired an attorney to handle the transaction so she wouldn't have to deal with Warrick. She was so emotionally dead inside that she hardly blinked whenever she heard his name on the news, which was often. She hadn't reacted even when she'd heard that he'd been romantically linked to yet another actress. She was completely numb.

Her family and friends were worried sick about her. Her parents and sister took turns making unannounced visits to her loft. To her credit, Reese had never said, "I told you so," though she certainly could have. She even went out of her way not to discuss her burgeoning romance with Dr. Carracci, not wanting to rub Raina's face in her happiness.

Raina had called things off with Bradford. She knew it was unfair to lead him on when she was in love with another man.

Trey and Tina, who now worked at different spas, also kept a regular vigil on Raina. They came bearing food, books, movie rentals—all the things she used to enjoy.

She now worked as an advertising consultant, although she didn't need the money. She could easily retire and live off the generous sum Warrick had paid for her property. But she didn't want his money, so while it sat untouched in the bank, she was putting her education and skills to good use—and keeping herself busy in the process.

One morning in early October, Raina was working on an ad campaign for a new client when her doorbell rang. When she answered the door, she was stunned to find Yolanda Mayne standing there.

Raina was so shocked to see her that for several moments she didn't speak, just stared at her old friend while painful memories rushed to the surface of her mind.

Because Yolanda had been blessed with her mother's youthful genes, her looks hadn't deteriorated during her twelve-year incarceration. But the brown eyes that stared back at Raina were unmistakably older, wiser. Filled with a humility that had never been there before.

"Hello, Raina," Yolanda said quietly. "Mind if I come in?"

Raina hesitated, then wordlessly stepped aside to let her enter.

"Nice place," Yolanda murmured, glancing appreciatively around the comfortably furnished loft. "You always did have—"

"What are you doing here, Yolanda?" Raina interrupted. She was in no mood for exchanging pleasantries, especially not with this woman.

"I came to talk to you about my brother." Yolanda hesitated. "Can we sit down?"

"I don't think—"

"It's really important, Raina. Please?"

That, too, was new. In the eight years they'd been friends, Raina could count on one hand the number of times Yolanda had said *please.*

They sat in the living room and stared at each other for a long moment, two strangers who'd once been as inseparable as sisters.

Yolanda smiled softly. "He said you were beautiful. He was right."

"Who said that?"

"Warrick. When he came to see me a few months ago."

Raina said nothing, though inwardly she was surprised that Warrick had discussed her with his sister.

Yolanda shook her head slowly. "You and Warrick…I never would have guessed it."

"There *is* no me and Warrick."

"That's not what I've heard. Everyone in the family has been talking about how heartbroken Warrick is over you, how he hasn't been himself in months. And I've seen it with my own two eyes. My family threw a big homecoming celebration for me last week, and even though I know Warrick was as ecstatic about my release as everyone else, he seemed subdued, like his mind was a million miles away. He's definitely not himself. Even his father's worried about him, and Uncle Randall never worries about anything."

"I don't know what to tell you—"

"My brother loves you, Raina. And I know the only reason the two of you aren't together is me."

Raina said nothing.

"You know, I've had a lot of time to reflect upon the past," Yolanda said somberly, "and of all the regrets I have, my biggest regret is what I put you through, Raina. You don't know how many times I've thought about that night and wished I could undo the terrible decision I made to get into that car with Tate. But I also wish, more than anything, that I hadn't asked you to lie for me. I put you in an impossible position, and for that I'm truly sorry. I don't expect you to ever forgive me, but I at least wanted you to know how I felt."

Raina stared at her hands in her lap, torn between conflicting emotions. Anger, vindication, sorrow, gratitude, regret.

"I plan to gather my family together this weekend and tell them the truth about what happened that night," Yolanda said. "It won't be easy, but it's something I should have done a long time ago. I let you take the fall for me, Raina, and that wasn't fair to you or my family. They're going to feel horrible for the way they've treated you all these years. Don't be surprised if your phone starts ringing off the hook."

"I don't want their apologies," Raina said coldly.

"That's understandable." Yolanda hesitated. "I've made so many mistakes, hurt so many people. But you and Warrick were two of the most important people in my life, and you both deserve to be happy."

"Yolanda—"

"I brought something I think you should read." Yolanda pulled an envelope out of her leather purse and passed it to Raina.

"What is it?" Raina asked warily.

"A letter. From Warrick." She paused. "He sent it to me on July sixth."

The day before Deniece's article was published.

Raina unfolded the letter and saw Warrick's bold, distinctive handwriting. Her hands trembled as she began reading:

Baby girl,

I know we're going to see you later this week, but since we won't be alone, I wanted to share some things with you that have been on my heart, things I've never told you before.

When Ma first called and told me you had been arrested, I was devastated. As I flew home from Philly, all I could think about was the night my father pulled me over for speeding and found drugs in the car. As you remember, he looked the other way and let me go home that night—after he kicked my ass, of course. It was the first and only time in his career that he'd broken the rules, and he made damned sure I realized how lucky I was that another cop hadn't pulled me over.

When I heard that you'd been arrested, it felt like bad karma. Since I'd escaped from my brush with the law, you had to make atonement. I know it may sound crazy, but I felt guilty, like I was responsible for what had happened to you. I've never judged you, baby girl. Were it not for my father, my life could have turned out so differently. It could be me serving time instead of you. I hope you know that my love for you will never change, no matter what may have happened that night twelve years ago.

Which brings me to the last—but definitely not least—matter I wanted to share with you. It's about Raina. I'm in love with her. I know this may be hard for you to hear, but it's the truth. I'm crazy about her. I think she's amazing. I'm even thinking about asking her to marry me. You're the only one in the family that I've told, because I thought you deserved to hear it from me first. You may feel that I'm betraying you, but believe me when I tell you that I never meant to hurt you any more than I meant to fall in love with Raina. I want to be with her, and I hope you and the rest of the family will support

my decision and welcome Raina back into the fold. But if you can't do that... Well, that's a sacrifice I'm willing to make.
See you soon.
Love always,
Warrick

Raina would have read the letter again, but she couldn't focus through the tears blurring her vision and spilling from her eyes. As she clutched the letter against her aching heart, Yolanda rose from her chair and sat beside her on the sofa. When Raina looked at her and saw tears shimmering in Yolanda's eyes, something melted inside her. The two women hugged each other and wept uncontrollably.

When the emotional storm finally subsided, they drew apart and smiled tremulously at each other. And in that moment Raina realized that although they could never erase the painful past and reclaim their old friendship, they could forge a new one.

One day at a time, Warrick had told Raina.

Warrick!

Yolanda laughed as Raina suddenly leaped from the sofa and began rushing around in search of her car keys.

"He's not here," Yolanda told her. "He went back to New Jersey after the party last week."

"In that case," Raina said determinedly, "I need to buy a plane ticket!"

Chapter 19

Raina was waiting for Warrick in the study when he returned home that evening.

Cyrus Gibbons and Evamay Watts had been so pleased to see her that they'd happily agreed to create a ruse to lure Warrick into his study as soon as he came home from work.

Raina was seated at his desk with her back facing the door so he wouldn't see her right away. But she had a clear view of his reflection in the window as he strode into the room, briefcase in hand, scowling as he impatiently jerked his tie loose. Her heart lurched at the sight of him.

"I've had a long day," Warrick said to his butler and housekeeper, a note of exasperation in his voice. "What did you want to discuss with me that was so urgent?"

On cue, Raina swiveled around in the chair and drawled, "Actually, Mr. Mayne, *I'm* the one with an urgent matter to discuss with you."

Warrick's eyes widened.

"Raina?" he whispered, staring at her as if he were hallucinating. "What are you doing here?"

"You have something of mine," Raina said, looking at the snow globe on his shelf, secretly relieved that he hadn't gotten rid of it in the aftermath of their argument.

Warrick frowned. "If you're talking about the snow globe, that's mine. You gave it to me."

Raina smiled softly. "I wasn't talking about the snow globe. I was talking about something else you have, something else I gave you a long time ago." She paused. "My heart."

Warrick's expression softened. "Are you taking it back?" he said with a husky catch to his voice.

"Even if I wanted to," Raina said, rising from the chair, "I couldn't. It belongs to you, and I don't think that's ever going to change."

Their gazes held.

Raina didn't know who moved first, but the next thing she knew she was rushing around the desk as Warrick tossed aside his briefcase and strode purposefully toward her. And then she was in his arms, wrapped in his fierce embrace, and it felt like heaven.

With gentle, conspiratorial smiles, Mr. Gibbons and Evamay Watts quietly left the room and closed the door behind them.

"I love you," Warrick whispered fiercely into Raina's hair. "I've missed you so damned much."

"I've missed you, too," Raina moaned, her face buried against his broad chest as she held him tightly, never wanting to let go. "I was crazy to think I could ever live without you."

"So was I!"

Raina lifted her face to his, and he seized her lips in a hungry, plundering kiss that she returned with equal passion.

Even as their mouths separated long moments later, they clung to each other, neither willing to end the embrace.

Gazing down into Raina's face, Warrick said feelingly, "I'm sorry for all the pain I caused you. I didn't want your property anymore, not like that."

"And I'm sorry for not believing you when you told me you had nothing to do with Deniece's article. I should have trusted you."

"I never gave you any reason to. Your reaction was perfectly justified."

"Let's not rehash the past," Raina said, echoing the words he'd spoken to her on that devastating morning. "From now on, let's look to the future. To you and me."

Warrick smiled into her eyes. "I like the sound of that. You know what else I'd like to hear?"

"What?"

"You saying *yes* when I ask you to marry me."

Raina closed her eyes for a moment, remembering all those childhood fantasies she'd had about marrying Warrick. The reality of this moment far surpassed anything she could have ever imagined.

Opening her eyes, she gazed into the unbearably handsome face of the man she'd loved over half her life, and she said simply, "Yes."

Warrick laughed, a full, satisfied rumble. Overcome with emotion, he lifted her into his arms and swung her around. Their lips met in a deep, lingering kiss.

As they drew apart, Warrick gently set her down and took her hand. "Come here. I want to show you something."

He led her across the room to a large glass-topped drafting table. As he opened a drawer and removed a stack of drawings, Raina asked curiously, "What are those?"

And then she saw.

The architectural drawings of his new office complex, which was already under construction at the site of her former spa. She waited to feel a twinge of resentment, but it never came.

Warrick spread the drawings across the table, and Raina leaned close to admire her first view of the sprawling, ultramodern facility Houston was abuzz about.

"This is what I wanted to show you," Warrick murmured, pointing on the page.

There, on the first floor of the main building, was space for a day spa.

Raina gasped, tears rushing to her eyes. She stared wonderingly at Warrick. "How…?"

"If you hadn't decided to forgive me," he said huskily, "my backup plan was to hire you to run the spa. I was going to make the offer too irresistible for you to turn down. And then I was going to do everything in my power to persuade you to marry me."

Raina's heart swelled. Awash with tenderness and gratitude, she curved her palm against his cheek. "Thank you," she whispered.

"Thank *you.*"

She smiled through her tears. "I'm going to hire Tina to be the spa director, and Trey will be in charge of customer relations."

"Whatever you decide, sweetheart. The spa is all yours. What else do you want?"

Raina said softly, "I want to marry you in the garden on a beautiful, balmy spring afternoon."

Warrick smiled. "I think we can manage that. Anything else?"

"I want a baby."

His gaze softened. "We can definitely manage that."

Raina gave him a sheepish smile. "But would you mind if we have dinner first? All they served on the plane were peanuts, and I'm *starving*."

Warrick laughed, kissing her forehead. "Golden girl," he said, his eyes shining with all the love and adoration she'd longed for all these years, "you can have anything you want."

"I know," Raina said lovingly. "I already do."